The Statement

Albert Stark

Albert Stark

outskirtspress
DENVER, COLORADO

The Statement

v2.0

Cover Illustration by Victor Guiza at Outskirtspress, Inc. All rights reserved - used with permission.

Outskirts Press, Inc.
http://www.outskirtspress.com

Paperback ISBN: 978-1-4787-7083-1
Hardback ISBN: 978-1-4787-7178-4

Library of Congress Control Number: 2016902226

PRINTED IN THE UNITED STATES OF AMERICA

Dedicated to James McCloskey
and the late Harlan (Bruce) Josephs

Prologue

Seventeen days after Martin Luther King was shot and killed in Memphis, Lester Gold sneaked into the Brothers of Israel cemetery on Cedar Lane where another good man was being buried—Julius Menachem Gold.

Moments before they were about to leave for the cemetery, his mother had even reached up to cuff him on the ear, hissing "you have to be strong," but in the end Lester had escaped. Fifteen years old and a freshman at Trenton High, and finally he had run away from home. He circled the block, watching, until his mother, Minnie, and her sister left, and then he slipped back into the house to retrieve his baseball glove, the one that had been signed by Robin Roberts, and took off at a trot. He took every shortcut he knew, even climbing a few fences, and arrived at Brothers of Israel just as the service was ending.

He crouched behind a stand of cedar trees as he watched, wiping hard at his tears. The mourners were clustered around the grave—at least he presumed it was the grave. From this vantage, what he could see were long black coats and black hats and the blue and white *talits* around the men's shoulders. And his mother, no bigger than a child, next to Rabbi Greenberg. She hadn't been to the beauty parlor, he could tell—her hairdo was dented in the back where she had slept on it. The death had been sudden, and no one, including Lester, had had any time to make sense of it. Not that any sense could be made.

Lester tuned in to Rabbi Greenberg's words. "Make no mistake—there shall be swift and righteous justice. With God's help."

"May he rest in peace"—he heard it repeated among the mourners, and then he heard his mother. "May he rest in peace."

Swift. Righteous? "There will be no peace," Lester muttered.

After the others left he moved quickly toward the plot where they had gathered. Standing at the foot of the grave, facing east, he began to say Kaddish. "Ehei shmëh rabba mevarakh lealam ulalmey almaya." He stopped and looked up. Across the street was a row of houses as ordinary as the one he would go home to. The sky was darkening and he didn't have much time. There was no *minyan*, only he, his father's only son. He stepped to the edge of the grave and stared hard at the coffin before he tossed the glove down into the dirt.

1
Sitting Shiva

Minutes before what seemed like the entire population of Jewtown was about to land on their doorstep, Lester was still shuffling around his bedroom, unable to choose a tie, or descend the stairs to greet the guests.

Ever since what Minnie had been calling "the accident," Lester's life had moved in slow motion and now, this silence—his mother had not yet scolded him for missing the funeral—was worse than the battle he knew was coming. As if on cue, he heard her coming up the stairs. He flung himself face down on his bed.

He heard her open the door. "We're sending you to Whispering Pines."

Lester buried his head under the pillow. "No," he said. "I won't go."

"You can and you will," she said. "It's a chance to mingle with your betters."

Lester froze. After a moment, he felt his mother's hands on his shoulders. "Do it for your father," she said.

He lay there until he heard her leave. It could be worse, he thought. It was comforting, actually, to know that she was still the same mother she had always been. The mother who never failed to take him aside and tell him The Story, the one she had been telling since before he could talk. The Golds were a link in the 4,000-year-old chain of Jewishness, but she and his papa didn't want their boy to be snared in the web of Orthodox Jewry's rigid tenets, to wear ringlets under his skullcap and a beard on his chin. Yes, he should go to *shul*, but he wasn't to succumb to it, to spend his days competing with the other men to see who could pray the hardest.

He was his father's son, and no one had to remind him of that. Every day after school he went, without reminding, to Gold's Kosher Cuts. Gold's, where two days earlier, on a Tuesday afternoon, as Lester swept up, Julius Gold was shot in the back as he hunched over a rack of lamb.

That was the day everything changed. The very next morning, for the first time in memory, he had not scrambled to the front porch and grabbed *The Trentonian* as soon as he heard the familiar *splat*.

When Martin Luther King had been assassinated, Major League baseball season had been just three days away, and Lester was anxious to read the paper, not just because King had been shot, but more importantly, because the paper's legendary sports sections featured the starting pitchers for opening day of the Major League season.

He had ripped off the plastic and flipped pages looking for the list of starting pitchers for the sixteen American and National League opening games. The next days had been busy ones as he handicapped the games, and typed and mimeographed Goldfinger's Picks, a tote sheet he sold for a quarter to customers who frequented Gold's.

Phillies' lefty Chris Short was facing off against the Mets' Tom Seaver and the duel between the Yankees' Mel Stottlemyre and the California Angels' George Brunet was sure to attract brisk business.

And then his father had asked, "Did you hear? The opening day games, postponed. Because of the funeral."

"You're kidding me," Lester said. "No way. They have to play. People have tickets. It's gonna be on TV—the networks will never let it happen. Did they stop football for Kennedy?"

Yussel had been behind the counter, as he nearly always was, trimming a brisket. He thrust his bottom lip forward and then shrugged. "I heard it on the radio." He put down his knife and reached for a broom, handing it to Lester. "Here. Sweep. Listen to your father."

That day they had not had a single customer, and so they had climbed into the Ford pickup, which Yussel kept parked out back, and driven the three blocks home, the streets empty.

Lester had turned on the television in the living room to hear the six o'clock news. A reporter was interviewing Roberto Clemente, who talked about how he admired King's courage, and the way he inspired the oppressed to speak out. "They started saying things and they started picketing, and that's the reason I say he changed the world."

As the sports segment was about to end, the announcer said, "It's final. The baseball commissioner has confirmed: since Cardinal pitcher Bob Gibson will not pitch, opening games will be played on April 10, the day after Martin Luther King's funeral in Atlanta."

Lester sidled over to Yussel, who had come downstairs after washing up. "You were right again, Pop."

Yussel put a hand on Lester's shoulder. "It's the right thing to do. Koufax wouldn't pitch Game One of the '65 World Series because it was Yom Kippur."

He had run upstairs and come back down with two gloves, handing Yussel one glove and putting his Robin Roberts glove on his left hand before heading out to the porch. It was the last time he would ever play catch with his father.

And now, after his mother's opening salvo, the mourners were arriving. He could hear them as they stopped at the bench beside the front door, poured water from the pitcher sitting there and dried their hands on towels Minnie had laid out.

Lester sighed heavily and then galumphed down the stairs

in time to see Aunt Myrtle waddle out of the kitchen as she and Minnie hugged the guests.

"What a wonderful man your Yussel was," Lillian Cala said as she came through the door. Lester had known Mrs. Cala his whole life: she was one of the sewing machine operators at the Gross Doll Factory, where his mother worked.

Minnie frowned. "His parents lived their last days in the camps, and, thank God, Julius survived. For this? For these *ganef* to . . ." She stopped, shaken, and leaned heavily on the arm of her friend.

Lester backed himself up against the dining room chintz. The *ganef* again—the ones who had murdered his father and in the process stolen Lester's future: tenth grade at Trenton High, playing second base for the Schroths, even the chance to make out with a girl like Carol Cala, who everyone said was "easy."

"Minerva," Myrtle said gently as she took her sister's arm and tried to extricate her.

But Minnie wouldn't budge. "Thirteen years I've worked side by side with Lillian."

Lester strained toward the doorway—yes, Carol was standing there between her mother and her father, Dino, the only non-Jews in the house. She was the new girl in school who had taken the seat next to Lester on his day at Trenton High. She had long, curly black hair and ebony eyes, and Lester still remembered what she had worn that day: a red silk blouse, short skirt and black ballet shoes, which were known as "slut slippers."

The Calas were Italian, from the Burg, where Catholic was pronounced "Catlick." Lester had seen them at Trionfetti's, where the mob ate spaghetti and meatballs and ravioli with forks and spoons at round tables for ten, napkins anchored under their chins.

"What's that you're wearing?" Minnie asked Lillian.

Lillian extended her hands to show off the long, flowing sleeves. "It's a caftan. I saw Carol Burnett wearing one on Johnny Carson."

She approached the dining room table, her sleeves grazing the tablecloth. "Look at all this *food*," she said, and Dino added, "Yowza."

Minnie took a breath—now she was in her element. "Let me tell you about Wenarski's," she said, pointing to the table. "It was a lot of things to a lot of people. Mama and papa —may they rest in peace—lived over the store. Sunday mornings it was so busy there was no rest: bagging bagels and rolls, getting the rye breads out of the slicer, bringing pickles and corned beefs and tongues and pastramis out of the basement."

She took a seat on one of the hard cane chairs near the table, settling in, and Lester knew there was no stopping her. "Never a time when you couldn't smell the sour pickles, never will I forget the taste of the creamed herring. My mother ran the kitchen while my father kibitzed with the men."

Minnie looked over at Lillian to see if she understood and Lester bowed his head. He couldn't even look in Carol's direction.

"Somebody said I have to try the *tzimmes*," Lillian said.

Minnie rose, grabbed Lester's arm, and dragged him toward the table. "Now my Lester, he knows from *tzimmes*."

"Ma," Lester said.

"Go on," Minnie said.

Lester sighed and mumbled through his explanation. "It's a traditional Jewish dish made from a variety of vegetables often combined with dried fruit."

"Seymour Bishofsky, he runs Wenarski's now, and his *tzimmes* aren't as good as my papa's, but it's not his fault because nobody's could be." She beckoned to Lester to come nearer and he dutifully took a step in her direction. "One time a customer complained. Papa told her that he was out of *tzimmes* and then she saw him serve the dish to a man at the next table. She was irate, naturally, and Papa told her, 'I didn't serve to you because you wouldn't appreciate it.'" Minnie gripped Lester's arm tighter and doubled over, her 4' 11" body shaking with laughter.

Lester yanked his arm away. People were staring—the widow was cackling in the midst of the Shiva.

"The sour pickles are better at Gold's," he said loudly. "Best pickles in all of Jewtown."

Carol glanced at him shyly. "I always wondered, is it . . . derogatory to say Jew—?"

"—Nope," Lester snapped. Everybody in Trenton knew that Jewtown was not a derogatory word. Friday night was *shabbas* dinner, Saturday was *shul*, and Sunday, when the gentiles went to church, the Jews ate. For boys like Lester, Jewtown was the world entire: The sweet smell of fresh rye and pumpernickel and rugelach at Kohn's bakeries. Louie the Barber cut hair and booked numbers. Herman Spiegel sold furniture. The sweet shop, the drug store, the tire shop, the plumbing supply house. Not a single church. Three *shuls*, all Orthodox. And the *Cheder* where Lester went until first grade.

And Gold's, where he spent every afternoon. What would he do with himself now? There was school, of course—he would have to go back to school. The day of King's funeral, things got weird—even his picks that day, Lester had been off, although he'd been in the middle of a lucky streak, calling all the wins, and Gold's customers were starting to take his advice.

April 9—the Stars and Stripes had been at half-mast when he arrived at Trenton High that morning, and the students, black and white, were in a state of shock. JFK, and now MLK. The black students had amassed at the front of the entrance, standing arm-in-arm, a human barricade, singing "We Shall Overcome."

"What's up?" Lester asked Santo Bassoni, a kid from the 'Burg.

"They want the day off 'cause of the funeral."

"It's the right thing to do," Lester said.

"You outta your mind?"

"Clemente won't play. Gibson either. Koufax didn't throw in the

Series. Jewish holiday."

"You expect school to shut down for two days for you?"

"Nah."

"Then why should they get a day off?"

William Miller, the vice principal, came onto the steps behind the black cordon. "School is open. All those who do not come inside will be marked absent and treated as a truant." He turned and went back into the building.

The crowd began to stir and Lester could hear their voices rising as they resumed their chant. "No, No, We Won't Go. No, No, We Won't Go."

Greg Pinter, a white student, joined in—he was in Lester's home room. Then another kid and another. A dozen more joined.

The clock on the bell tower above the school entrance read 9:20 when Miller reemerged, this time with a megaphone, and announced, "School is cancelled for the day. You're dismissed."

Lester followed a mass of students as they headed down Greenwood toward downtown. Everyone seemed to be talking at once. When they hit State Street, "Dance to the Music" by Sly and the Family Stone, a big hit on the radio, blasted from a record store, drowning out the jubilant voices.

But Lester had peeled off, making a left on Montgomery and heading over to Front. It was a beautiful sunny day and the maples on Mercer Street were budding green.

Yussel looked up as Lester opened the door to the store. "Playing hooky?"

"Nah."

"Don't tell me they sent you home, I don't want to hear my son is breaking the rules, and he's only a sophomore."

"School got closed for the funeral."

"That's a good thing. The blacks, they deserve respect."

Lester headed to the back room, grabbed *The Trentonian* from a chair and sat down with his rosters, pouring over his notes for Goldfinger's Picks. Lately, he'd been gravitating to the Mets. They'd been 61-101 last year, finishing tenth in the National League, forty games behind the Cardinals. But they'd brought in Tom Seaver and Steady Eddie Kranpool and Bud Harrelson. Tommie Agee was a great outfielder. Sure, they were at the bottom, but with their new manager and new pitchers—he had a good feeling about the Mets.

Lester heard sirens and he walked through the store to the front window. Police cars and fire engines raced up Market, past Gold's. Yussel put his carving knife on the cutting table and wiped his hands on his apron. Standing on the sidewalk next to his father, Lester could see flames in the distance, downtown, where he had passed the record store less than a half hour ago.

Officer Bert Randolph approached Yussel—Gold's and the surrounding businesses were part of his beat. "You'll be okay. They have it under control. It's a real mess up there. They broke into Teddy Snyder's. They got golf clubs and hit some balls through the store windows. 45 arrested so far." He pointed to the Mercer County jail across the street from Gold's. "It'll be standing room only in there real soon."

Later Yussel and Lester had stood in the doorway, eyeing a crowd of blacks gathered in front of the jail. Three boys with Afros picked up some bricks and held them in their upraised hands, and then, a moment later, charged across the street. Yussel turned and ran to the meat counter, grabbed his cleaver and stomped to the doorway just as the windows shattered. Lester cowered as he heard the glass breaking, and then moments later cursed his cowardice. The boys had succeeded in making far more work for him. He would spend the rest of the afternoon sweeping up the glass, moving faster with the broom, as his father exhorted him. Lester could see the tension in his father's round, gentle face as he wiped his hands on the blood-stained apron and muttered, "For this we came to America?" They taped up the windows and headed home.

"A regular Kristallnacht it was. So much broken glass," Julius said to Minnie, once they were at the dinner table that evening.

"How many times have I told you? Move to Hermitage, like Wenarski and Shulman, get out of Jewtown," Minnie said. "You took our Lester out of the Cheder. And look..."

"Always you're tcheppening me! Wenarksi, what a schande he should vacate Jewtown. Over my dead body we move to Hermitage. I won't hear of selling to the Havesons."

Minnie shuffled out to the kitchen and then back to the table. "You could have been killed. Then where would we be?"

"Meshugaas. That's what the insurance is for."

"And our son—you wish for him too a brick—schbam!—right in the keppe? Jewtown, nothing for us here. When did business start to go bad? I'll tell you when. When the black hats, the huyots, stopped shopping at Julius Gold's. Why? Because they thought the Golds were becoming too uppity. That's right. Because we wanted more for our Lester, so we weren't Jewish enough. That's the emmis, the truth."

Lester had run up to his bedroom, slammed the door and flopped onto his bed. He knew what was coming next—his parents had been fighting about his future for weeks.

"This summer he is going to Whispering Pines," Minnie vowed, her voice rising. "He's going to meet his betters. You can stay where you are. But my son is not."

"So he should go to the Jewish high school."

"You're not listening to me."

"There's no baseball at Whispering Pines."

"There is."

"But not like the Schroths. He has his heart set on making the Schroths."

"You tell him he should go, he will go. For you he will do anything."

Lester roused himself from his reverie and glanced over at Carol, who was sitting primly on one of the hard chairs. He closed his eyes. *Yes, he would have, he would have done anything for his father.*

And now the Catlicks had to come to Jewtown, because Lillian had no choice—after all, her friend's husband had been killed. But why had she dragged her daughter along?

Carol looked in his direction and gave him the barest hint of a smile. Lester couldn't smile back, though. Before the guests had arrived, Minnie had hissed at him "smile—don't let them pity us!"

Rabbi Greenwald stepped into the room and began to pray, chanting *yisgidal,yis gadash,* as he rocked forward and back. The mourners joined in, some sitting, some standing. After awhile, a line formed and people grabbed napkins and paper plates, but Carol just sat there.

Aunt Myrtle hustled in and out of the kitchen as the guests worked through the spread she had spent so much time preparing. Then she began cleaning up, huffing and puffing into the dining room with a dish towel over her arm, clearing plates and glasses and platters. At one point, she leaned over and hissed to Lester, "That girl will never understand what it's like to be Jewish."

"What girl?" he muttered, but he knew who she meant. Was he that obvious? He glanced at her and then turned away: his glasses were taped together—Minnie's handiwork—and he couldn't face Carol. He squeezed his eyes shut and prayed to disappear, to vaporize right through the chintz wallpaper, but when he opened his eyes there was no way to avoid Carol's stare.

"My Lester," Minnie announced, "I always told him to marry Jewish."

"Ma," he pleaded, "*stop*."

Minnie ignored him. "My mother would say, 'You don't have to socialize with *them*. There are enough Jewish kids to be friendly with. You have more in common. It's hard to believe. We didn't know any better."

Minnie leaned over and touched Dino softly on the knee. "It's great to see you. Just like yesterday. When you're good friends you can just pick up where you left off."

Lester had resisted for as long as he could, but there was no way to avoid it any longer: he was going to have to do some damage control. He went over to where Carol was sitting. She was picking at a piece of apple cake.

"I have to go to camp," he said.

"Whispering Pines?" she asked, taking a bite of cake.

"Oh, God, do you have to *whisper* when you say it?"

She smiled shyly but he couldn't read her at all.

"It's sleepaway camp," he moaned. "Kill me now."

She looked at him, her eyes wide, as Lester slowly realized that that was something you weren't allowed to say when your father had just been killed.

"Oh, that was a joke," he said, forcing a chuckle. "We Jews, we exaggerate."

She put her fork down and he figured that he had succeeded in the very thing Minnie had feared most: Carol pitied him, she was so struck with horror at what Lester had failed to do that she couldn't make herself take a single bite more. Here was a boy who had let his father be slain in the middle of an ordinary Tuesday, and then hadn't even showed up for the funeral service.

Lester leaned in. "Did you go . . . ?"

Carol blinked rapidly. "I . . . you mean the . . .?"

"Funeral."

She shook her head, back and forth, back and forth, unable to stop.

He began to nod "yes" to counter her "no's." "I went," he said. "I mean, naturally, I was there. And I was called on to say a few words. Which again, naturally, as his son. . . ."

He knew she wanted to ask, he could feel how badly she wanted him to say it. He had heard the shot and come running from the back room, slipped on the sawdust, and hit his head on the counter. He hadn't been any help at all, and to prove it, ever since "the accident," Minnie and everyone else had treated him as though he were a helpless child.

Carol began to nod and he matched her again, and they sat there nodding in unison until Carol jarred the fork off her plate and onto the floor. Lester lunged to pick it up as Minnie advanced on him.

"Lester, come and help."

He spent the rest of the night boxing up food—not a single guest left empty-handed. The Calas were among the last to leave. Lester stood with his mother in the doorway, intoning, "May God comfort you among the mourners of Zion and Jerusalem," as Carol balanced a container of kugel. Inside was the fork—Minnie would be down one when she checked her silver collection, and for the moment Lester relished the idea that she would not miss what she didn't know she had lost.

"Ma," Lester said, as he trudged exhausted up the stairs. "Enough already." He went into his room and shut the door, but before he could sit down she was knocking.

"Go away!" he shouted.

He knew that would only make her knock harder, and she did. He got up and wrenched open the door. She was standing there holding Aunt Myrtle's striped hatbox, the one Minnie kept on the upper shelf of her bedroom closet. The lid was embellished with elegant antique script: *Miss Elaine's*.

"I've got something for you," she said.

"Ma," he groaned. "Whatever it is, I don't want it."

"This you'll want," she intoned as she handed him the box.

He eyed it suspiciously.

Minnie shook her head. "Open it."

Cautiously, as if there might be a bomb inside, he peeked under the lid.

Inside was the glove—there was no mistaking it, as the signature was clearly visible—or what was left of it, anyway. The lower case letters had faded, but the stems of the two "R's" still spiked along one of the fingers. Lester gaped and then shook his head. It could not be. *How could a glove levitate out of a grave?*

Minnie grabbed the glove, brandishing it. "What is this—bupkis? No! It's perfectly good." She took a step back and crossed her arms. "So who should call me but Seymour Lehman."

"Who?"

"The manager at Brothers of Israel. One of the caretakers found it when he was . . . ."

"Dumping dirt on him?"

Minnie frowned and then gave him her fiercest stare. "It's meshuggah—you don't come to your own father's funeral! This is how you honor him?"

"Ma, *stop*. I know, okay?" Lester said, shaking his head miserably. "It was . . . it was supposed to be a tribute."

"A tribute! A tribute is, you *attend*. You bow your head, you say the prayers."

"No, I mean, the glove. A tribute, not for him—for *me*. Because we played catch since I was three. Since he took me to every game, and he waited hours so I could get Robin Roberts' signature. How he loved Hank Greenberg, and Sandy Koufax." He sighed and softened his tone. "And if not for him, I wouldn't be the player I am today."

Minnie nodded. "And now the glove is back. Just in time. We're sending you to Whispering Pines."

He shook his head fiercely. "I'm playing for the Schroths this summer—we're a championship team!" he said, his voice rising. "From there, the majors." He said the last part with less conviction, but still, he had spoken it out loud.

Minnie plowed ahead. "They've got baseball—"

"No!" he shouted. "Absolutely not. Either the Schroths or baseball is out."

"Well, then they've got tennis."

"Tennis is for sissies, Ma."

He swallowed hard. "You don't understand. My life is over—"

"—so you don't play baseball," she said with a shrug. "There are worse things." And then she moved in, grabbing his arm. "It was your father's wish that you go to camp."

He stared glumly at the floor—Minnie had played her trump card.

2

Whispering Pines

Lester put up a good fight and he won the battle, convincing Minnie that even though it was during the Shiva he should be allowed to attend the tryouts for the Schroths. *Baseball is the American game*, he told her—*who knows from tennis? Isn't that what you want for your son? Eisenhower, he was a big baseball fan. Always throwing out the first pitch. He loved the Senators*. She caved.

For the tryouts, he couldn't bring himself to use his Robin Roberts glove, so he borrowed a glove from a friend. When it was his turn he fingered the brim of his Phillies baseball cap, and then fiddled with his glasses—he was wearing the old ones, the ones that had broken in half and which Minnie had mended with glue and duct tape. He wiped the sweat from his forehead with the back of his hand, crouched, and let his glove hang in front of his knee just like Phillies infielders Roberto Peña, Cookie Rojas, and Bobby Wine. He knew them not only by name but also by number.

His mother's voice came flooding in—*You know every baseball score and all the batting averages, but you can't remember who killed your father?*—and he squeezed his eyes shut. He opened them when he heard the crack of the bat, and was on his toes, sidestepping to his left toward the bouncing ball as Billy thundered up the baseline toward first. He stabbed the ball, snatched it from his glove, cocked his arm and threw, a wild misfire that caused him to go down. The ball sailed over the first baseman's mitt. Billy rounded first and was heading to second as Lester got up and brushed the dirt off his glasses. At least they'd stayed in one piece.

"Over here, Lester." He jogged toward the bench, following the coach's instruction, as Jimmy trotted past him to second base. "Good try. Have a seat."

Minutes later, the coach announced, "Pitcher, Al. Catcher, Fred, First base, Carl. Second base, Jimmy."

Lester got up and walked behind the bleachers, where his eyes flooded, and he struggled to remove the strap that held his glasses in place so he could wipe away his tears. He tried to tell himself that it wasn't his fault—his mother's voice invaded his mind at the crucial moment, and even as the ball rolled toward him, it was already too late. It was the Schroths or nothing and now baseball was over, for good.

Four weeks later, after school let out, he arrived at Whispering Pines. The boy who had the bunk below Lester snored like a buzz saw, and so he lay awake night after night. By the time he got to breakfast all that was left was muesli and so he didn't eat, and that meant he hadn't excelled at any sport so far. At least no one mentioned his father—that was a big plus.

On Tuesday the coach insisted that Lester try out for the Blue Team, but he knew he wouldn't make it—he had no intention of playing. He forced away thoughts of his mother, how he would never forgive her for making him come to camp. *So you failed at baseball. So try tennis. Try swimming. Look how beautiful the lake.*

He was learning Minnie's lessons well. "Surviving, you put nothing before survival!" she had said over and over, "You see in the movies. The brave ones—always they end up dead, but the cowards, they live!" He had long ago figured out how to be the right kind of coward, a sensible one, not a weak-kneed sniveling one, but one who used cowardice as a shield to protect himself as he kept foremost in his mind a more pragmatic goal: self-preservation.

A few days later he sat on a rock beside the campfire on the bank of Sunrise Lake, where the campers gathered every evening. He scuffed his shoe in the dirt and decided that he could last one more day. And then he would put in place his backup plan—faking a protracted bout of food poisoning, which would surely send him home. He had to admit that the tennis lessons weren't so bad. The pro had said, "you're a natural," and he had won his first match easily—but still, if he couldn't play baseball, he wouldn't play tennis either.

He looked up as one of the counselors tossed a log on the fire. Through the shower of sparks, he saw that Carol Cala was standing near an oak tree watching him.

He got up and walked over to her. "Don't tell me you're a Jew."

She shook her head. "Catholic."

"But they sent you here."

She shrugged. "We're not really very religious. Mass and all that. My dad wanted me to learn horseback riding. He thinks if I learn dressage I'll marry a count or something."

She was wearing shorts and her legs were long and slim. Her dark curly hair was pulled back with a bandana. It occurred to him that there might now be a reason to stay.

"Yeah, well, I might be going home"—he glanced up at her to see if he could detect any disappointment, but her face was serene—"but my mom wants me to learn tennis. So I can be the next Dick Savitt."

"Who's that?"

"He's from Jersey and he never had a tennis lesson in his life. He won Wimbledon. From my ma's perspective, all that matters is he's Jewish."

"My dad always says, salt and pepper, salt and pepper. We moved from the Burg to Hermitage last year and there's Scots, Poles,

WASPS, Jews and Negroes."

"And the bakeries sell white bread."

"And rye too."

She wasn't letting him get any points in for all he had suffered—in fact, she seemed to have forgotten the tragedy altogether. "I, uh, well, it's hard to have fun when you're . . . you know." He gave her his best tragic stare.

She nodded.

"I'm up for being distracted, though," he said, trying to give her a winning smile. "And I heard that there's a makeout tree—like, back by the cabanas, near the lake."

She didn't flinch. "That's just an old wives tale."

"And how would you know?" he asked, arching an eyebrow.

"How would *you* know?" she retorted. She pursed her lips and then quickly changed the subject. "You know that girl Naima?"

Lester shook his head.

"Tall? She's on the track team at school."

"Oh. Naima." Of course he knew her—everyone did. She was a Negro with a big reddish Afro and a sprinkling of freckles on her nose.

"Well, she's here, and . . . we're in the same cabin, and I really like her."

"Why would a Negro want to come to Whispering Pines?"

Carol glanced around, and then lowered her voice. "Actually, she's Jewish."

"No way. She's a heeb?"

"Her mom is Jewish."

"Wow, never would have guessed." He paused. "I've never seen her sitting with the Jews in the cafeteria."

"Is there a Jewish table?" Carol asked.

Lester rolled his eyes. "Uh, I guess I tend to be resistant to the . . . uh . . . the tribe mentality." He twirled the lanyard that held the key to his locker. "My ma, she wants us to move out of Jewtown, since . . . *you know.*" He paused dramatically, trying to detect any hint of the pity she had displayed at the Shiva. "She wants to buy in Hermitage."

Carol held up a small poster with the words *Modeh Ani Lifanecha* spelled out in red and silver glitter. "I made this in Arts and Crafts today. It means, I gratefully thank you."

"I know what it means," he snapped.

She smiled at him. "You're a mensch, Lester."

"Is that your first try at Yiddish? You're a quick study."

"How'd you break your glasses?"

"Oh, this?" he said, trying to yank them off, but succeeding only in getting tangled in the strap. "Yeah, I have to wear the strap now. I did it, I broke them. He began to bounce on his toes. "So what cabin are you in?" And before she could reply he blurted out, "I'm in a cabin of *machers.*"

"What?"

"Big shots, every one. I'm the only one who isn't Class President or some shit. Or US Olympic backstroke champion." He shrugged. "It's enough just to take a swim, know what I mean?"

"I love swimming in the lake. No chlorine."

"Sometimes you just want to be doing the backstroke, without having to imagine you're flailing in the Red Sea."

"You sound like you're not having a good time."

Lester grimaced. "I guess I'm feeling successfully indoctrinated. My bunkmate recites *anu lavan, yesh lanu ruach* in his sleep."

"What's that mean?"

"We are the white team, we have spirit."

She giggled and he felt his heart lift. "I didn't see you at *hora* practice last night."

"I'm not much of a dancer."

"Neither am I."

"But I will concede—if you can't dance the hora, it's like an insult to all Jewry."

Carol paused. "I saw you on the court the other day. You're good."

"Yeah, I'm the littlest guy out there, so I have to try harder."

"Lester. I mean it—you're really good." She flashed him a wholesome smile.

"I gotta go," he said suddenly. "I have canoe duty." He couldn't stop explaining himself around her. "You have to stack 'em. Upside down, only I guess that's obvious."

She gave him a little wave and turned to go, and he felt suddenly bereft. "What's your camp name?" he blurted out.

Carol took a couple steps back toward him. "Scout, I guess. On account of I can find my way out of the woods. I mean, blindfolded."

"Oh God, they *blindfold* you in the woods? Kill me now."

"Lester, you've got to stop saying that," she said gently. "It's not . . . appropriate."

"Right."

She paused and then pushed ahead. "Were you . . . my mother said you were . . . ."

"*There*."

"And did you . . .?"

"You gotta tell me, what are they saying at school?"

"Nothing," she said quickly.

"That I didn't *do* anything, right?"

She stared glumly at her shoes.

"I was sweeping up."

She stood there staring at him, her dark eyes brimming.

"I have to testify," he said nervously, "tell what I saw."

She nodded gravely, and then smiled. "Dramatic—I've never been to a trial. Except Ironside—I mean, on TV."

"Yeah, I like that he's in a wheelchair—he's got to be crafty, figure out ways to outsmart the criminals."

Carol started toward the woods, but then called over her shoulder.

"You never said what your nickname is."

"Kike. What else?"

She stopped and looked at him. "No, I mean *here*. It's a Jewish camp, so we're all kikes, right?"

Lester laughed. This girl, she was including herself right in with the Jews. "Goldfinger they call me."

The next afternoon Lester had canoe duty once again, and he arrived early to meet the swimming instructor and get the canoes ready for the campers to paddle to Mohican Island, a half-mile across the lake. As the campers assembled, he saw that both Carol and Naima were in the group called the Turtles. He immediately volunteered to be one of the guides—he was a strong swimmer and he could easily maneuver the canoes.

Carol waved to him from where she was standing near the shore. She had on a yellow one-piece bathing suit and her hair was tied up with a bandana. Naima was standing next to her looking out at the water, a tall girl in a blue plaid two piece. Her hair was as big as it always was—she had made no attempt to tie it back. The girls got into one of the canoes and laughed nervously as they picked up the paddles.

"Life vests!" barked Jim Nelson, one of the counselors, and the girls strapped on vests, still giggling and whispering.

Lester got into another canoe, along with Alfred, a boy from his cabin, and they set out behind the girls. The lake was calm and there was a light wind, just enough to ruffle the waves a bit. Lester had paddled across to Mohican Island a half-dozen times before, and it was an easy trip. He and Alfred were well-matched and they began to make good progress across the water. He looked back to see the two girls laughing and clowning. Carol was paddling, but Naima was just sitting there like a queen. Then she began fidgeting, turning back and then forward, struggling out of her life vest.

"C'mon, Naima!" Carol shouted, "let's go!"

"How come you're in front?" Naima yelled, laughing. She stood up, balancing on her long, thin legs, and began to step toward Carol.

Lester stopped paddling—he was maybe 200 yards from the girls, and something told him to wait. Sure enough, the tall black girl with the big Afro lost her balance and plunged into the lake. He had been so attuned to her, so sure she was in danger, that he jumped in almost at the same moment she did, and then he started swimming as hard as he could. The girl started to flail, crying out, but the more she struggled, the deeper she sank.

"Naima!" Carol shrieked.

Only her head was above water and she was gulping down big mouthfuls of lake as she flailed; he could see that it took all of her energy to keep from going under, and she was too panicked to cry out. Lester kept his head down and swam hard, and when he got to her, he shouted, "Float on your back! Just float!" But she couldn't—he was close enough now to see the fear in her eyes. He reached for her, but she grabbed at him, flailing, pulling him down with her. He pushed away and shouted, "Stop! Stop fighting."

Jim Nelson was paddling furiously toward them and was nearly on them.

"I'm gonna push you into the boat, okay?" Lester yelled. "Don't fight me." He could see that she was exhausted and barely able to speak. He reached for her, he grabbed handfuls of her hair and then got his arm around her throat, and began to swim backward, dragging her along. And then Jim was there, reaching down to pull her up into the boat. She lay gasping in the bottom of the canoe and closed her eyes. Lester swam back to Carol's canoe and clambered over the side. He sat there, spent and panting.

"Oh my God," Carol said.

"What were you *doing*?" Lester demanded.

Carol looked up guiltily. "I didn't . . ." she began. "She . . . she said she was going to be Pocahontas."

"Shit, that girl almost drowned," Lester said.

They paddled back to the shore. Jim Nelson was on his walkie-talkie, giving their location to the first aid monitors. Lester walked over to where Naima was sitting on the sand, her arms wrapped around her knees. She was shivering, her lips tinged with blue. Water droplets sparkled in her big hair, and he had never seen anything like that—a girl wearing a crown of sparkles.

She looked up as he approached and nodded.

"Why'd you stand up?" he asked.

She shook her head and looked down. Her long legs were covered with sand the same color as her skin; she was sprinkled with fine grains, as if she had been dusted with gold. Earlier, when she had been sitting in the boat, he had thought, *She's sitting there like a queen*. He knelt down next to her.

"What are you doing?" she asked, annoyed.

"I just wanted to make sure you're all right," he muttered.

"Sure. I'm fine."

"Pocahontas, she was the guide," he said softly.

She leveled a stare at him. Her eyes were a warm caramel gold, not dark, the way he had imagined. "I know," she said. "I got an A in American History."

3

Green Meadows

Lester watched as Minnie took a pack of Camels from the pocket of her rayon housedress and lit a cigarette, nodding with satisfaction. She shuffled through the living room, the dining room, and into the kitchen, where she turned on the gas stove to boil water for tea.

Lester had started the new school year—he was now a sophomore—and Minnie had managed to move them out of Jewtown and into Hermitage, where the streets were wide enough for two cars to pass with parking on both sides. She had sold the store to the Haveson brothers, who used to work for Julius.

Lester was trapped at a tiny linoleum table that Minnie had managed to squeeze into the kitchen at their new place, a semi-detached, which in Trenton was called a "Siamese."

"You know who called me yesterday?"

"Ma. Enough already. Not the policeman again?"

"Not the policeman."

"Nobody you know."

"Nobody I know," Lester intoned, slumping a little lower in his seat.

"Mrs. Underwood."

"Who?"

"Dorothy Scudder Underwood," Minnie said, repeating the three names triumphantly. "She invited you to play her son, Charles, at Green Meadows. On the Har-Tru courts, she said. And she told me, not those slippery sandy courts at Cadwalader Park."

Lester slumped a little lower and muttered, "I know this is your big dream, but it's not mine."

Yussel had tried to intervene about the tennis lessons a year ago when Minnie had wanted him to go to a tennis clinic offered at the city park. *Let the boy play baseball,* he had said. Lester tried not to think about it, but the truth was that his father had always been on his side.

As the tea kettle began to whistle, Minnie got up and turned off the flame. Then she turned to Lester, sighing heavily. "For nothing did I endure April 14, 1942?"

"Oh my God, ma! Not the *shtetl* story—" He tried to stand up but he was boxed in by the table.

"—On the *shtetl* playground and I don't know nothing. I'm six years old and the Germans come for my mama and papa. If not for the Zaburskis next door taking us to their farm, hiding us for three years until the war was over. . . ."

He scrambled to his feet, finally managing to break free of the padlock made up by the table and the sideboard. "You're going to invoke the *Nazis* in order to get me to play tennis at a country club?! This is what I put up with—"

Minnie advanced on him as he retreated into the dining room. "What do I always tell you?"

It had been six months since Yussel died, and his mother hadn't let a day go by without invoking his memory. *Your father, God rest his soul, he wanted you to be the first Gold to go to college. Your father, God rest his soul, he wanted you to marry Jewish and give us grandchildren.*

Lester could see there was no winning this battle. "The Golds are a link in the 4,000-year-old chain of Jewishness," he intoned.

"What's that even *mean*?"

"You know perfectly well what it means. It means you have a *responsibility*."

He flung his hands in the air. "I know, I know, it means I'm not going to grow up like the Hasidim. With ringlets under my skullcap and a beard on my chin."

Minnie looked around the room, as if she might be overheard, and then lowered her voice. "Your father, God rest his soul, the saint he was, to put up with those Services . . . not a word of English spoken! And all of them competing to see who could pray the hardest."

He sunk into an overstuffed chair and covered his face with his hands. He had renounced baseball at Whispering Pines, and now it was final: tennis was his game. Since he had come back from Whispering Pines, his refuge had been the Strand Theater, a half-block away. He regularly escaped there to stroke ball after ball against the Strand's back wall, day after day, as he fantasized about being Ken Rosewall. At the Park, Lester played older boys and men twice and three times his age. Two weeks ago, he had won the City of Trenton's tennis championship for boys fifteen years old and younger. He was quick and the other boys had started calling him Mighty Mite.

Minnie came and stood over him. "Some people had resentments against your father," she continued, advancing on Lester. "On account of he was a businessman—successful, and so they wanted what he had."

"Seriously, ma? Why would somebody kill him just because he was a good businessman?"

"To cheat him, that's why! You tell me, was it one of us?"

He shook his head.

"No *hasid*?"

"Ma—no! Don't you think I woulda seen if it was some Hasidim with side curls who came in and shot him?"

"Well, you don't say what you did see. And so how do you know it wasn't?"

"It wasn't."

"So it was the Negroes then. The schvartze, they killed your father." Minnie banged the table. "You're afraid of the schvartes!"

"My God, why would you say that?"

She moved toward him and he could see her face was drawn and her eyes flinty. "Ever since the riots . . . . It was everybody running, everybody robbing, everybody shooting, and no respect for a good man trying to earn a living. They thought they could take everything, and they don't have no respect for their betters."

Lester sighed heavily. "Ma, it's 1970 practically—you can't say that anymore. We're all the same, they have just as much right as we do to start a business and earn a living."

"Who's saying they can't?" she demanded. "The way they dress—those robes in the street. And they're congregating now."

"What robes?"

"And you," she said, eyeing him, "when you go out you should wear a sport coat."

"Where am I going I need to dress up for?"

"To show you got class." She walked over to him and smoothed his hair. "So help me, you're going to college."

"Right, Ma," he said wearily.

"Harvard. Or Columbia. Miriam's boy—"

"—Irv?"

"He got bad marks this semester—"

"How would you know?"

Minnie paused. "The walls, they're paper thin."

"So you're eavesdropping on the neighbors now?"

"God knows I don't listen."

He shook his head and then laughed. "Don't you worry, ma. I'm gonna be as big as Wrigley's, as Campbell's Soup."

"Your father, God rest his soul—"

He stood up and squeezed himself through the narrow space behind the sideboard. He moved over to Minnie and spoke softly. "Wasn't I helping, making a little extra, telling the customers what ball team to bet on? Weren't they coming more and more because your Lester studied and figured out the odds?"

"And he put it all toward your college fund." Minnie paused and then smiled. "You're smart, a good boy, and your mind is top-notch. None better. Your mind's gonna take you far."

He put a hand on his mother's shoulder. "I'm gonna buy you a fur coat, ma. And then I'm gonna buy GM."

Minnie settled into the sofa and crossed her arms. "Do you remember your first day at John A. Roebling?" she asked, smiling at him. "You were such a sweet boy, but not a fighter. You were barely four feet tall and so skinny I could count your ribs."

"Don't remind me, ma." He stood up and moved toward the dining room table.

"You went out for recess. A boy was climbing on the jungle gym, and he yelled, 'Hey Joo.'"

Lester smiled. "That was Santo."

"Giovanni. And you dropped your lunch box, ran over to the jungle gym and tried to punch him."

"Yeah, and missed."

"And that was how you broke your glasses the first time. Because you were a mensch even then and that boy jabbed you good, you never had a chance. And you came running home, crying, 'Mommy, he broke my glasses,' big fat tears rolling down."

"Ma, I was six."

Minnie frowned. "Always I had to sit in the balcony with the women, and don't think I didn't question God. Mama and papa survived. They worked every day. And then papa, his heart, and then two years only before mama passed." She looked up at Lester and smiled. "I grabbed your hand, and I dragged you the six blocks back to the school yard. And I marched up to that boy and said, 'Why'd you call my son a Jew?'"

He bent forward, his hands on his hips, mimicking Minnie. "Why'd you call my son a Jew?" He smiled. "And poor Giovanni, he was like, I was just sayin' 'Hey you,' but it came out 'Joo' cause of his accent."

"I heard that and I grabbed you by the collar and dragged you over there and made you apologize."

"Now, boys. Shake hands," Lester said, in his Minnie voice. "And now me and Santo both have Mr. Gugliemi for math."

Minnie reached down to gently touch his face. "Boychik, I was your protector then, but now you've got to do it. I moved from Jewtown so you could go to a good school, to speak good English. Now you're going to meet the nice people."

"It's Green Meadows, Ma, it's not like I'm gonna meet the President."

"Dorothy Scudder Underwood, a woman like that doesn't make an invitation every day. Maybe she only does that once. No boy in his right mind would turn that down."

"Maybe I'm not in my right mind."

As if on cue, Lester heard a motor in the driveway and he peeked from behind the curtain to see a huge black Cadillac idling, a Negro chauffeur at the wheel. Lester ducked away from the window and headed toward the stairs, where he froze.

"They're *here* for you," Minnie shouted.

"Shit," Lester muttered as he took the stairs two at a time.

"He's coming!" Minnie shrieked, as she rushed toward the door.

Lester realized in horror that the Negro chauffer was walking toward the front steps. He darted back to his room and grabbed his bag, and then descended the stairs slowly, as if he were about to face a firing squad. He stood at the door and turned back gravely, giving

Minnie a look of desperation. He hoped she might clutch him to her breast like she had done the day Jerry Stanhope had threatened to kill him after Lester won a flipping contest and had rightfully taken all of Jerry's baseball cards: Willie Mays, Babe Ruth, and Stan Musial.

But Minnie just handed him a faded green towel. "It's hot," she said as she bent over, cradled his head, and whispered in his ear. "Now, go kick his *tuchas*."

He forced himself out the door and down the steps, as the Negro nodded and grabbed Lester's bag. He approached the door of the Cadillac, but it wasn't over yet: Minnie scuttled out to the street in her housedress, tossing her cigarette onto the macadam.

Lester climbed into the backseat, but then turned and stared out the window. God, if only she would disappear, he thought, as he stared at his mother standing at the curb. The Cadillac pulled away and to Lester's satisfaction the figure of Minnie receded a little more each second until he could no longer see her at all.

He glanced toward a stylish woman in a soft yellow suit and patent leather shoes, who sat regally in the rear seat, her posture erect.

"Hello, dear," she said, extending a soft hand.

He nodded and grasped her fingers before turning away to stare out the window at the Siameses, the scrubby patches of lawn, and the modest driveways. He switched his prayer: it was no longer his mother he wanted to vaporize, it was Mrs. Underwood. He spoke not a single word on the drive and he never once looked in her direction.

As they turned into the entrance of the club, Lester saw the sign—"Green Meadows Country Club. Members ONLY"—and his throat closed up. The Caddy bounced over a speed bump and Lester got a good view of a white manor house with tall pillars, the front porch lined with boxwoods. The men from Hermitage who worked for "John A," the man who had built the Brooklyn Bridge, always said he lived in a house that was "out of this world." It had to be Roebling's place!

Mrs. Underwood led Lester around to a cottage where a boy with straight blond hair was sitting on a lounge chair. His white collared shirt and crisp white tennis shorts were impeccable.

"Charles, this is Lester Gold," his mother said.

Charles looked at Lester and muttered, "Hi."

"Are you boys ready to play?"

Lester turned toward an older man in a white sweater with red and blue stripes along the V neckline, white slacks and white sneakers. He was as dashing as Bill Tilden, the World No. 1 tennis player for seven years.

"They'll be right there, Mitch," Dorothy said to the man, and then turned to her son. "You're ready, Charles?"

It was too late to run, or be sick, or disappear: he, Lester Gold, baby-stepped onto the tennis court, his shoulders slumped like an old man, wearing white shorts that looked like boxer undershorts.

Charles faced him across the net. He grabbed a Jack Kramer Autograph racket strung with cat gut that leaned against the net, and then picked up three new white tennis balls, handed one to Lester, and headed for a baseline.

"You ready? Let's get this over with," Charles snapped.

"I've never played on a court like this. Let's hit a few so I can see how the ball bounces."

Mitch strode onto the court and exchanged a few words with Charles, and then Charles spun his racket. "W or M?"

"M."

Charles bent over. "W. I'll receive. You'll serve."

Lester backpedaled to the baseline as a ball bounced in front of him. He swung, pure reflex, and the wooden throat of his racket drove the ball into the net.

He tossed a ball above his head and smacked a serve. Charles returned it. Lester hit a backhand into a corner. Point after point,

Lester stroked the ball back. Flustered, Charles sprayed shots that landed outside the court.

Ahead four games to love, Lester served at game point. A bright sun rose over the tall oak trees that lined the court, blinding him. Three double faults later, he tossed the balls to Charles. "Four to one," he called out. Charles began to lob returns, and Lester lost the moon balls in the sun. Perspiration dripped onto his thick glasses.

He began to mis-hit serves and Charles' returns, and the strong sun made him boil. Why had he hurried to get out of the Cadillac, forgetting the towel Minnie had given him? Why hadn't he insisted that they change sides on odd number games after he had won the first game? He wiped the sweat from his burning eyes with the back of his hand.

It was four games to four when Lester hit a short ball. Charles scampered forward, just getting his racquet under the ball before a second bounce. Lester lobbed the ball over Charles' head, and he could see a puff of white chalk as it hit the Har Tru.

"Just out," Charles barked.

"Are you kidding me?"

"No. I'm not kidding. The ball was out."

Lester advanced toward the net. "It was in. Look at the ball. It's got white on it from the lime. That's proof."

Charles folded his arms. "It's my call."

Lester glanced at Mitch, who regarded them in silence.

Tennis was his game—it was all he had now that baseball was over. He wanted to show Charles Hart Underwood that he was the better player, and make his mother proud. This kid wasn't one of the Catlicks, those sweaty garlicky boys with zits as big as nickels on their faces. Charles went to Lawrenceville Prep, where they probably didn't even know about the boy whose father had been killed.

Lester slammed a serve into the net. Two double faults later, it was five games to four in Charles' favor.

Lester slammed his racquet on the court—the set was over.

At the net, Charles sneered at Lester. "Choker."

"Cheater," Lester snapped.

Dorothy Scudder Underwood put her hand on Lester's shoulder. "I saw what Charles did," she said, and then said something to Mitch that Lester couldn't hear, before retrieving his racquet and handing it to him.

"Charles, apologize to Lester," she said, shooting her son a look.

The boy said nothing.

On the drive back, Lester curled up in the back seat, as far from Charles as he could get, and covered his eyes with his towel.

As soon as he opened the screen door, Minnie was there. "How did it go?"

"I never want to play that boy again. He's a liar!" Lester yelled as he stomped up the steps to his bedroom.

As he shut his bedroom door, he heard her mutter, "Those kind will do anything to win."

4
Columbus Park

After Julius died, nothing changed, and everything changed. Lester attended Trenton High every day, just as before, and except for Carol, no one said anything about the murder. He saw her in the hallways or in the cafeteria, but he was too shy to walk right up to her. She was part of a crowd of studious, dark-haired girls who played clarinet or violin in the school orchestra.

One day during lunch in the cafeteria she smiled at him, and he went over and stood next to her, too nervous to actually sit down.

"I see you got your glasses fixed," Carol said.

"Oh, these? Well, actually, I got new ones."

She nodded. "Me too. I couldn't see the board."

He was surprised that she was wearing thick glasses—she hadn't been wearing them at camp. But camp seemed as if it had happened in another lifetime, a time when he had had a routine—working in the store—and a purpose: becoming a major league player. "I'm on the tennis team—I guess you knew that," he said nervously. "You're the student manager?"

"Yeah." Carol took a bite of her meatloaf and asked Lester to sit down. When he did, she pushed her tray aside and leaned her elbows on the table.

Just seeing her name printed on the roster as the manager

had lifted his spirits—for weeks now. "The game coming up, with Lawrenceville Prep. I have to play this princeling—"

"Charles Hart Underwood—"

"—That's the one." He scooted nearer to her and lowered his voice. "See, I already played him, over at Green Meadows—"

"—You played over there?"

"My ma, she was crazy for me to go. I would sooner have drowned myself in the bathtub."

She scowled at him and he nodded, closing his eyes. "Sorry, I forgot. Inappropriate." He opened his eyes and glanced up at her. "This place, you would not believe. A manor house with big pillars, and a *lawn*. I swear, I saw a sycamore that was probably there before the Mayflower." He stopped and shook his head in wonder. "It was like some kind of purgatorial netherworld where . . . every serve, every volley I made, it was just a little bit off. I think God was angry that day, probably angry 'cause a Jew was on the courts."

Carol folded her hands and smiled. "Lester, you can beat Charles."

"I know, I know, but that pissant cheats."

"But he won't be able to—the referees and all. They'll keep things honest." She leaned toward him and her long dark hair swung forward. "Tell you what. I'll keep my eye out during your match—so we can rat him out if he pulls any fast moves."

Lester was emboldened by the way she smiled at him. "I'm a sports reporter for the Spectator now. At one of the games, Amos Sullivan—he's the sports reporter for The Trentonian—he said he'd pay me five bucks a story if I cover the suburban games."

Carol leaned toward him. "I thought I saw you in Mr. Jackson's office working on the paper."

He inhaled the scent of her hair, and resisted the urge to bury his face in her nape among the fragrant strands. "I saw that you made band," he whispered.

She nodded. "I'm second clarinet. Naima, she's first chair." She took a deep breath. "She's *really* good." She cocked her head toward the table near the wall. "She's sitting over there—with the other Negroes." She stopped and laughed nervously. "Only I guess we're supposed to say 'blacks' now—that's what Naima says."

"So you're playing by the rules." He looked over at the table of blacks and then glanced away. Naima had shown no signs that she recognized him, and she had not spoken to him since the day at Sunrise Lake.

Carol glanced over her shoulder and then lowered her voice. "We're sort of friends now," she said, and then laughed. "Well, she's really popular, and I'm not in her crowd, but we really hit it off in band." She leaned toward him. "My father, he would *kill* me."

"Oh, you mean, if he knew . . ."

"Yep. He would have a conniption fit. Or maybe a heart attack," she said, giggling. "But I don't see what's so wrong with it."

Lester could think of a lot of reasons why Dino Cala would disapprove, especially since the race riots had practically destroyed downtown Trenton, and since the Negroes were becoming more militant. Now that Minnie had moved them to the Hermitage, Lester wasn't at all sure where he belonged anymore. There were no *shuls*, only churches. The blacks jumped up and down when they prayed—he knew that much. He'd seen the ladies in their outlandish hats and the men in their brightly colored sport coats congregating outside Mt. Cavalry Baptist on Sundays.

For the first time in his life, Lester had stopped observing the Sabbath. Minnie didn't know, of course, but now on a given Saturday he might head over to Columbus Park, where he could find a bunch of other sophomore guys from Trenton High. Since Minnie had sold the store to the Haveson brothers, Lester was at loose ends every afternoon. Columbus Park had turned out to be the perfect place, in that he could be idle there, or he could just linger at the edges of the group.

The gatherings at the park had taken on an almost sacred tenor ever since the riots. The blacks' looting and burning of downtown Trenton had changed the city, and none of the Columbus Park boys had any idea how to match that kind of destructive power. Hot-wiring cars, running away from home, or filching a paperback from Bob's corner store—this was now quite literally child's play. Even the seniors, who sat in the dirt smoking cigarettes and drinking sodas from Porfirio's, seemed chastened. Their games were Poker, Catch-Five and Gin, and the piles of pennies and nickels tossed into the dirt grew ever larger—nobody wanted to take the pot.

The kingpin of the park was Santo—Giovanni Bassetti, the boy who had beat him up on his very first day of school, the boy Minnie had made him apologize to. Lester knew him and all his cronies because they had homeroom together, and he heard their stories.

After his conversation with Carol at school, Lester walked through the park—it was a crisp fall day and he was wearing a new jacket. Santo was there as usual, regaling a group of boys about just what exactly a man had to endure if he picked up the clap. Later Lester had gone home and looked up what it was—gonorrhea—but at the moment he knew only that this information was crucial to improving his reputation at Trenton High. So he stopped and stood at the outer edge of the circle.

"They stick a probe up inside your johnson," Santo was saying, with a grin.

Tony Martini, who was known as The Wanderer, and who had run away from home more times than even he could count, snickered. "You're payin' for it, that's your problem."

Joey Salmastrelli, who was called Giggles, on account of he never smiled, rolled his eyes. "Now you know he would never have to go to those kind of extremes—he's got Angela, and Maria." He turned to Santo and smiled broadly. "And aren't you boffing that girl Naima?"

The boys hooted loudly.

"Whoa!" Santo said, holding up hands. "Are you suggesting I got a taste for *African* pussy?"

It was the second time that day that Lester had heard her name—Naima—and he began to envy her a little. Nobody talked about him that way, nobody would ever mistake him for popular.

"That girl with the red-headed Afro," he said, almost to himself.

Santo stopped and looked over the heads of the other boys. "Maybe *you're* the one who's takin' a walk on the wild side," he said to Lester.

Lester shrugged. "I should be so lucky."

Santo snorted and some of the other kids broke up laughing. That emboldened him and he stepped over to Santo. "You remember me? I'm 'Hey Joo.' You beat me up in kindergarten."

Santo smiled and clapped him on the shoulder. "Hey Joo! Of course I remember. The skinny kid with the glasses. How you been?"

"Decent," Lester said. "Excellent."

"They call me Santo Bassoni. On account of I got these big ears, like a basset hound, and I'm a hound dog for pussy, see?" He brushed his dark hair back to reveal a floppy earlobe.

Lester nodded, and the other boys stood there, silently staring at him. He knew what was coming, and he braced himself.

"Of course you do. You see these big ears. And you got big ears, too, doncha? Sittin' there in homeroom every day. Bet you know a lot."

"I know the neighborhood," Lester said. "Gold's Kosher Cuts—I been working there since I was six years old."

And just like that it was as if he had drawn a dark cloak around him—just the mention of the store meant they were all thinking of Julius, and how he had been killed right by the cash register.

Santo was the first to recover. "Right," he said. "You know Jewtown like nobody else."

"Yep. And I know also that you work at Louie's."

"Very observant."

"On account of it's in Jewtown. And my dad—well, he . . . ."

Tony Martini looked over his shoulder at Lester. "We was in the streets during the riots, trying to keep the blacks from destroyin' Jewtown, and every other part of this town. Where were you—pussy!"

Lester shrugged and turned his palms up, as if to say, *What do want from me?* It was exactly what Julius would have done. "My pop—I gotta help him at the store." He hesitated. "Or, I did."

He trailed off and stared up at the others. Ever since what he and Minnie had been calling "the accident," he sometimes found himself choked up, unable to go on, and he had no control of when this feeling would overtake him.

Santo leaned down and put a big arm around Lester's shoulder, the thick leather of his jacket enveloping Lester's thin windbreaker. "Tell you what. You're gonna come over to Louie's and start working with me."

"I am?" Lester gulped, and then wisely said no more because he couldn't trust his voice.

"Sure. We got some guys over there just don't know how to pick up the slack. You follow me?" He stepped back and regarded Lester. "I seen you in there, in Gold's, how you was always sweeping. Well, we got a need for somebody knows how to push a broom."

Lester hesitated. It would mean he'd be back in Jewtown—but he couldn't tell if Santo was razzing him, or if he was serious. Besides, working at Louie's might not be such a good idea.

"Walk with me," Santo said, and they began to move toward the north side of the park, leaving the other boys behind. "Now I don't imagine that what you need is simple cash. Am I right?"

Lester quite liked the idea of some cash, but he decided it would be best to shake his head, and then nod.

"What you need, my friend, is a distraction. And I'm gonna bet that you have certain skills we could use."

Lester wasn't sure what Santo meant, so he nodded again.

"Your pops, he had something going under the table, am I right? Impossible that some of that didn't rub off on you. Am I right? So this job I am speaking of, it includes some collection."

Lester smiled to himself. So Santo knew about the Picks at the store and he was offering Lester a chance to stay in business. At Gold's it had been playing the numbers, women coming in with nickels and dimes. "That's an offer I can accept."

Santo grinned at Lester. "You see, I got all kinds of income from my business. Me and my cousin, Anthony, we're artists in the automotive realm, shall we say. I specialize in Chevys and Buicks—10 seconds it takes to cross the wires, and then I rent them out for a buck an hour to any boys in the Burg who want a joy ride. And in my business, there are, shall we say, risks. When things heat up, Uncle Louie steps in, for me and Anthony. And in exchange I sweep the floors and deliver the winnings." He clapped Lester on the shoulder. "Lester Gold, you are one lucky Jew. That's what I hear over at Louie's."

"Lucky? Louie's?" Lester had never thought that they were talking about him over at the barbershop.

"Everybody knows that the blacks did all the damage. Spooks stole more stuff in one night than I ever got in my whole career," Santo groused.

"Yeah, but they recovered a lot of it." He looked over at Santo but he looked away. His response had been far too practical, but it was too late to take it back.

"Listen," Santo said, keeping pace with him. "Once we had the riots and people was everywhere, it was just . . . mayhem. And things ain't been right since. I mean, it could have been anybody who shot him, right?" He stopped and stared intently at Lester. "But it wasn't . . . it wasn't just anybody."

Lester waited. He wouldn't say it wasn't and he wouldn't say it was. Officer Randolph from the Trenton police had interviewed him. Minnie had asked him a hundred times, she had nudged him in the way only she could. *It's your mitzvah, Lester*, she told him. *You have to say.*

"Great minds think alike, am I right?" Santo asked.

Lester nodded.

"And even if your mind ain't so great, it don't take genius to figure—it was a Negro. They got this pent-up anger, right? And so they start tossin' bricks, lootin' every store in town. They lost their respect for law and order. And it spooked all the shop owners. Naturally. But shooting a hard-working man like your father, now that is a crime that cannot go unpunished. For that, for shooting a man in the back, the perpetrator of such a crime, is going to have to pay."

Lester stopped and then sank down on a park bench. Santo was right, of course. Somebody had to pay. He couldn't remember a time when Yussel wasn't in the butcher shop. Soaking, slicing, prepping in the back room, and then managing the front counter, kibbitzing with the customers. He'd peer over his wire-rim glasses and say to Mrs. Shimonsky or Mrs. Meyer, "for you, only the best."

"I got an idea who it was. A Negro *gentleman*," Santo said, suppressing a smirk. "Some cat who plays the bongos. Can't say he's on his way to Carnegie Hall anytime soon. But he's got a thriving business over there at Uhuru."

"That furniture shop on Spring Street?"

"Used to be. Now it's a front, right? He's running a head shop, and they're smoking hash in the back, but he sells guitars and instruments out of the front."

"How come you know so much about this guy?"

"I got ears, that's how. Over at Louie's, the word is he's one of them organizers, see what I mean. He's an unsavory character. A black radical." Santo leaned down. "My uncle, he said the dude was usin' 'H.' Probably one of them Commie pinkos." Santo muscled in and put a big arm around Lester's shoulder. "You was there when it went down. So I heard."

Lester nodded sheepishly. "I was sweeping up."

Santo shook him gently until Lester looked up. "They shot him in the back," he said grimly, and gripped Lester's shoulder a little tighter.

Lester pulled away, his head down, and stood up. "I didn't see."

"Is that what you told the cops?"

Lester stood there, frozen. Officer Randolph had been mild in his questioning, maybe even a bit distracted. He had gently asked and Lester had gently demurred. "I said that I heard a shot." He looked up and Santo gave him a grave nod. "And . . . he fell . . . and I went over to him."

"So you didn't see nothin'."

"I saw . . . ." He shook his head and began to walk away, toward the north side of the park.

Santo followed him, still asking questions. "You say anything else?"

Lester turned around and then shook his head.

"So what did the cop say?"

Lester forced the image out of his mind: a helpless child seated in a wooden chair as the officers bustled around him. He cleared his throat and spoke up. "Usual cop stuff, you know." He glanced over at Santo, and he seemed genuinely interested, like he cared. "I guess, well, it was weird, but he told me that he knew how I felt, and that your mind, it can't really cope with bad news when it comes all of a sudden like that, and so your mind tells you it's a mistake, or maybe it just says it's a story that's not really true."

"You believe that?"

Lester shrugged. "Maybe." He forced himself to make eye contact with Santo. "Yeah, I guess so. I keep waiting for it to be true, but so far it still seems like a mistake."

5
Louie's

Lester started going to Louie's every day after school, just as he had always done at Gold's. Louie, in his white tunic, cut hair and lathered cheeks all day long. It was always a cut and a shave at Louie's, and all the while Louie kibitzed about the Yankees, the Giants, the Phillies, or a race at Monmouth or Yonkers. As Lester swept the floors and did general cleaning, Louie would bark, "Gold, you got a tip for today?" and Lester would give his prediction.

"The Yanks have lost three in a row. No way they'll lose four." Or, "The Phillies are on a streak."

Between April 11, when the season began, and the 23rd, when his father had been killed, Lester had called 85 percent of the picks. He had dropped everything—Goldfinger's Picks, his school work—after the murder, but now he was getting back up to speed with his tote sheet.

After a customer won a bet, he would show his appreciation with a fiver or sometimes even a ten-spot. The place was small, but Lester felt right at home there, and he liked the privacy—the windows were covered with big movie posters, so you had to come inside if you wanted to know what kind of action was going on. Lester's favorite poster was the one for *Goldfinger*—his nickname—with a lady painted gold in the background and Sean Connery looming in the foreground.

One day he found himself staring at another poster—one with *Bonnie & Clyde* in bold stylized red letters and Warren Beatty and Faye Dunaway laughing behind a windshield shattered by bullet holes. The next day that poster had been taken down and replaced with one he was a lot more comfortable with: *The Dirty Dozen*—Lee Marvin charging ahead with serious firepower and a slogan that read "Turn Them Loose on the Nazis!"

In the late afternoons, Lester and Santo would walk home together, but Santo began to insist that they walk the half-mile or so to the Battle Monument neighborhood. The main street was mostly black businesses now—the whites were moving out—and they proceeded slowly, checking out the used furniture stores, the pawn shops, the Salvation Army. It didn't take Lester long to figure out that Santo lingered the longest outside Uhuru—the music shop. "I got no reason to go in there," Lester said.

"You do if you want to finger him."

"Who? You never even said who it was."

"Name is Salim. Salim Johnson."

"He's not going to admit it," Lester said, rolling his eyes.

"No, but we go in artful like—we get him talking. Get face to face with him and you'll know for sure."

"What you got against him?"

"Hey, it ain't me—you're the one who saw what you saw."

And so Lester caved—he agreed to Santo's plan to go by Uhuru at night and spy on Salim. "He'll never know we're there," Santo insisted.

Santo had cased the back alley where Salim often relaxed in the evenings with his friends. On a chilly Wednesday, a school night, when Lester was supposed to be doing homework under Minnie's watchful eye, he and Santo crept into the alley and crouched behind a fence. Santo wore his usual black turtleneck and black leather jacket, but Lester owned only one article of black clothing: a Batman sweatshirt, which he had turned inside out, so the Batman figure was on the inside, next to his chest. He didn't want Santo to think he was still interested in cartoon figures.

Three men were seated in lawn chairs on a concrete patio, clustered around what looked like a big clay pot, in which they had a campfire going.

"He's the one in the caftan," Santo whispered, pressing his face into a gap between the slats.

"That's called a dashiki," Lester hissed. "Naima wears one—it's some kind of Africa thing." He edged closer to the fence and peered through. "He's wearing a yarmulke!?" he said, turning to Santo in disbelief.

"It's called a skullcap, dumbshit. The Black Muslims wear it."

"What's a Muslim?"

"Shut up," Santo said. "Now you focus on the dude in the caftan and you see if that isn't the one."

It was nearly dark, but Lester actually had a pretty good view of Salim, given that he was sitting next to the fire. Of the three, he was the only one with a big Afro, and he was wearing flat brown leather sandals. "Cyril, he's out on bail," he was saying.

One of the other men nodded. He had on a jeans and brown Beatle boots. "Don't do you no good to be above the Mason-Dixon line—Chicago, Detroit, it's all the same."

"It's worse in D.C. and Newark. Just a more efficient form of lynching," a third man said. He was tall and skinny and had a Fu Manchu moustache. "Just shoot you in the back."

"I heard Bobby moved out to San Francisco, joined an ashram," Salim said.

"Hey, if I had a little more scratch, I'd head out there, make the scene," Beatle Boots added. "What's a brother to do stuck here in Trenton?"

"Hell, my old lady is here, I ain't leavin' unless she's down with it." Fu Manchu reached toward Salim. "Give a brother a hit."

Salim got up and handed Fu Manchu a pipe. Lester noted that he was a small man, probably not much taller than he was himself, and his skin wasn't dark—it was a light brown.

Salim resumed his seat. "These dumbasses think the future is gonna be some kind of happy rainbow. I got some news for the citizens of the United States of Give it Up for the White Man: the future is coming and it's called One Nation, Under Black. To the Republic of Free Blacks, I pledge a musical toot, cause I'm a free man, once and for all."

"Hallelujah! Forty acres and a mule," Beatle Boots said with a chuckle.

"Look away, look away, Dixieland." Salim's voice had gotten heavier and richer as he spoke, and his comment ended in a rumbling laugh. He looked around at the other two and then continued. "The honkys took the golf courses, the plantations, and every patch of green, and said to the colored man, darkie, how come you ain't satisfied with them bars on your windows, them cesspools and slums, them privies and prisons? You ingrates, you better straighten up and fly right or you're goin' down to Parchman Farms!" Salim shook his head. "You won't catch my ass in no Mississippi."

Beatle Boots stood up. "My cousin Clive was down there. A regular plantation. And I'll tell you, he got himself out right-quick. Said they got men workin' on *chain gangs*—for real." He took a few steps toward the fire and extended his hands, warming them. "What's whitey more afraid of than anything else? *Mis-ceg-e-nay-shun*, that's what. Yet these ofay overseers done raped our women—took 'em whenever they wanted, you hear?" He moved over to the fire and stood there chucking some twigs into the clay pot. "Here's what it comes down to: just by breathing oxygen, we scare the shit outta these crackers. And that's the whole ball of wax right there: straight up, if that ain't power, I don't know what is."

Lester's knees were aching and he was freezing. He got up and walked back toward the street, and after a moment, Santo followed.

"So? Was it him?"

Lester shrugged. "I can't say. Too dark."

"Ha!" Santo said, "the darkie was too dark."

Lester shook his head. "Not *him*, the scene—how can I tell anything when he's forty feet away?"

Santo jammed his hands in his pockets. "You remember what Randolph told you about remembering? I read this article a while back by some cat who says we're all in a state of future shock. He says it's due to something called 'information overload.' And this is what I'm saying here: I got information overload about how the whites are all a bunch of racists, all the harm we're doing to the black man. Blah blah blah. They's lazy Mandingos and they want us to do all the work for them."

"Was that grass they were smoking?"

Santo ignored his question. "You don't see them piling into boats or marching down to Mexico, do you? Why? Cause this is the freeest country in the world and they got it good here. Plenty of 'em don't work at all, they just get a handout. Hey, I sleep good at night. They got as much right as me to make it. If they're stuck in the ghettoes, it's cause they didn't have the initiative to get out."

Lester walked a little faster. "I gotta get home before my ma goes on the warpath. You going—"

"—Carol's."

Lester headed toward the bus stop. He knew Santo had been spending nights sneaking out with Carol Cala, and he was afraid to get too deep into a conversation for fear that he'd have to admit he wasn't getting any action.

"Hey," Santo called after him. "She said for you to come over to her house on Thursday night to study for the English midterm."

Lester turned around and came back toward Santo. "Serious?"

"That's what she said."

"*Me*? She wants to study with me?" Lester considered that maybe his overtures at Whispering Pines had paid off after all.

Santo punched Lester in the arm. "Just go over there, okay? She's, like, behind, right? She was out sick for all of eighth grade. She says you're the smartest kid in English. I think she wants help figuring it out, whatever it is."

Lester could hardly wait for Thursday evening. He had seen Carol at school and she had confirmed that he was invited over to her place to study. He showed up at the appointed hour in a blue button-down with khakis and penny loafers. Dino greeted him at the door and directed him to go down to the rec room—a small wood-paneled space with a wet bar at the back. Carol was seated on a brown plaid couch, her books spread out on the floor. Lester had brought his textbook and he got right to work, reviewing the chapter and the study questions.

"So Cicero was the greatest orator in Rome," he said, pushing his textbook aside. "All right, I'm impressed. Statesman, lawyer, inspired the founding fathers of the republic. Blah blah blah. Some guys just don't know when to quit." He looked up and Carol was regarding him with a bemused smile. "Hey, you gotta like his style. His last words: 'There is nothing proper about what you are doing, soldier, but do try to kill me properly.'

Carol giggled. She was wearing a pair of dungarees and a light blue shirt tied at her waist. "I'm stuck on Fulvia."

Lester nodded. "The tongue thing?"

"Yeah. I mean, there's his head up there and she grabs it and rips out the tongue."

"Leave it to a girl to use a hairpin."

She shrugged. "Probably all she had—she used the only weapon available to her. I get it, though—I mean, he was the master rhetorician, the one with the silver tongue. And he plotted against her husband." She looked over at him and sighed. "Santo's not even studying for the midterm."

Lester leaned back against the couch and started to relax a bit. "And that's why he's failing English."

"And you're getting an A."

He shrugged. "He's a natural-born businessman and I'm more the intellectual type."

Carol let her textbook slide off her lap and onto the floor. "Truth is, I hammered my Dad trying to convince him to let Santo be my study partner, but I got nowhere."

"Right," he said slowly. "But he was fine with me being your partner."

She gave him a mysterious half-smile. "My Dad says he trusts you."

"You mean, not to make a move?" He looked over at her, but she was staring hard at her notebook. "I see, so Santo's Mick Jagger, and I'm Whistler's Mother or something."

She looked at him, puzzled. "You're weird, Lester."

He stood up and began to pace. "I got moves. Dino thinks I'm just a scaredy cat who'd never try anything with his daughter."

Carol looked up, and then flipped her hair back. "So. He's right."

He came and stood over her. "Okay, now my reputation's on the line. I've been with plenty of girls, you know."

She folded her hands and gave him a patient stare. "I thought you liked Naima."

"I do." He started pacing again. "I mean, did she tell you that?"

"No."

He came and stood over her, waiting.

"I *said* no."

"I don't believe you."

"She never said anything."

"Even about camp? She never said that I—"

"—look," she said, sounding exasperated. "When my Dad said, 'study with Lester,' I said 'fine.'"

"Because . . . you think I'm such a brain?"

Her smile was contained, but he noted that it was ever so slightly flirtatious. He went over and sat next to her on the couch. She stared intently at her textbook, but she didn't move away when he put his hand on her arm.

"I think it's time to shake up ol' Dino's world a bit."

She turned her face to him and he kissed her. He felt a great placid weight lifting and then he was straddling her, his hands in her hair. Inwardly he braced himself for the moment when she pushed him away, but it never came. He couldn't read her—she sat there primly, she was completely contained. She did nothing to encourage him but neither did she pull away. He reared back, staring into her eyes—brown eyes whose velvety depth he had imagined, but which now seemed flat and dark as buttons.

"What?" he said.

"You," she said. "Why did you—?" She tugged on the hem of her blouse, and then ran her fingers through her long hair.

"I didn't."

"My mom said you know who . . . ."

She trailed off, and Lester grimaced, shaking his head. He waited a moment, but he knew it was over. Perhaps there had been an opportunity, but he wasn't sure.

"Thanks for coming over," she said primly. "I've got a B-minus average, and I really want to get it up to a solid B."

The next day Lester showed up at the barbershop in an apple green shirt with a Nehru collar, jeans the color of sand, and a pair of Jesus sandals.

When Santo saw him, he said, "Lester, you're one funky heeb."

"I'm expressing my inner hippie. I needed some new threads."

Santo took a few styling steps toward him, flipped out his palm and said, "Lay it on me."

"Peace," Lester said, slapping his palm. "Shalom. After last week at Uhuru, I realize there's a whole new world out there."

"You was inspired by the jigaboos? Maybe you should head out to San Fran and live in an ashram. I myself, I think I'll start a commune."

"I'm not going anywhere they don't have pastrami," Lester said, taking a seat in one of the barber chairs.

Santo selected one of the combs from the beaker of blue liquid and began to slick back his hair. "Hell, who am I kidding? My old man falls asleep on the can with Readers Digest."

Lester continued to spin the chair around. "My Uncle Hiram, he's still so afraid of The Bomb he's spent the past seven years in an underground shelter with packets of Lipton Soup and a stack of *Exponents*. I think he comes out to go to synagogue Fridays, but only if it's a good day."

"My sister, she's going with a Mexican."

"Wow. How'd that happen?"

"Some guy from her job."

"They got Mexicans on her job?"

"Hell if I know, maybe he cleans the toilets. Anyway, I told her, she gets herself pregnant, she's dead to me. I ain't gonna have no spic for a niece or nephew." Santo walked over and put the comb back in the beaker. "You know, Anthony—he enlisted."

"No shit?"

"Yup. And so . . . we got a job here . . . that you might be asked to do when the time comes."

"Legal or illegal?"

Santo rolled his eyes. "Yeah, dumbass, what we need is for you to tie the shoelaces of the little boys when they sit up in the barber chair get their hair cut." He stalked over to the front window, picked up a copy of *Life* magazine and began to thumb through it. After a minute he glanced up at Lester. "You deliver the envelopes, see? You and me."

Lester looked up to see that Officer Randolph was standing in the doorway.

"Hiya," he said. "Can you come outside a minute?"

Lester looked over at Santo, who shrugged. He followed the officer outside and they stood in the shade of a maple at the edge of the sidewalk.

"Your friend says you might have recovered your memory."

"Shit," Lester said. "He told you that?"

"Said you two paid a visit over to Uhuru."

"That fink." He could see Santo hiding behind Sean Connery, peeking out from behind his silhouette. Santo stuck his head out the door and yelled, "He won't say on account of he's chicken."

"I'm not!" Lester plopped down on the edge of a planter and put his elbows on his knees.

Officer Randolph smiled indulgently at him, and nodded, as if to say, *I know you're trying your best to remember*. He wore his full uniform with his badge and gun and his cap still on, and he sat down on the sidewalk, cross-legged, smiling up at Lester. "We got plenty of time."

"I don't know."

Officer Randolph nodded.

"He had an Orioles cap."

"What color?"

"Yellow. It's the Orioles."

"You told us that already. So what else?"

"Nothing else."

"You saw the Orioles cap but nothing more," he said, and then he gave Lester a stern look. "Lester, you don't have to be afraid of this individual. We do a very good job on the protection front, you know."

"I went over there, didn't I? I mean, that's what Santo said."

Officer Randolph sighed. "I know you want to help us catch this guy."

Lester nodded wearily. "My *mitzvah.*"

Santo stormed out the door, grabbed Lester by the shirt and pulled him to his feet. "Just say, you dumbshit."

Lester yanked himself away. "I don't know!" he shouted. "Okay???"

Santo turned to Officer Randolph. "He knows."

Officer Randolph lurched to his feet, his belt and shoes creaking from the strain. "Lester, you'll be doing us a favor. And once we've got him, he can't do any harm to you. He'll be locked up."

Lester turned to see Minnie come hustling down the street in a pair of Yussel's old slippers. She had obviously left in a rush: she had a kerchief over her hair and a slash of red lipstick on her mouth.

Lester turned to Santo in disbelief and Santo gave him a sheepish grin. "I called her from inside."

"Are you *crazy*?"

Minnie came over and shook Officer Randolph's hand. She looked up at Santo—she was barely taller than his belt buckle—and patted his beefy arm. "You're a good boy." Then she turned on Lester, her eyes narrowing to a tight squint. "You need to tell the truth."

Lester took a few steps away from her and then turned back. "This is insane."

Officer Randolph spoke slowly, as if he might defuse the situation. "Now in cases like these when your ability to recall . . . is *fuzzy*, shall we say. A little something to jog it can't hurt."

"What he needs is some truth serum," Minnie barked.

Lester had read about truth serum, and he knew that spies sometimes used it, people like Goldfinger.

"I got a case of Manischewitz leftover from the shiva," Minnie said with a sly grin.

The thought of Minnie force-feeding him Manischewitz was so preposterous that Lester began to giggle and the giggle blossomed into a yelping laugh and then he wasn't sure if he was laughing at her or himself. He turned to her, frowning. "He had an Orioles cap, okay? That's what I saw."

"You saw the cap, so how come you didn't see the whole person?" she said, cuffing him lightly. She turned to Officer Randolph. "He's going to realize that he saw a black man, this Salome or whatever he's called."

"*Salim*," Lester said angrily.

Officer Randolph nodded and took out his notepad to scribble a few words. "Now don't you worry, Lester. We've had our eye on this fellow. You have no reason to feel sorry for him. This is a criminal element and we'll all be safer once he's locked up."

Lester sank back onto the planter and buried his face in his hands.

6
Uhuru

Less than twenty-four hours later Lester and Santo stepped gingerly into the foyer at Uhuru. As they opened the door, a bell tinkled and a thick curlicue of smoke encircled them.

"Incense," Santo whispered, nodding toward six thin brown sticks smoldering in a long wooden tray.

The place was tiny and it was jammed with glass cases filled with big silver and gold water pipes and ornate jewelry. A huge red, black and green map of Africa filled the entryway. One wall was plastered with album covers: Peter Paul and Mary, Stevie Wonder, The Grateful Dead, Roland Kirk, John Coltrane, Herbie Hancock, Nat King Cole.

Lester took a few bold steps into the store. He was here to prove to Santo that he wasn't afraid. A moment later Salim approached them and Santo jabbed Lester, hissing, "Just follow my lead." When Salim was standing there, Santo pointed to a poster of Martin Luther King at the Lincoln Memorial and said somberly, "He was a great man."

Salim took a step back and frowned. "Don't tell me. You boys here to *apologize* for slaying Martin Luther King?"

"My ma's got a recording of the 'I Have a Dream' speech," Lester added eagerly.

Salim crossed his arms, and the long fringes on his jacket swung wildly. "I suppose you boys are a couple of freedom riders, is that right?" He turned to Lester. "Tell me, what's *your* dream, young man?

Lester gave him a sheepish smile. "I've been thinking about the law."

"Oh, the law. Of course. You leisure-class whiteys gonna grow up to be leisure-class whiteys. You gonna defend the rights of the oh-pressed?? No, you ain't. You're gonna line your pockets! Cause the system, all them beautifully oiled cogs and wheels, they turnin' just for you. Ain't that right?"

Santo stepped forward. "Hey, my friend, we just come over to see about—"

Salim assumed an exaggerated pose, his hands on his hips. "My *friend*, you callin' me *friend*? Really, have we met? Scuse me cause I don't remember. You a *friend* to the black man?"

"Hey, like my pops says, it takes all kinds. Am I right?" Santo countered.

Salim narrowed his eyes. "All kinds a what?"

Lester had expected that up close Salim would be blue-black, what Santo called a "Mandigo," but he had light skin and eyes and a sprinkling of freckles on his nose.

"Let me tell you about a most honorable brother, man by the name of Stokely Carmichael. Now what do you think he said about the assassination of Dr. King? He said it was the state's war against *us*. An eye for an eye."

Salim had a crazy jitterbug energy and he bounced up on his toes while he talked. "You boys listen to your daddies? You get an allowance?"

"Hell no," Santo replied, "I got my own income."

"You work over there at the hamburger stand?" Salim propped one hand on his chin, an exaggerated gesture, and Lester could see that his fingernails were ridged and yellowed from nicotine.

"Nah," Santo said, "I'm a part of the underground economy."

"What're you, Christian?"

"Catholic."

"So you got your pope," Salim said, smiling. "Now lemme ask you, suppose he came down off his throne and he says to you, if you a true believer, young man, you're gonna have to suck my dick."

Santo took a step back, opened his mouth, but then just stood there. Lester had never before seen him lose his cool, but it was clear that he was undone by Salim's comment.

Salim laughed. "You rattled now, ain't you? See, that's my point. Here's the best advice you boys will ever receive. You got to stand up for what you believe in." He shook a finger at Santo. "If you believe it, then get on in there to Mass and get down on your knees, and you follow everything Pope Paul says, even if it's way out there. You dig?"

He pointed to a poster behind the cash register—George Foreman and Muhammad Ali facing off against a green map of Africa superimposed on a bright yellow background. *The Rumble in the Jungle.* "Now you take Muhammad Ali. Cassius Clay. He refused to be inducted into the Army, refused to go kill our brothers in Vietnam. And what did Uncle Sam do? He stripped him of his heavyweight title—now ain't that a lowdown thing to do to a brother? Just following his conscience and look how they do him." He took a few steps across the room and leaned against one of the glass cases. "You take Emmett Till's mama, she had an open casket for her boy—so all of America could see what the white racists do to any black man they perceive as a threat—and Emmett, he wasn't no man, he was a boy, right about your age. You know how many black men down south been strung up from trees?"

He moved toward them, coming uncomfortably close, and Lester could see that Salim's eyes were gold, like a cat's. "Now, you a Jew, am I right?" he asked, but he didn't wait for Lester to reply. "The Nazis, they exterminated the Jews. Why? Because they did not see them as human, they did not confer on them any humanity. And we got the same situation right here in the U S of A. The white oh-pressors want to deny the black man his humanity. And this is a situation that cannot stand, this is a situation for which all right-thinking persons will rise up and bring justice *by any means necessary.*"

When he said the last part, he gave them a fierce glare, and Lester began to wonder if maybe they shouldn't leave.

Salim nodded at Santo. "If you boys is so fired up about Martin, I suggest you go on over to the memorial service for the brother that got killed by the fuzz the other night—that would be one Vernon Josephs. And what do you think he did to get hisself shot? Not a damn thing! Because you know they shot him in the back. Poor Negro was runnin' for his life, runnin' from the racist pigs who cut him down, like a dog in the street. Just because he walked into Columbus Park, whitey's turf."

When Santo glanced over at him, Lester imagined that they shared a moment of guilt—Columbus Park, their turf.

Salim ducked behind the counter and Lester heard him say, "I bet you boys could use some reading material." When he stood up again he was holding a battered paperback—and he was wearing the Orioles cap.

Lester gulped and then sat down hard on a big wooden drum with an animal skin stretched over it. It was the same cap—yellow with the black "O," the one the killer had been wearing. Trenton was chock-full of Phillies fans and Yankees fans and they'd found the only Orioles fan?

"Get your candy ass up off there," Salim commanded. "You're gonna warp the drumhead."

Santo stepped toward Lester. "He's anemic. It's his heart."

"Is that yours?" Lester blurted out, staring up at Salim, and pointing to the cap.

Salim took a step back and regarded him suspiciously. "Why—you want it?"

Lester shook his head. He tried to get up but he stumbled and fell to his knees. Salim paused and regarded Lester, and then his demeanor changed. He seemed like he was taking Lester's illness seriously. "I got some carrot juice in the back—that'll fix you right up."

"Juice of carrots?" Santo said. "That'll probably kill him."

But Salim was already out of the room and it was only a few seconds before he reappeared with a glass, which he handed to Lester.

Lester accepted the sticky glass gingerly and peered suspiciously at the orange liquid. "Actually, I feel better."

"How you know if you like it you don't even taste it?" It was a father's question and Lester, a now fatherless boy, responded immediately. He raised the glass to his lips and took a tiny sip. It tasted like soap, orange soap.

"You finish that you're gonna feel like a new man."

Lester took another sip and then he really did start to feel better. He stood up and put the glass on the counter, and then took a deep breath. "Actually, I'm here because I want to buy a gift . . . for a girl."

"Okay, now you're talkin'. You wanna impress this chick. What kinda person is she—quiet, studious? Or more the life of the party type?"

"Uh, she's kind of both, actually."

Salim turned and began to regard the contents of the store as if through new eyes. "Hmmmm, a gift for a young lady."

"Well, she plays clarinet in band at school."

"All right, then, that makes it easy." He went over to a case and selected an item, bringing it back and handing it to Lester.

It was shiny brown hollow tube with holes along the body. Lester held it, surprised at how light it was. He studied the hand-painted pattern of red and green hummingbirds.

"Now that there is called a washint. It's an end-blown wooden flute originally used by the Amhara people in Ethiopia."

Lester turned it over. "This girl is kind of like a hummingbird," he said slowly.

"It's made from the rare African baobab tree."

"How much?"

"How much bread you got?"

"Seventeen dollars."

"You can have that for seventeen."

Santo glared at Lester, and he realized that he had been stupid to tell Salim the truth about how much money he had. "Would it be possible for you to discount your price?"

Salim laughed. "Oh, I get it. You're of the Hebrew persuasion. Gonna Jew me down, are ya?"

Lester smiled. "Like you said, I'm a kid, right? I got a job sweeping floors over at Louie's and it takes me weeks to earn seventeen bucks."

"Okay, for you, I'm gonna give you a special price."

Lester broke into a huge grin. "You sound just like my dad."

"Well, you tell your dad he's a smart man, 'cause you always want the customer to go away satisfied."

"Actually, his dad is deceased," Santo said, narrowing his eyes at Salim.

"Well, I am sorry to hear that," Salim said evenly. He put a hand on Lester's arm. "Tell you what, I'm gonna let you have the flute for seven ninety-five. How 'bout that?"

Lester handed over the money and fled the store. As soon as they turned the corner he and Santo broke into a whooping, full-out run, and they didn't stop until they reached Louie's.

"Shit!" Santo shouted, as they stood panting in front of the store. "He's got the Orioles cap. It's a sure thing now."

Lester leaned against the wall, his hands on his knees. "So what? It doesn't mean that's *the* Orioles cap."

"How many people you seen wearing that cap—huh?"

"So it's not that many. But it's still . . . it's not scientific."

"Fuck science. He practically gave us the noose to hang him with."

"I dunno. He seems okay—he gave me a good price on the flute."

"Puh-leeze. You could get that piece of junk at Kresge's for ninety-nine cents."

"Yeah, I figured."

Santo took off his jacket and dropped it on the bench in front of the store. "How come you buyin' her a gift, anyway?"

Lester shrugged. "I don't even know. I mean, she won't even look my way, and . . ."

Santo shook his head. "I don't think any good can come of it, mixing with the blacks."

Lester giggled. "Thing is, my friend, she's a Jew."

"Serious? But she's got that big Afro and she's always hanging with the Negroes."

"Half and half—that's the beauty of it. She's both."

"Wow. You could take that girl to a Hillel and then to the NAACP." He went over to the entrance, opened the door, and held it for Lester. "You never gonna get to ball her, though. She's too fine."

7
The Statement

The next afternoon, as Lester approached the barbershop, he felt himself tackled from behind. Gravel bit into his skin as he landed hard on his right elbow and shoulder. Was it possible that they were going to kill him too? First Yussel and now his son? But then he caught a whiff of Brylcreem and sensed the heft of the body that had hit him. It was Santo.

Santo scrambled to his feet and Lester lay there, panting.

"Carol says that Dino kicked you out of her basement."

Lester got up and leaned against a dumpster, breathing hard. "No way."

A kernel of righteous anger began to glow inside of him: the satisfaction of knowing he was being falsely accused. Then the wheels began to turn. He could not imagine that Dino had any inkling of what happened in the basement. So Carol must have made up the story about her father kicking him out. But why? It was her cover. She didn't want Santo to know, and she didn't trust herself to spend any more time alone with Lester in her rec room. So that meant she liked him. In spite of himself, Lester began to smile. "My friend, I swear to you on all that is sacred—"

"—the Talmud," Santo muttered.

"—on your nonna's red gravy. I never saw Dino, never heard from him. It ain't true." There was something reassuringly familiar in his claim—a lie by omission. The same sort of omission that was at the center of the murder case. What he didn't say wouldn't hurt anybody.

"Why did she say it then?" Santo demanded.

"You in love with her?"

"What kind of question is that? That girl is gorgeous. And she's willing."

Lester walked over and punched Santo good-naturedly. He held up his right hand. "Look at this, you dago moron. My wrist is *bleeding*." He reached down and brushed off his new jeans. "And this schmutz better come out in the wash or you're gonna have to buy me a new pair."

Santo sighed heavily. "Randolph caught me and Carol at the quarry in my car. And I mean I was *in her,* man." He shook his head. "For a while I was ballin' her in the back room here. Didn't take nothin' to jimmy the lock. But then I think Louie got wise. Showed up one night and I'm facin' a king-sized deadbolt."

"What's that have to do with me—"

"—I told him that I had some, uh, information, about the murder."

"You mean, *me*?"

Santo nodded.

"But I don't," Lester said evenly.

"Doesn't matter. Just need to keep Randolph out of my business is all. And Carol—she needed a cover story."

"Cover story?" Lester bristled at the thought. "You ask Carol about Fulvia."

"Wha—"

"—Not what, *who*. If you ever showed up in English, you'd know she was the wife of Mark Antony." Lester took a few steps toward the back of the alley and then turned back to Santo. "So they nail Cicero's head and hands on the wall in the Forum. And this lady comes and rips out his tongue and stabs it with a hairpin."

"Sounds like she was one crazy bitch."

"Nah. For her, it was the right thing to do."

They headed into the shop and Santo conferred with Louie while Lester watched the front. When he came out of the back, Santo had urgent news. "Guidotti hit big and my uncle says he will be very appreciative if we get the delivery over there by 2:00."

"So?" Lester said. "You be the delivery boy?"

"Pretty big hit," Santo said. "A grand."

"Nice payoff."

Santo's cousin Anthony came into the store. He was slim and wore his hair slicked back. Lester nodded at him and then grabbed a broom and began to sweep.

"You finish up. I'll get the baggage." Santo nodded at Anthony and then moved toward the beaded curtain behind which Louie monitored a bank of telephones. A moment later he emerged and motioned to Lester. "Let's go."

They headed out of the shop, but instead of crossing the street Lester grabbed Santo's arm. "Is it true he volunteered?"

"Anthony? Sure."

"Dumbass," Lester said, shaking his head. "Didn't even wait for his number to come up."

Santo shrugged. "Somebody's gotta serve."

"Shit," Lester said. "Maybe if my number was 1A, then I'd volunteer."

Santo dragged Lester along for a few feet, but then Lester pulled away. "What about the delivery?"

"Delivery can wait. Important business to discuss."

"My friend, let it go, I got no reason—"

"Not that," Santo snapped. "You did me a solid. Carol says she aced the midterm."

Lester put his hands on his hips and scowled at Santo. "Really?

That's what she said?"

Santo shrugged. "Well, she *thinks* so. Like I give a shit, anyway."

"I bet she said I was a great study partner," Lester said, rolling his eyes.

"Yeah, yeah, whatever."

Santo leaned against the dumpster and took what looked like a cigarette out of his shirt pocket—except Lester could tell it was grass.

"This here's our new product. I figured, you know, with me and Carol . . . and you with . . . ." He looked at Lester and raised his eyebrows. "We're both going to need some more cash. You want the snatch, you gotta have some scratch, you dig?" He slid the marijuana cigarette under his nose and inhaled deeply.

Lester leaned against the wall. "Legal or illegal?" Lester asked, smirking. "Thing is, you haven't factored in . . . that I'm not your typical—"

"—You're a classic kike."

"—I'm not—"

"—You're square. That's your problem."

"And since when are you some flower child?"

"All I'm sayin' is, there's a market, and we can tap it." Santo struck a match. "Anthony, he's dealing this shit around town. It's just weed. Won't hurt you."

"The delivery. Louie's going to be pissed."

"Fuck Louie."

Santo fingered the weed and inhaled, closing his eyes. He grinned and held out the joint to Lester.

Lester glanced toward the end of the alley. "Shit, look who's going into the shop."

He hadn't recognized Officer Randolph at first—he was wearing dark slacks and a sport jacket. What was he doing here and why was he out of uniform? He knew it wasn't a bust. Louie's wasn't

Randolph's beat, and besides, the blue shirts that trolled Jewtown cast a blind eye. Louie gave out generous Christmas presents, what he called his "*in*surance." No, it had to be that he was following up on the bullshit line Santo had fed him the other night.

"Jesus," Santo said, tossing the joint. As they headed toward the shop, Santo fumbled in his pocket for some Binaca, sprayed a couple pumps into his mouth, and began to cough.

As they came into the shop, Officer Randolph turned. "I thought I'd find you boys here."

Lester glanced at Santo—he had ratted him out once again.

"Lester," Officer Randolph said. "I've spoken to your mother. She told me you were here. I've got some good news for you."

Lester eyed Santo. "Good news?"

"Cough it up," Santo said, and winked at Lester.

Officer Randolph chuckled. "Just between Lester and me."

"It's time for me to vamoose," Santo said, and disappeared behind the beaded curtain.

Lester thought of the baggage tucked in Santo's pocket, waiting to be delivered to Guidotti. Why hadn't they headed out on that delivery? Officer Randolph would never have known where to find them.

Randolph took a seat in one of the barber chairs and smiled at Lester. "How about coming down to the PD?"

"Good news? I'm not sure I like the sound of that." Lester hadn't smoked any of Santo's marijuana cigarette, but he felt almost as if he had. His heart was racing and he felt giddy. "Let me ask you . . . . I mean, I expect when I see a cop, I expect a uniform."

"I'm sure you do," Officer Randolph said, smiling even harder at Lester. "You boys have been doing some investigating. So have I. We need to talk."

"Can't we just talk here?"

"I had a nice cup of tea with your mother earlier."

"She wasn't there. She has no idea."

"Lester. I understand. You have every right to be afraid, afraid of retaliation. When you testify, that is."

Lester wondered if maybe he should take a seat in one of the chairs, sit down with Officer Randolph, make out like they were having a heart to heart. *I've told you everything*, he imagined himself saying. And the officer would see that in fact he had and would leave him alone.

Officer Randolph crossed his arms and gave Lester a condescending smile. "I know you're not the kind of guy to get someone else in trouble."

Lester stared at the floor.

"Am I right, Lester?"

The patient, indulgent tone—Randolph was playing him and he knew it, but he couldn't swallow the lump in his throat. He looked up, trying to put on his best poker face, but it was no use. Officer Randolph was right.

"What time are you finished work?"

Lester looked at a wristwatch. "In an hour."

Officer Randolph stood up. "Tell you what. Go on home. Talk to your mother. I think after you have a conversation with her you'll come see me." He nodded and then took a couple steps toward Lester, sticking out his hand.

Lester hesitated, but then he shook the officer's hand. What else was he going to do?

At a little before 5:30 that afternoon, Minnie and Lester Gold entered the Trenton Police headquarters. They approached a glass window and spoke to the blue shirt, who told them that Officer Randolph was expecting them, and then instructed them to take a seat on a wooden bench across from the glass window. After a few minutes a Negro woman came towards them. "Mrs. Gold?"

"Yes."

"And your son?"

Minnie nodded.

"Come with me, please."

The matron ushered them into a room. She offered Minnie a chair in the far corner behind a wooden desk. Next to the desk was a hardback chair. The matron turned the chair so that it faced the door, and then she beckoned to Lester. Of course—that was his chair.

They waited in the silence, in the tiny windowless room with beige walls and no lock on the door. This is where they interrogated people—that much was obvious. And it was a different room from the one in which Officer Randolph had interviewed him the night his father was murdered.

Lester closed his eyes and gripped the hard wood of the chair—the room was closing in on him, Minnie seemed to have shrunk into the walls. The visit to Uhuru caromed into his brain. Why had he let Santo talk him into spying on Salim? And the bold move of walking right into the store—how stupid was that? He had been sure that it wasn't Salim—and then Salim had screwed it up by putting on the Orioles cap. Wasn't that the same as making a confession? But then, why would he confess? Maybe he was innocent. Maybe he was just an innocent Orioles fan who knew how to help a boy choose a gift for a girl he wanted desperately to impress.

Minnie stirred and seemed to come to life. "Lester. You remember when you were just a boy." She stopped and shook her head. "A big imagination—that's what you had. The stories! And your father and I believed them."

Lester crossed his arms. Santo had ratted him out, and now Minnie was in on it too.

"The one you told about Miss Tobish—that was bubbe maseh."

Lester smiled. "A big one."

"Imagine, a boy says his fifth-grade teacher slaps him across the face and breaks his glasses." She smiled at him. "His mother is going to get to the bottom of that. And what do I discover? Miss Tobish did indeed have a reputation for hitting."

"I was pretty crafty for a ten-year-old."

Minnie chuckled. "Crafty you've always been."

"And dad had to take the belt to me."

Minnie held out her hands. "How he suffered! Hitting, it caused him such pain."

Lester smiled at her. Just thinking about Yussel calmed him. "Imagine, a butcher who—"

"—A pacifist, he was. No harm to be done, to the animals, to the people. And never to his son."

Lester started to choke up, but he pushed through it. "And he had to beat me, 'cause I wouldn't say . . . ."

"How you got into a fight in the schoolyard."

"How's it going?" Officer Randolph came bustling in, a thick red file in his left hand. He grabbed a hardback chair near the wall and slid it to four or five feet in front of Lester. "Thanks for coming over." He seemed huge in the tiny room, as if he could barely be contained in it.

Lester sat up straight and gave Minnie a look, one that said, *don't make this any harder than it already is.*

"So, Lester," he said, his face impassive. "You've had some time to think, and I'm interested in your thoughts."

Lester shrugged. "Thoughts? Like, maybe who I think is gonna win the World Series?"

The officer frowned. "Lester, have I been out to your house? Have I been over to see you at the barber shop?"

Lester nodded dutifully.

"What does that indicate to you? You take a look at my actions—not my intentions, my *actions*—and you see that I take this case very serious. Is that right?"

Lester nodded again.

"And we've asked you down here tonight on a very important errand. And your mother—is she a very busy woman? Yes, she is. And here she has come down to the station, hasn't she?"

Lester sighed. "But I told you already, I told you what I know."

The officer matched Lester's sigh, and then folded his hands. "I guess you're not going to be doing your father any favors."

"Lester," Minnie began. He could feel it coming, the onslaught, and he bowed his head.

"Your father—"

"—May he rest in peace," Lester said, in unison with Minnie.

"He would have wanted—"

"—Ma! Don't say. I've heard it a thousand times."

Officer Randolph stood up and beckoned to Minnie. She hesitated, but then stood and came over to the door. He turned to Lester. "C'mon, we're done here."

The officer escorted them to the door of the station and out onto the sidewalk. "Mrs. Gold, you have been so helpful. Go home and get some rest."

Minnie nodded and took Lester's arm, but Officer Randolph reached for Lester's other arm. "Lester and me, we're gonna have a little heart to heart."

Lester glanced at Minnie and then back at the officer. "Okay," he said, but then he just stood there, waiting to see what Randolph would do next.

Randolph tightened his grasp on Lester's arm and escorted him back to the room. As they entered, Lester saw him flip a switch on the wall, and a green light came on. They resumed their seats, Lester on one side of the desk, Randolph on the other.

The officer leaned back and crossed his legs, cradling the file. "I hear you tried out for the school newspaper this year. You're an 'A' student, am I right? And quite a tennis player."

Lester grimaced.

"You ask me, you got a great future."

Lester narrowed his eyes at Randolph. He wasn't sure where he was going, but he sure didn't trust it.

"Now I know all about you, and I know about what you and Santo are up to. I know what you're doing with Louie and you ask me you're headed for an 8 by 10. You know what I mean?"

Lester leaned forward. "What Santo told you—"

Randolph grimly shook his head. "—I knew about your father's business, and I turned a blind eye. You get me? Here's what tonight's all about. If you come clean in this room, I'm gonna forget what I know. I'm gonna go right back to believing in Lester and Santo, two boys from good homes who work hard in school. You understand?"

"I—I wish I could say, but the truth is—"

"The truth is," Randolph said, raising his voice, "is that you're gonna stop bullshitting me right now." He stared hard at Lester and then picked up his pen and began to take notes. "I'm just going to write down what other people have told me." He jotted some more and then looked up. "I've interviewed lots of people. I have a good description of the person who shot your father. You know the jail down the street from the store. It has a camera. On the afternoon of the murder, there is a shot of a person that fits the description several witnesses have given me."

"Witnesses? I thought I was the only one who—"

Officer Randolph patted the file. "Now Lester, you let us be in charge of all that."

Lester raised his eyebrows and tried to swallow the lump in his throat. "I thought I was coming down here tonight to tell you what I saw at Uhuru the other night."

"Who told you that?" Officer Randolph asked, keeping his eyes fixed on Lester.

Well, Minnie Gold, that was who. Her voice filled his head.

Forgive me, Lester. I told you a lie, but only a white lie, and only for your own good. Now Minnie was the crafty one.

Officer Randolph cleared his throat. "Salim at Uhuru is into drugs. We know that."

Lester nodded.

"And your father's murderer did not steal any money from the store. Isn't that right?"

"Yeah, but his money clip is gone. And he always kept money in it—maybe a couple twenties."

Randolph spoke deliberately. "The *cash register* was untouched—that means the murderer was not after money. And we know that Salim was a riot leader. True?"

"If you say so."

"He wants to go to war against whites. He wants power."

Lester fidgeted in his chair.

Officer Randolph fingered the file in his lap, and then stood up and moved to the door. Lester started to get up, too, but Randolph shook his head. "You stay put. Take some time to think on this matter. You need to be absolutely sure of everything you say to me. I want the truth, the whole truth, and nothing but the truth."

When Randolph left, Lester slumped in his chair. Why couldn't they leave him alone? Sitting in the tiny, airless room wasn't going to blast the truth out of him—or *into* him, for that matter. If he knew, he would tell, but he didn't, so what more was there to say?

The only thing to look at was the clock on the wall, its sturdy black hands, and the red minute hand sweeping the face—was it really every 60 seconds? Was the clock fast? No, Lester determined that it was slow. He sat there blinking at the red needle as it made its painstaking revolution until his head was heavy with the ticking. He leaned on his elbow, dozing, as visions of his father and his cronies at the smoke shop seeped into his consciousness: fat bellies and fat cigars, a gruff old guy with an eye shade, the men tossing hearts and diamonds onto the green felt; then the midway at the State Fair, the alligator man in a glass box behind a tent flap; the race track with his father, the boardwalk at Atlantic City. At some point, he fell asleep, and then awakened with his right arm completely numb. He got up and counted 5,280 steps backward around the room; he called the final games of the World Series, meting out the runs, the scoreless innings, the Tigers breaking through with three runs in the top of the seventh of the last game, and then he walked through Mickey Lolich's winning pitches. Finally, he called for help. But no one came, nothing happened at all, until four hours later, when Officer Randolph came back into the room.

He solemnly took his seat behind the desk and sighed heavily. "Lester, my job is to discover the truth. I've talked to a lot of people. As I told you, we have a witness who saw Salim enter your father's store the afternoon of the murder and leave it, heading up Market to Broad." He stared intently at Lester. "You had a limited opportunity to see the perpetrator, correct?"

"Limited," Lester repeated

Officer selected a photo from the file photo and pushed it across the desk. "Do you recognize the man in this photo?"

It was a dark-skinned man in a windbreaker crossing the street—that's all he could tell. It didn't look like Salim but it didn't look like anyone else either. "No," Lester said.

Randolph sighed. "You are white. And the man in this photo is of a different racial group. Are you biased? Scared of blacks?"

"But—"

"—No 'buts,' Lester."

The officer stood up, and Lester wished that he were dressed the way he had been when he came by Louie's—in his casual slacks and sport coat. After the endless empty hours, the uniform was distracting; he couldn't concentrate with all that brass in the room.

Randolph perched on the edge of the desk and crossed his arms.

"You don't want to fail your father . . . and your mother," he added, glancing at Lester. "All you have to do is go along with the crowd. These folks who signed these statements are good citizens. What they need you to do is see what they saw and the case is closed. It's that easy."

Officer Randolph leaned toward him, waiting for him to do the right thing.

Lester uncrossed his arms and slumped toward the desk. The thing was—he had already failed his father. Surely Officer Randolph knew that, and Minnie—she wouldn't admit it to herself, but deep down she probably knew it too. If only he had been sweeping out in the store instead of in the storeroom behind the counter—then maybe he could do what they wanted. If only he had x-ray vision, like Superman; if only he had the cunning of Goldfinger.

Officer Randolph stood up, his belt creaking, and placed a typed letter on the desk. "Lester. Here's what I am going to do. I have here the statement from you. After you sign it, I will make sure that if Salim doesn't plead guilty, all you will have to do is watch the good citizens testify and then agree with them."

"Plead guilty?" Lester asked, the haze lifting. "Why would he do that?"

"To avoid the death penalty. That's why."

"That's not possible," Lester said, shaking his head again.

"Well, not if you do the right thing it isn't." Randolph stared hard at Lester.

"What?" Lester stood up and took a couple steps toward the wall. "I can't."

"Can't?"

He took a deep ragged breath. "I can't . . . I mean, I can't understand, what bothers me in all of this, is . . . he had a money clip." He stared hard at Randolph. "My dad always carried it in his right front pocket, always had money in it. And it was gold—it had this sun on it, a rising sun."

Randolph waited a moment before returning Lester's stare. "I can tell you that we carefully inventoried the scene and we examined the contents of the . . . uh . . . deceased's, his clothing, and his person. And there were no personal effects. Except his glasses, which were given to your mother. As you know."

"I remember that money clip from the time I was a little boy—"

"—Lester," Randolph said, taking a decisive step toward him. "It's time. All you have to do is sign this paper," he said, handing Lester a gold pen.

Lester edged toward the table, his legs aching. "Promise me," he said, his guts roiling. "If I sign this, it isn't forever. I can change my mind."

Randolph nodded gravely, but Lester couldn't tell if he was nodding "yes" or if he was just indicating that he should sign.

Lester felt himself weakening—his body, his trunk, his skeleton, his flesh, his breath. It was as if he was being electrified, as if a slow fuse had been lit inside him and it was burning down to this moment of the pen boring down through layers of papyrus. If that was even what paper was. How was paper made? They shredded up trees, they ground them down. "I'm not . . . sure. I need more time," he said wearily.

Randolph dragged a wooden chair over to the table and sat next to Lester. Randolph's chair was gigantic next to his, and Lester's chair—it was a child's chair, one that would fit under a child's desk.

I'm not a child—he almost said it, but the words wouldn't come. Instead, he thought to himself, *It doesn't matter*. It doesn't matter what a child thinks or what he signs. He had failed his father already—what difference did it make if he gave in now?

He grasped the pen and bore down on the paper. What else was he going to do?

8
Calvary Baptist

On Tuesday night Lester went alone to the Mt. Calvary Baptist Church. He figured that Naima would be there, and he had carefully wrapped the flute and put it into his backpack. The church was huge with big columns in front, and Lester milled around among hundreds, maybe thousands, of people, most of them black. After a while, he stood on a bench near a sign that read "Memorial Service, Vernon Josephs, Jazz Vespers, Roland Kirk," and searched the crowd. When she came in his direction along the sidewalk, it was easy to spot her—few girls were as tall as she was, and there was no way you could miss that big red Afro.

"Hey Jew," he called out. She stopped and turned to him with a dumbfounded stare. "What'd you say?"

Lester giggled. "It's your fellow heeb from Trenton High," he said triumphantly.

She gave him a bemused look, which turned into a smile. "My mom's Jewish. My real name's Frieda. Naima's my middle name."

Lester jumped down and went over to her. She had on a lavender Poorboy sweater and a short velveteen skirt. She was taller than he was and even just standing there, shifting edgily, she was elegant. He had watched her with her friends. The boys wore sherbet-colored shirts—lime and raspberry—and had pics in their Afros. The girls had high cheekbones and dark eyes and they wore swirly patterned dresses in fuchsia and orange. "You seriously don't remember me?"

She sighed. She seemed to be considering saying that she did not.

"Just so you know, if you say no, I'm gonna start following you around the hallways and telling everyone about Sunrise Lake." He gave her his most winning smile.

She tipped her head back and stuck out her bottom lip. "You think I'm some kind of Nubian princess, I can tell."

"Didn't I just say, 'Hey Jew'?"

"Yeah, but you act all *respectful* around me, like you're in awe or something."

"Really? Cause it's more like I think of you as someone who can't swim. Some dumb broad who fell in the lake."

She smiled. "No, you don't."

"Well, what I really think is that you're a JAP."

"A Jap?"

"Jewish American Princess. Well, half-JAP. And the other half, whatever you said—Nubian?"

"My dad, he's African. He lives in Paris. On account of he can get so many gigs—Amsterdam, Berlin, they love us over there."

Lester frowned. "By 'us,'" I don't think you mean *our* 'us,'" he said, drawing an imaginary line between them with his pointer finger. "The tribes of Israel."

"Let me ask you something," she said, crossing her arms. "Abraham Lincoln. What do you think of?"

"Four score and seven years ago."

"What else?"

"He freed the—"

"That! That right there." She pounced, pointing two long brown fingers at him. "Seriously, how realistic is it to think that some white dude freed tens of thousands of people? Every man is born free. Now you can enslave him after he's born, which is what they did to the Africans. But nobody can give anybody else his freedom. My people freed *themselves.*"

"There's that 'my people' thing again."

She shrugged.

He moved a little closer and put his hands on his hips. "Okay, *my* people? Golda Meir. She's gonna be the Prime Minister of Israel—that what my dad says. *Said.*" He glanced guiltily up at her. "Or Totie Fields—"

She giggled. "Totie Fields. She's so roly poly."

"My ma just dies every time she's on Ed Sullivan. Or Abbie Hoffman. The Chicago Seven."

"You know why they're Seven instead of Eight—because they separated out Bobby Seale, on account of he's black and one of the Panthers."

"Wait a minute," Lester said, narrowing his eyes. "I don't get it—what's Lincoln freeing the slaves got to do with you and me at the lake?"

"You think you're some white massa come along to set the Negro free."

He laughed. "More like Moses parting the Red Sea."

"More like you think you walked on water."

"What?"

"I'da saved myself," she said, and gave him an insouciant smile.

"No way! You would have gone under if I hadn't been there. I saved your black ass."

She burst out laughing, and then cocked a hip at him. "Little Jewboy up in my face talkin' bout, 'I saved your black ass.'"

Lester stood there beaming at her.

It was now nearly 7:30, the time that the service was beginning, and people streamed past them. Some of them disembarked from rows of buses at the curb, and others got out of cars, or rode up on bicycles. A few glanced at the tall black girl and the antic white boy talking earnestly on the street corner, but most just pushed forward toward the church.

A large black woman with her hair wrapped in layers of cloth approached Naima. "Sister, the program is about to begin," she said sternly.

Naima nodded to the woman and began to move, dragging Lester by the arm. "He's with me," she said hurriedly. When the woman was out of earshot, she said, "That's Mother Makeba. She looks out for me. My ma's here somewhere," she said, turning her head in all directions. "She's probably inside already. C'mon," she urged, dragging him toward the entrance.

There were already hundreds of people seated in the pews, but Lester and Naima inched along the carpeted aisles until the woman who had spoken to Naima earlier beckoned them over. They squeezed in beside her and Lester sat quietly, trying to take it all in. Black ladies dressed in white nurses' uniforms patrolled the aisles. A tiny man sat behind an enormous Hammond organ down near the front, and Lester's heartbeat thumped along with the music. On the stage, four men in dark glasses played tall bongos and the rhythm sounded like a war cry.

A choir in vermillion robes was assembled on risers. As they began to sing, the audience stood, joining their voices.

Woke up this morning with my mind, Stayed on freedom. Woke up this morning with my mind, stayed on freedom. Hallelu, Hallelu, Hallelujah.

They resumed their seats as the Reverend Horace Abrams, a big man in a navy blue suit and red tie, came out and addressed the crowd. He introduced Vernon Josephs' parents, who were seated at the far left of the stage.

"When God gets ready to do a thing, he don't hesitate. I don't know why God chose this young man, but we his people can hold him up to Heaven today. We aren't going to hold up Vernon as a martyr for all the black boys and men who have been slain, cut down in their prime, cut down senselessly and without reason. No, Vernon Josephs was just a man, an ordinary boy who was taken from us too soon. God lit a fire in this young black man, this young lion of our community. Brothers and Sisters, Vernon was one of us, a boy from down the block, a loving son, a dutiful worker, a *nobody*, you might say. And yet because of the events that have come to pass in this year of our Lord, nineteen hundred and sixty-nine, he has now been made a *somebody*. God took an ordinary young man and made him into great light to shine upon us all, black and white, to show us the way. God has intervened in this young man's life, and set him up on the Mount to show us the riches of one *decent* life, the treasures that lie dormant in the human breast. Before this moment any one of you might have given up on Vernon, and certainly the leaders of this nation would not have singled him out, but now he has been lifted up to the highest heights, to show us the way. One common man, a *black* man. We might never have thought that God would choose Vernon, but he did, and we are here tonight to light the lamp that burns in a young man's breast, in the breast now of every young black man in America. Vernon Josephs was guilty of nothing. He was guilty of studying hard in school, and loving his mother and his father, and extending the hand of friendship to his neighbors. He departed in glory. He has been appointed by God to show us the way, to rebuild our commitments, to love harder, to reach higher. Amen!"

When the Reverend finished, a Negro in dark glasses came out, guided by another man, and they approached the microphone. The Negro had on a dress—what Minnie had called a robe—over a pair of dungarees, and the same kind of crocheted skullcap that Salim had been wearing.

"That's Roland—he's blind," Naima whispered. "But he sure can blow."

The man held a saxophone, and he set it aside for a moment

and leaned into the microphone, shouting, "THEY SHOT HIM DOWN! THEY SHOT HIM DOWN TO THE GROUND! But we're gonna say a little prayer for him anyway." And then the band launched into a powerful tune with Kirk wailing on the saxophone and shouting at the same time.

Moments after they finished the first tune, Lester saw Salim step out onto the stage and walk toward the microphone—it was unmistakably him, and he moved in the same antic way he had the day at the store. He stood silently before the crowd and then began to speak in a sonorous singsong, in very much the same tones the preacher had used.

"Brothers and Sisters, I come before you tonight to speak on a topic you might not have spent much time studyin'. And that is *resistance*. Now you've all heard that the way we do, the right way, is to forgive and forget, *to say a prayer*." He turned and bowed to the saxophone player. "And you have just heard one of the greatest prophets we have here in the U S of A, you just heard him blow. Am I right?" He grinned and the audience cheered. "Now I'm all for prayer. That's a powerful thing, you dig? But let me right now ask you to cogitate on what it means to be prayerful. Prayer is more than just speaking to God, beseeching him. I need a new car. Please don't let me get fired from my job. Help my old sick mama to get back on her feet." As he spoke he paced the stage rapidly, his boots clacking against the wood. He wore the same sort of long dress that the saxophone player wore—only Salim's was patterned in yellows and golds. Along with his usual skullcap he wore a long scarf. "Now I'm here to tell you that prayer is also a way to talk back, am I right? It's a way to speak your mind, like a chant, or a song. It's something we often do in unison, and that's part of the power. Tonight I want you to understand what it is to speak a prayer of resistance. Yes! Because our people, the African people, we are masters of resistance. We have had to be. We didn't just bear up under the yoke—*we shook it off*. We stepped around it, we stepped *over* it, we found a way to thrive, to *be*, even when the manacles were cutting into our flesh. Ain't that right?" He stopped and gesticulated to the crowd, and Lester heard shouts along with the applause. "And one way we got up and over was through prayer. We resisted our oh-pression, we resisted in every way you can imagine. Now you might be asking yourself, what is this *resistance* I'm asking of you? What does it look like? And what is the path we must walk to reach it? My people, we do it through *love*. As my brother Stokely Carmichael says, *our people* first, *our people* first. It is through a black united front—that's what I'm talkin' about. Do not let the white man define this resistance for you, do not let him dictate to you how you should be. And by that I mean, do not let him dictate how you should eat, how you should walk, how you should talk.

"You must insist on White America cashing that promissory note that Martin spoke of, that note that was defaulted on. America has written you a bad check, a check marked insufficient funds—that's what Martin said. Five long years ago, he spoke of the 'urgency of now'—and *now* it is 1969 and what has changed? We got innocent black brothers off in Vietnam killing our innocent yellow brothers—that's what!"

Lester glanced over at Naima as the crowd roared. She was watching intently and her eyes were wet. He suddenly felt more out of place than ever—he had not resisted, not even when his father was murdered. What was there to resist? How could he undo such a senseless act? He looked over at Mr. and Mrs. Josephs sitting quietly on the stage with their hands folded. Had they resisted?

Lester began to feel squeamish and he glanced toward the back of the auditorium—could he slip out unnoticed? No, of course not—hundreds of people would see him marching up the aisle. And then there was Naima—what would she think if he walked out? He sat stiffly in his seat until the rally was over.

After the service, Lester and Naima wended their way through the crowd and stood in front of the church. He could feel the gift burning through his backpack, warming his shoulder blades, making him itch with the urgency of bestowing the only beauty he could muster, purchased at $7.95, upon her. A moment later Lester looked up to see that Salim was walking right toward them, moving with that quick jerky step, the way he had hustled across the store on the day of Lester's visit, wearing the Orioles cap, the way he had danced up on the stage just now, a marionette with invisible strings. Lester turned and tried to move away but Naima grabbed his arm.

"There's my brother."

"Your *brother*? You mean—"

Salim kept on coming, and then he walked right up to them. Lester stood there, frozen, but Salim showed no sign that he recognized him.

"You goin' to your mom's later?" he asked Naima.

"Yeah."

"Stop by after that. Calvin and Leona are in town."

"Cool."

Salim barely glanced at Lester and then he was gone. Lester turned immediately to Naima. "You said you got a car? I'll follow you anywhere, just let me sit. I gotta sit."

"Sure," she said, and she grabbed his arm once more. They walked a few blocks until they came to a powder blue Plymouth Valiant. "It's my mom's car, but she's riding home with my Aunt Esther."

Lester nodded and slid across the bench seat, leaning against the passenger side window.

"What's wrong?" she asked as she slipped in behind the wheel.

Lester could feel his mouth trembling and he didn't trust his voice. Finally, he whispered, "I might of said something . . . ." He glanced over at her and she seemed completely relaxed. "You know Santo Bassoni—"

"Big-mouth wop kid?"

"That's him."

"You mind if I smoke some grass while you're talking?"

"Help yourself."

She took out a marijuana cigarette and held the twisted end in her delicate fingers. "Gold's—that was your dad's store? You're the boy whose father . . ."

Lester nodded vigorously, and waved her off. For this one night, he needed to be someone else with this girl, someone you didn't have to feel sorry for.

She shook her head and gave a low moan. "Uh . . . uh . . . uh. I just don't understand. How you could shoot someone in the back. No respect."

Lester took a deep breath. It was the first time he had talked about it with someone who didn't seem to have an agenda. "You know," he said, "we keep kosher—at the store, I mean." He pictured his father doing computations on scraps of brown paper bags, lugging the big sides of meat back and forth to the walk-in. "And how you kill a creature—it's a ritual, you know. The *shocet* has to have the steadiest hand, so the animal, he never feels any fear." He glanced over at her and she was taking it in, her eyes soft and liquid in the light of the streetlamp. "If you're gonna take a life, make it humane."

She offered him the cigarette and he took several deep drags, holding in the smoke in the same way she had.

"Look at the moon," she said. "It's gotten so fat." And she laughed in her sultry throaty way, the music bubbling up out of her.

"I almost forgot," he said, rummaging in his backpack and handing her the instrument. "It's a . . . flute. I forget the name."

She held it in her open hands, smiling down at it. "It's a washint. It's from Ethiopia. My brother carries these in his store."

"I figured 'cause you play clarinet and all."

"Gosh, it's beautiful. I love it." She turned to him. "But . . . why . . ."

He felt his face burning and he looked away. "I just . . . I dunno, maybe a peace offering."

"Peace?"

"Yeah, shalom. You know, from one Jew to another."

She turned to him and he thought her eyes seemed moist, like she might cry, like the flute really mattered to her, or maybe it was him, maybe he mattered. A big bubble of laughter erupted from his throat—he couldn't hold it down. It was a good thing he didn't want to stop smiling, because he couldn't. Her frizzy hair and her fizzy laugh—he was beginning to feel an effervescence rising inside him, as if he were carbonated. "*Gurllll,*" he said, stringing it out the way she did, like music, a slow sweet saxophone blowing on the syllable.

"You are one crazy Jewboy," she said, shaking her head. She suddenly pushed out her hands, raising her palms up toward the roof of the car, and then slowly shook her head, turning to him. "Screw all this confession crap. Okay, here's the thing. I can't swim."

"That's obvious."

But . . . I mean, I never go in the water." She paused and shut her eyes, then opened them again. "Cause of my hair." She turned fiercely to him. "*Okay*?"

"What? What'd I say?"

"I guess . . . you're right . . . you were there . . . and it was just the right time and all."

"I saw you, I was watching you, I could feel you about to go in, like you were some beautiful bird about to take flight."

She gave him a sleepy-eyed smile. "You some kind of poet? I got a poem for you. I recited it for the talent show last month. Ready?" She turned to him, her eyes shining. "To fling my arms wide/In some place of the sun/ To whirl and to dance/Till the white day is done/ Then rest at cool evening/Beneath a tall tree/While night comes on gently/Dark like me— That is my dream!" She stopped and looked down. "That's Langston Hughes."

"Wow, you're good. You could have been up there on the stage tonight." What she had said—*dark like me.* She didn't seem dark at all, but lit up, golden, and in his smoky dream he moved toward her and kissed her full mouth, the roses of her lips. She smelled like sandalwood and she tasted like a reed, like the reed from her clarinet, like balsam. "I saw something," he whispered. "The night it happened. I mean, I *didn't* see something—"

Her eyes were closed and she was leaning against him. "What?" she mumbled.

"I . . . tried . . . but . . . my glasses . . . I couldn't really see." He felt that he might cry and the possibility that he would break down in front of this glorious girl sobered him up. "I broke them," he said stoically. "I fell and they broke."

"Okay," she murmured, and he knew that she didn't really grasp the enormity of his confession. After a minute she gently pushed him away, and he arranged himself in the passenger seat so that he was staring out the windshield. It was crystal clear to him now: he had not told the truth on the night that Officer Randolph had interviewed him, and the statement he had signed, that wasn't true either. The truth—that was a gift he had just given this girl, and only to her. He had heard a shot, and he came running from the back of the store, but he fell as he rounded the corner, and his glasses ricocheted into the refrigerator case. He had seen nothing more than a figure in an Orioles cap. And then his father, down.

Lester pushed the hand crank to open the passenger side window and then cleared his throat. He needed to come back from the confession he'd just made. "You're half and half, right?" he said casually. "Lemme ask you, how come you don't choose the Jewish side?

"It's not a choice."

"You ask me, you favor the black side."

"But that's how I'm *seen*. You understand? That's how the white system sees me."

"Well, one thing I think I can say is, I don't see why dark is bad, I mean, just cause some people are light."

"Dark is what troubles them."

"But you play into it—wearing the dashiki."

She smiled and handed him the joint. "So you know what a dashiki is."

He took a deep drag and held the smoke in for few seconds. "I looked it up." He watched as she held in the sweet smoke and then released it all at once in a big gray plume. She turned to him, her eyes shining in the light of the streetlamp. "Lester, they killed the finest human being on this planet. How can I stand by and just let that happen? How can *you*?"

For a moment he thought she meant Yussel, and he wanted to tell her that the only thing that mattered was another chance to sit at the card table his father set up for him in the back of Gold's, to sit and do his homework while his father kibbitzed with the ladies, Sylvie, Ruth, Miriam, and how after a while he didn't even hear what they said anymore because they all said the same thing, every time, but it didn't matter, what mattered was the sound of their voices, and he never wanted it to stop.

He moved a little closer to her. "Martin, you mean. You're saying, join the revolution."

"No. I'm saying, *Je responderay*."

"What's that?"

"I will respond."

She was so lovely and it was enough just to sit next to her, but he slid over a bit and gently took her hand. He had never heard anything so beautiful as those French words in her mouth. And what it meant—do the right thing. She understood—it was her *mitzvah*, and it was his too.

9

Town Crier

Lester ran all the way to Chestnut Avenue, to the apartment that Santo shared with his father. It was 11:30 by the time he got there and Pops was probably asleep and maybe Santo too, but Lester didn't care. He didn't bother to go around to the front door—you could knock but they'd never hear you, and the doorbell had been busted forever. He went straight to the alley behind the rowhouse and picked up a handful of stones. He had just left the most remarkable girl he had ever known—kissed, held—and the weight of that, the weight of her words—*je responderay*—propelled him straight to 1421B Chestnut Avenue. He began to ping the stones at Santo's window. Three, four, five. Nothing happened. He waited and still nothing. He kept tossing more stones.

"Santo!" he yelled. "Santo!"

Pops came to the window, opened it and shouted, "Stop that racket!"

Ordinarily, that would have been funny, but in light of the significance of his errand, nothing was funny, and so Lester just stood there staring up at the dark window.

Pops walked away and still Santo didn't appear. "What the fuck?" Lester muttered to himself. He wasn't about to give up. He ran down to the corner and over to Romeo and Juliet's, the bar on Whitaker, where there was a pay phone out front. He dug in his pocket for some change and came up with two nickels. The phone rang six times before Santo picked up.

"For fuck's sake, I was just over there tossing pebbles at your window!"

"I was asleep, you dumbass," Santo mumbled, his voice gravelly.

"How come you answered, then?"

"Thought it might be Carol."

"Shit, this is way more important than a chick."

"Front door in five."

Lester hung up and headed back to Santo's, walking around to the front. Santo let him in and they headed back to the kitchen. The house was small and dark, even in the daytime, and the kitchen didn't have a single window.

"I got some cappicola," Santo said, as he stuck his head in the refrigerator.

"How come you never have pastrami?"

Santo turned. "You show up at midnight and you want pastrami?"

"Sorry," Lester mumbled. "I got problems. Big problems." He leaned back against the counter as Santo unwrapped the lunch meat. "I was just over at Calvary Baptist—for the memorial."

"What you doin' over there with all them jigaboos?"

"Naima. I knew she'd be there."

Santo, bleary-eyed, wearing boxer shorts and a t-shirt, plunked himself down on a rickety chair as he began to wolf down the slices of cappicola.

"Geez," Lester said, raising his voice. "You gotta have some respect."

"Shut the fuck up, you'll wake up Pops."

"Already did that," Lester hissed. "I'm plotzing here. Seriously, my life is over. As of tonight."

Santo rolled his eyes. "Thought you said it wasn't about a chick."

"I said—"

"—My life is over!" Santo whined, mocking Lester. "You start with that bullshit I know it's about a chick."

Lester went over and sat down on one of spindly kitchen chairs, facing Santo. "Yeah. Naima, it's about her. But . . . I think, I just . . . ." He stopped and buried his face in his hands.

"You're killin' me here," Santo said, as he chomped on the lunch meat.

Lester looked up at him. "You're not even gonna make a sandwich?" He shook his head. "My friend, you're in trouble too."

"What? You flunked English?"

"No, fuck face. *Salim*. You're the one who got me to go over there."

"So? I didn't do nothin'. You're bugging out about nothin'."

Lester stood up and walked over to the counter, his legs shaking. "He was at Calvary Baptist. He was on the fucking *stage*. He's some kind of guru or leader or—"

"—I coulda told you that. He's one of them Panthers. He'd shoot you just as soon as look at you." Santo stopped chewing and looked up at Lester. "Shit."

Lester began to pace. "Yeah, now you said it. How do you know he shot anybody?"

"I—"

"—Don't you get it? He's her *brother*!" He was shouting now. "Her fucking *brother*!"

And then Pops was on the stairs in his bathrobe. He leaned over the banister and scowled at Lester. "I got a good mind to call your mother. What kind of a boy comes around past midnight, makes such a racket?"

"It's okay, Pops," Santo said.

"I'm sorry!" Lester shouted.

"This fuckin' kid goin' crazy?" Pops asked.

"Nah, I got this. Go back to bed," Santo said, getting up.

Lester bolted for the door. "I gotta go," he shouted.

And then he was running again, and it wasn't aimless running, running to let off steam, to keep from going crazy. It was running for his life, or maybe it was Salim's life, running to the Trenton police station, down Sakson and back to Ludwig and past the school and over to where the sidewalks were wide and there were streetlamps on every block, running right up to the door, and down the hall, and into the squad room, where Officer Randolph was watching the 76ers' Archie Clark shoot a free throw.

"Would you look at this guy?" Randolph said, pointing to the screen.

Lester stood there panting. "I gotta talk to you."

The officer got up and came over to Lester. "Okaaaay," he said, squinting at him. "Shouldn't you be home? It's a school night."

Lester knew why Randolph was suspicious: he, Lester, was the star witness, as they kept saying, and without him, they didn't have a case. "I want to withdraw my statement."

Randolph frowned at him, and then nodded. "Come back to the room."

Lester knew what room that meant—the same windowless box where he had been kept for hours, where he had clocked a backwards mile, 5,280 steps, and then had stopped counting. Officer Randolph opened the door and took a seat in the hardback chair at the desk, and indicated a smaller hardback chair for Lester. The same clock with the bold black hands stared back at him.

Lester took a breath and leaned across the desk. "I made a mistake. It wasn't him."

Randolph folded his hands. "Now how you would know that, Lester?"

Lester looked glumly at him. "Okay, I don't know who it was. That's the truth."

"Well, as you may remember, we have other witnesses who ID'd Salim. Are you prepared to say that they're wrong?"

Lester miserably shook his head. "Whatever they say, it's their right, but I can't say what I don't believe."

"Have you spoken with your mother about this?"

Once again Lester shook his head.

"You seem very worked up tonight, Lester. Are you having problems at home?"

"No! I just . . . I don't want this on my conscience, okay?"

Randolph adjusted his weight in the chair, and his belt creaked as it strained against his belly. "It's too late for any pangs of conscience, Lester."

Lester stood up and walked to the door. His heart was bursting out of his chest, but he tried to arrange his face to show that he was calm. He struggled to modulate his voice. "It's simple. I just want to retract the statement. I'll go on record, okay?"

Randolph leaned back, lacing his fingers behind his head. "It's not that simple, Lester. You see, then you'd be guilty of perjury."

"But—"

"Giving a false statement to a police officer." Randolph stood and leaned against the wall, crossing his arms over his gut. "You're on the debate team, isn't that right? School newspaper? An 'A' student, so your mother tells me. You've got a bright future, young man. You don't want to mess that up, do you? Think of the disgrace to your parents—well, to your—"

Lester slammed his hand against the wall. "Don't say it!" He felt the tears welling up and he fought to regain his composure. "My dad—he was a pacifist, did you know that? He would have protested the electric chair. You know it doesn't always work the first time? It's not like how the *shocet* does it, not at all. My pop, he had the utmost respect for life, humans and animals too. You take a life you have to do it in a humane way, see? Even Eichmann—"

Lester stopped as tears began to run down his face, and images from his World History textbook paraded through his head. "When they were about to hang him, he refused the hood, right? He said, 'I don't need that.' And then that same night they cremated him and scattered his ashes in the Mediterranean Sea, in the dark."

He put his hand on the doorknob as he wiped away the tears. "That's what I'm saying. My father, even for one of the most evil men in the world, he would have said his killing should be humane." He opened the door and stepped into the hallway. "You said Salim could get the death penalty, and that means the electric chair. My father, he wouldn't have been proud of me, not for this. He wouldn't have wanted this."

Lester started down the hallway and he could hear Officer Randolph following him, he could hear him saying, "Now, Lester," and so he began to run. He ran out the door, into the dark windy streets, as the boat with Eichmann's ashes bobbed in the sea, and Lester tried to picture just who would have scattered the ashes and if they had said anything, if there was a prayer. He began to say Kaddish as he had done every day since his father's death, muttering the words to himself. "Blessed and praised, glorified and exalted, extolled and honored, adored and lauded be the name of the Holy One, blessed be He, beyond all the blessings and hymns, praises and consolations that are ever spoken in the world; and say, Amen."

He slowed down to catch his breath, muttering as he walked. He didn't know where he was; there were no streetlights, no signs. The cold wind knifed through the narrow streets and for all he could see he was alone in the world: there wasn't a single lit window, not a single open door. He started running as the words burst from his aching lungs. "May His great name be blessed forever and to all eternity!" He shouted it at the top of his lungs and he didn't stop, all the way to Hermitage, all the way home.

10
Old Sparky

Nothing happened. Summer came and then it was fall and a new school year. Lester was a junior now, and he had worked out a circuitous route through the hallways, enabled by the fact that the black kids didn't mix with the white kids. It was surprisingly easy to avoid the one girl he wanted to see more than anyone, the one person he would have given anything to talk to.

He was still working at Louie's, really picking up some cash now—his Picks had taken off. He had earned a reputation by picking the Mets to win games. On October 11, Orioles had won Game 1 4-1 at Baltimore, and it looked like the Orioles would prove all the prognosticators right and Lester Gold wrong. But on October 12, the Mets won 2-1. And then the Miracle Mets won the next three games to win the series. He was golden.

He devoted an editorial to the Mets in the *Spectator* and the principal had stopped to shake Lester's hand. He loved being editor of the school newspaper and he took his deadlines seriously, which meant that he spent a lot of time in the office. He had figured out a way to work right up until he had to be in class. Or if there was an assembly, he had mapped out a route that allowed him to cut across the parking lot and come in a side door right next to the entrance to the auditorium.

One day right around the time of the Mets' win, he came through the side door to line up for assembly and there she was—standing at the edge of the crowd, her back to him. She was wearing a blue shift with white polka dots and a matching blue scarf tied in her hair. He flattened himself against the wall, and then faded back toward the door, stepping into the vestibule.

Pretending to tie his shoe, he bent double, nose to knees, gulping air. It was several minutes before he was able to straighten up and peek into the hallway. Hundreds of kids were lined up, waiting to go in, and she was still there.

He edged out of the vestibule and inched along the wall, poised every moment to bolt, in case she turned around. He forced himself to breathe and that allowed him to calm himself enough to observe—the way the editor of the school newspaper would. Objectivity, a nose for a story: that was what he needed right now. She was talking with Geoff and Samuel, boys who were in her group of friends, and she seemed at ease; at one point she tossed her head and laughed at something one of the boys said. Maybe it was as he had so fervently hoped—maybe his statement had been forgotten, or maybe Randolph had figured out they were wrong and had just dropped the whole thing.

All these months of waiting and they still had not arrested Salim. Lester had even crept over to Spring Street a couple of times at night, wearing his inside-out Batman sweatshirt and a knit cap pulled so low he had stumbled into utility pole and banged his nose. If he hid behind an elm across the street, he could see inside the lit space of Uhuru: he was in there, bopping around at his usual pace. Business was good, or it certainly seemed so.

Her brother was still in business, and Naima was still attending the eleventh grade at Trenton High, she was still going to assembly. Standing there, as close to her as he had been that day at the lake, the night in her mother's car, Lester allowed himself to wonder:

did she even know what he had done? For a moment, he imagined that Randolph had torn up the paper he had signed. He had spent his entire sophomore year and the summer torturing himself about whether she knew. A thousand times he had convinced himself that the whole thing would blow over, and a thousand times he was certain he had consigned her brother and the entire family to a life in hell. He burned to apologize, to respond to her. In his head, he begged her to believe him: *I didn't see, I couldn't see, I don't know, I still don't know*.

He wrote her a long letter of apology, which he then tore up. But the next day he wrote another, and then another. Soon enough he found himself writing to her nearly every day. 632 pages, single-spaced. He typed them out in the *Spectator* office, because that way he didn't have to pay for paper or ribbons. He smuggled the letters out of school by laying them flat and tucking them into his waistband.

Once he had casually mentioned to Santo that he was thinking of sending Naima a letter.

"Are you nuts?" he said in disgust. "You wanna get locked up, man?"

He hid the letters in the suit his Aunt Myrtle had bought him for his bar mitzvah, layering them inside the pant legs and sleeves, stuffing the coat and buttoning the pages inside, and then laying the entire suit into the bottom drawer of his dresser, like a dressmaker's dummy, a dummy that could say everything he, Lester, could not. In the breast pocket of the coat he placed another keepsake, this one from the day he had saved her—a single orange wooden bead from the lanyard she had worn around her neck. The bead was about the same size as the letter "o" on his typewriter.

One day when he was feeling hopeless he had typed up instructions, in case anyone ever found the pages he had crammed inside the bundled suit. *In the event of my death*. He requested that the letters be mailed to her, and he made sure the letters were in proper order, oldest on the bottom, most recent on top. At first he had typed out her address, but then he thought better of it, put a fresh sheet into the typewriter, and simply put her name.

He never reread the letters and it was because he didn't need to. The early ones were long, elaborate apologias, explaining that he had been railroaded, that he had never meant to implicate her brother or do any harm. But with each successive letter, as they piled up day by day, week by week, month by month, a crumpled stack growing taller, he gradually dispensed with formalities, niceties, and even punctuation. His speeches turned into pleas, and the pleas became suicide notes, mash notes, Morse code, scribbles, signs and symbols, and inside jokes that piled up in the bottom drawer, a stippled, battered confessional.

It had been easy to find her address (another perk of being the editor of the *Spectator*). And it seemed natural to begin spending evenings parked on Beale Street, watching as dusk outlined the trees, and the lights came on in the houses. Yussel's old Ford truck was his now—Minnie didn't drive. Lester always parked well down the block. He leaned an elbow out the driver's side window—just a boy killing time, not bothering anybody, a straight "A" student, editor of the school newspaper, dutiful son. Sometimes he would wave to a passerby, or offer a nod. And he had a story ready: he was there to pick up his little brother from his piano lesson.

Her mother usually came home around 6:00, in her white nurse's uniform, a cardigan over her arm. He was never able to figure out Naima's schedule—sometimes he waited for hours and she never showed. Other times she might pull up in her mother's Dodge Dart, or maybe walk home from the bus stop. He played a game with himself—whatever song was playing on the radio when he saw her, that was their song, the story that would make sense of the crazy world they found themselves in. The Beatles' "Lady Madonna": "*Friday night arrives without a suitcase, Sunday morning creeping like a nun."* That meant that this was their moment—no suitcases, just a pair of lovers on the run, waking up on Sunday morning in another town, a world made for them. If it was Tommy James and the Shondells' "Crimson and Clover"—*Now I don't hardly know her, but I think I could love her*—it was obvious: She knew, and he wouldn't have to explain.

The first couple times he saw her he ducked, and then peeked over the wheel to watch as she climbed the steps.

But then one day as he was slouched in the seat, he saw Salim come out the front door and come bopping down the steps, hustling, as if he were whistling a tune. Lester scrambled to the floor and hugged the gas pedal for a good 15 minutes before he dared raise his head. He was safe, but that was the end of his stakeouts on Beale. He couldn't risk an encounter.

And still, nothing happened. He was never caught, and there seemed to be no repercussions. He began to believe that as long as he carried the weight of his guilt, berated himself for his weakness, and wrote to Naima every day, nothing bad would happen.

And then Salim was arrested on a sunny Wednesday in November. All that day Minnie manned the phone, chatting with well-wishers, two words on her proud lips: "my son, my son." Lester cowered in his bedroom, trembling, weak-kneed, cringing when she called him a hero.

"Your papa would be so proud," she said.

Lester had come down to watch the news. Ross Bernstein, the prosecuting attorney, smiled on the courthouse steps in front of the TV cameras and announced that "justice would be done." He fled back up to his room. Why couldn't they leave him alone? He hadn't told the truth, but neither had he lied—he didn't have to: his statement had won the day. He had signed a document—nothing more and nothing less.

Minnie fed him bits of gossip: they had taken Salim away in handcuffs, the family had watched, his mother had fainted, on and on. But when Lester asked if she knew anything about Naima, Minnie just shrugged.

The very next day, first thing Thursday morning, Lester headed back to Trenton High. He was a junior now, the editor of the *Spectator*, but on the way to school he had to stop on Elm Street and vomit in the bushes.

He could have played hooky—it would have been so easy to simply join Santo in Columbus Park, or jump a train and head to the shore. But his conscience wouldn't let him: this appearance at school, it was his sentence. And sure, it was nothing compared to what Salim would probably get, but he had to serve it nonetheless. He knew better than to think that Naima would let him explain or even that she would talk to him ever again, but the slimmest hope shimmered at the back of his skull: maybe she didn't hate him, maybe she pitied him instead, for what he had been forced to do.

Santo hadn't attended classes in months, and was well on his way to having to repeat the eleventh grade, but he had agreed to make a special appearance that morning to act as Lester's bodyguard. As soon as Lester walked through the front doors, Santo was there.

"She ain't here," he said.

Of course, Lester thought. Her brother had just been arrested and charged with capital murder, so it made sense that her family was in mourning. They were holed up in their house on Beale Street, shuffling silently from room to room, clasping hands, folding and refolding their handkerchiefs.

Lester closed his eyes and leaned back against one of the trophy cases as a wave of relief crashed over him. "Shit, why do I feel disappointed?" he asked, opening his eyes.

"Uh, cause you're *crazy*?" Santo ran a hand through his dark hair. "It's not like you're ballin' her."

"What's that got to do with it?" Lester snapped. He glanced around at the kids who were coming through the doors into the lobby, and lowered his voice. "Bernstein, he said he'll probably get *the death penalty*."

"A date with ol' Sparky," Santo said happily.

"Old what?"

"Old Sparky," Santo said, crossing his arms. He smiled and nodded at a girl with long blonde hair, and then turned back to Lester. "Spook's gonna fry."

Lester grabbed Santo and dragged him out to the front steps. "No. No." He turned around, threw up his hands, and then faced his friend. "That cannot happen. Not on my watch."

"Your *watch*? My friend, you did the right thing."

Lester smiled weakly at a girl who brushed past him, and then moved closer to Santo, lowering his voice to a whisper. "No, I did the *wrong* thing. Randolph railroaded me." He stared hard at Santo. "*You* railroaded me."

Santo held up his hands, and gave Lester a blank, innocent look. "Me? I did nothin' that wasn't what any red-blooded American would of done. You should *thank* me."

Lester looked dejectedly at the flagpole that was planted at the entrance to the school. It was a windy day and the Stars and Stripes whipped hard against the metal pole. "But now she hates me. I mean, she'll never talk to me again. Hell, she won't even ever look at me again."

Santo shook his head. "She don't matter, man. Justice has been served, that's the point." He clapped a hand onto Lester's shoulder. "I'm here, see? I came to make sure nobody fucks with you. I got your back. See?"

Lester followed his friend inside but Santo was immediately caught up in talking to a girl with a ponytail, and Lester went on to History class. But then, as he was hustling from Geometry to

English, he spotted Geoffrey and Samuel. They were part of Naima's inner circle, boys who wore piks in their big Afros, tight pants, and platform shoes. They were tall slim boys, and they appeared suddenly, like apparitions, in the hallway, each taking an arm, as they escorted Lester down to the area where Shop class was held. Lester knew what that meant—the Shop was in the most remote wing of the building, where there would be all kinds of cover because of the noise. Someone was always running a saw or using a blowtorch.

He tried planting his feet, but they simply dragged him along the polished floor. He slid, whimpering, toward his doom. And then he saw Carol, coming toward him, chatting with her friend Lisa. Lester calculated: surely this girl, the one who never resisted, who had let Santo go all the way, at the shore, in her bedroom, in the attic at her grandmother's place, she wouldn't resist. This girl—she'd let him throw his arms around her, she'd pretend she was his friend, she wouldn't let on that he was the biggest pariah in the school.

He wrenched himself free and plunged into Carol's arms, bumping Lisa and shoving her toward the lockers. "Hey!" Lisa shouted, as she began to pick up her books.

"Lester," Carol hissed, "go home! You're in big trouble"—she glanced around and lowered her voice—"with *the blacks*."

He looked back at Sam and Geoffrey, who were standing there, watching him. They were like two eagles scoping a rabbit: they knew they'd get him, and it would be so easy, and they didn't mind watching him scurry around, digging a deeper hole, before they pounced. Lester decided that in this moment maintaining his dignity was not a high priority. He tore away from Carol and ran as fast as he could, and he didn't care that everyone was staring at him. He went for the one place of sanctuary he could count on: the library. Mr. Lyman, one of the hall monitors, was in there, and Miss Washburn, the librarian. The boys didn't dare follow him into the hushed, almost sacred space. Lester slipped into a seat at one of the dark burnished tables, and he let the whole library experience envelop him: the card catalogue, which ran the whole epic length of the room, the buzzing fluorescent lights, wall after wall of encyclopedias with gilt spines, the Dictionary of Literary Biography, which he loved, and every single Shakespeare play.

He sat near Miss Washburn's desk and kept his head down. After a few minutes he looked around, trying to figure out what his next move should be. He eyeballed the shelves, hunting for the most colossal and imposing book the library owned. For months Minnie had harangued him about trying out for the debate team ("You'll learn to stand up for yourself, you'll learn not to take any guff from the big shots") until he had finally relented. A mock trial was scheduled for that afternoon, and the question was, "Should mercy killing be allowed?"

Lester knew he wouldn't stay—he was going to sneak away as soon as Sam and Geoffrey were safely back in class—but researching the subject seemed a welcome distraction. He stood up, his legs still shaking, and headed over to the shelves. The library had some legal books—nothing fancy, but they had summaries of some of the major criminal cases back to the 1800s, and Lester lugged a huge tome back to the table and began to leaf through the glossy pages. He looked up "death penalty" and there were the Rosenbergs, along with a bunch of commentary. *Treason, treachery, spies, Commies.* There were photos of the two, Julius in his spectacles and dark suit, and Ethel in her cloth coat and hat. He had died quickly, it said, but Ethel died harder, and they had to administer the shocks several more times until "a ghastly plume of smoke" rose from her head. Lester covered the photo with his hand. Julius, that was his father's name. He had been executed too, shot in the back. There had been no mercy in that killing.

Lester kept reading. There was a long story on Bruno Hauptmann, the Lindbergh Baby killer, and a photograph of the electric chair.

Old Sparky, it said. So *that's* what Santo had been referring to. A big wooden chair with leather straps. Empty. He read on for a description of Hauptmann's execution.

His head, which had been shaved, titled slightly to one side. His face was yellow; his features were drawn. He glanced neither to the right nor to the left. He walked past the chair, and would have collided with a physician had not a guard stopped him. The guard turned him around, and maneuvered him to the chair. He gripped its broad arms with his hands, staring straight ahead as he was strapped in. His lips did not move, and he gave no indication that he wished to speak. I placed the head electrode on him, and helped to adjust the mask. At precisely 8:44 o'clock . . . .

Mercy killing—Lester decided he was against it. What was merciful about it? If anybody had mercy for him, they would take him out of his misery, they would exempt him from coming to school at all. He looked down at the photo of the Rosenbergs, and he covered Julius's face with one index finger and Ethel's with the other. *My people.* They hadn't done anything wrong. And neither had Salim. Or maybe he had done bad things, but had he killed a man? Or had he killed the man who mattered most—Julius Menachem Gold? Lester couldn't imagine that he had.

He pictured Salim being strapped in to Old Sparky and then the image morphed and it was Lester sitting there as they attached the electrodes. But then Naima rushed in at the last moment. "No! You cannot kill an innocent man!" She would save him because she knew, she had to know, somewhere deep down, under the layers of resentment and maybe even loathing, that Lester was a good man. He hadn't meant for it to happen this way. He slammed the book shut and Miss Washburn looked up, startled. "I'm sorry," Lester whispered, and then he said it again, louder. "I'm sorry." She nodded brusquely and put a finger to her lips, in perfect librarian fashion. Lester jumped up and began to move toward the door. The books lay on the table; he hadn't put them back the way you were supposed to, but he thought that Miss Washburn might forgive him just this once.

He had remembered something, a clue, something Ross Bernstein had said. Right after the arrest, Bernstein had come by the house to shake his hand, and Lester wanted to protest, to explain that he didn't deserve all the compliments. He had asked Bernstein about the witnesses, and he had turned to Lester, put a hand on his shoulder, and smiled. He had that slick lawyer look—the expensive suit, the crown of hair—and it was clear that he felt Lester could be easily dismissed. But Lester asked again, louder. Who were the witnesses?

"No witnesses," Bernstein said.

Lester knew that had to be wrong. Bernstein had started down the steps toward the street and Lester followed.

"Wait up!" he shouted.

Bernstein turned and laughed. "You're our star witness, you know that."

"But Randolph, he said there were others, he brought in a list, back when . . . you know . . . when I gave the statement."

"Right," Bernstein nodded. "You're right. There *was* somebody else." He hoisted his briefcase and began to rush away, but he turned and called over his shoulder. "Lillian Somebody."

Lillian Somebody. It could only be Mrs. Cala. Had she been there in the store that day? Lester could not remember. And why hadn't she come forward? As far as he knew, she hadn't spoken of it to Minnie. Apparently, though, she had signed a statement, just as Lester had.

He had to find out what she knew. He ran down the hall toward the front door, and even though the hall was empty, he kept running. He ran past the trophy case, and the Trenton Tigers pennants, and the stuffed Trenton Tiger, the school mascot. He ran past the big flagpole, and he didn't stop until he got to Kraft's drugstore, where there was a pay phone. He dug in his pocket for a dime, and there it was, one dime, all he had on him that day.

11
Freedom Riders

As Lester stepped through the glass doors of *The Trentonian*, he tried to imagine that he was coming home. Being back in Trenton was a step down, for sure, but only in terms of his career. The main thing, he told himself, was that he had an interview—a real-world, post-college interview.

A huge clock with bold black hands loomed over the newsroom, which was a warren of partitions and cubicles. A dozen men were seated at big metal desks, hunched under fluorescent lights, pounding away at typewriters. Lester approached the receptionist, a plump middle-aged woman. She announced him and a few minutes later he was ushered into Amos Sullivan's office.

Sullivan was the News Editor and his office was even more chaotic than the main room had been. His huge wooden desk was covered with two in-baskets overflowing with papers and two black telephones with every button lit. On the counter behind Sullivan's desk was an array of phone books, an overflowing ashtray, and a mini-TV. A photo of a smiling JFK presided over the mess.

Sullivan, a big fellow with a ruddy complexion and a mustache, looked like a man who had been caught in a gale—his face chapped, shirt open, sleeves rolled up, tie askew. His voice was hoarse, as if he had been shouting into the wind.

As Lester took a seat, he glanced at the red, white and blue bunting festooned around the walls of the office, and Sullivan seemed to spring into action.

"Watsa matter? You're not a patriot?" he barked.

"I am—" Lester began, but Sullivan held up a finger, as he punched a button on one of the phones.

"Elizabeth! Get in here."

A moment later the woman from the receptionist's desk came into the office. "How many times do I have to say? Get this shit off the walls!"

"Yessir," she said and hurriedly left the room.

Sullivan plopped into his chair, and then turned to an oversized wall calendar covered with red x's and circles. "Barely a month after the Bicentennial and feels like we're well into the next hundred years." He shook his head. "I was thinking, what a helluva thing it would have been: Watergate and the Bicentennial in the same year. You gotta love this country." He glanced over at Lester. "You believe in freedom of the press?" he asked, and then let loose a booming laugh. "Good one, huh? That's my opener." He swiveled his chair, lowered the volume on the TV, and turned back to Lester. "You read Harvey Samuels? He's my crime reporter, but the bastard just won himself a Pulitzer Prize, and so he's taking his hoity-toity ass up to the New York Times." Lester noticed that Sullivan could barely get out the name of the paper without smirking.

He didn't mention that he had just spent four days in the Trenton Library spinning microfiche on the past three years of *The Trentonian.* Maybe Sullivan would think he was a little too desperate, doing that kind of research, but Lester wasn't about to reveal why he had been holed up in the library. He had read about Samuels' Pulitzer Prize in investigative crime reporting, and how he had worked with Detective Bertram Randolph. He scanned a story on the murder of a coed who had been abducted and killed as she got out of her car in the parking lot of the Capitol Club.

And then finally he had stopped scrolling, as his hands began to tremble. It was a front page photo of Naima, which he realized as he stared at it he could not have prepared himself for. She was shouting amid a group of protesters, all of whom wore signs claiming, "Down with the Death Penalty!" and other slogans. She was picketing against the reinstatement of the death penalty, which was being considered by the New Jersey Legislature and supported by the Governor—and for a moment that didn't matter at all.

This bright star of a girl—she and he had been in alignment all this time, shouting the very same slogans: that was all that mattered. They were against the same thing—*death*—and for the same thing: *life*. June 29, 1972—that was the day everything had changed, as he paced in front of the courthouse waiting to hear the announcement of the Supreme Court decision in *Furman vs. Georgia.* And when they finally heard that the death penalty had been ruled unconstitutional, he leapt off the steps, and felt himself floating, weightless, for the few seconds it took to come down into the arms of a girl with curly black hair, who gleefully hugged and kissed him, and only later, much later that night, told him her name: Flora Klein.

Lester tuned back in to Amos Sullivan. "And I got another guy, Joe Earl—pushy bastard—moving up to the State House political beat." Sullivan flipped open a folder on his desk, and Lester saw his resume covered in red circles, just like the ones on the wall calendar. "I'm two down here, so I'm well-disposed to, uh . . . let's just say I need to hire a guy round about yesterday." Sullivan stabbed the paper with a meaty finger. "I pulled some articles from the archives, just following up on your resume here." He stopped and narrowed his round blue eyes. "Wonderin' how come you aren't trying for, uh, shall we say, a paper with a bigger circulation."

Lester nodded. He had sent out resumes up and down the eastern seaboard, starting with the *New York Times*. Not a single bite.

But there was a much more important reason why he was back in Trenton, and why he had spent the many hours at the library, although he couldn't share it with Sullivan.

"You grew up in Trenton, so I suppose you read the Trentonian?"

"Only the sports section."

"Back in the day, you made the papers a lot for winning tennis tournaments."

"It wasn't just me who won." Lester winced: he had been striving for humility but he had ended up sounding petulant.

Sullivan leaned toward him, lowering his voice. "What happened in the state junior singles tournament in your senior year?"

"I choked." Lester glanced up at Sullivan, whose face revealed nothing. "The boy I played was the brother of a Davis Cup player. I was ahead 4-1 in the third set. I couldn't believe I was beating him. I wasn't supposed to win. He was the heavy favorite."

Sullivan flipped through his Rolodex and then grabbed for the pencil behind his ear. "Frank Ciccolella."

Lester grinned. "Yep. He was our adviser the year I was editor of the Spectator."

"You won awards?"

Lester nodded. "Mr. Ciccolella was a great teacher. And he sold me on being a journalist."

"And you won a scholarship to Rutgers?"

"I did."

"Rutgers is my alma mater," Sullivan said, puffing up a bit. "Wrote for the Targan."

"Then we have something in common." Lester could feel his confidence building. "I read the New York Times," he said, and then paused.

"And?"

"The local news I get from the Times," he said, and when Sullivan gave him a stern glare, Lester meekly added, "The Trenton Times."

Sullivan traced his finger down the page of Lester's resume, muttering. "Okay, let's see. Objectives: make sure loopholes are closed, expose the underbelly." He looked up at Lester. "You on some kind of crusade?"

"Nah, I just . . . I work against the system is all."

Sullivan grinned. "So which one are you—Woodward or Bernstein?"

Lester laughed. "Bernstein, of course—he's the Jew."

"All this pie in the sky crap on your resume. You get hired, you're the new guy, you're gonna get the crime beat. Morgue, autopsies, street walkers, the numbers racket, that type a thing." Sullivan leaned back in his chair, rubbing his chin. "You ready for the crime beat? I assume you know what you're in for?"

Lester closed his eyes for a moment, but then opened them and focused on Sullivan. "What about the Statehouse beat?"

"We have an understanding with the boys at The Times, the Trenton Times. No exposing of politicians. We do the juicy stuff here at The Trentonian. See?" He held up a packet of Juicy Fruit. "This is our mascot," he intoned, and then gave Lester a wicked grin. "Drug dealers, junkies, cat burglars, gamblers, pimps and hookers." He winked. "Lions, tigers, and bears—oh my."

Lester nodded. He didn't have the slightest idea how to read Sullivan. "Columbia Journalism School was a great learning experience," he began, but then Sullivan frowned, either annoyed or distracted.

He glanced up at Lester and said wearily, "Name your two best qualities. As a reporter."

"Let me see . . . ." Lester said, leaning back in his chair.

"Ten seconds," Sullivan intoned.

"Uh, patience and perseverance." He could say it with conviction: Salim had been in Trenton State for six years, seven if you counted the months of the trial. And Lester had been doing his own time, plotting, replaying the events leading up to the bomb that had blasted him out of his life.

He had kept going to school, which is where you're supposed to be if you're a senior and playing by the rules. And it hadn't been as hard as he had imagined because once Salim's trial began, Naima dropped out and disappeared.

Until the day when he couldn't anymore. Math class, Mrs. Sargento. Vice-Principal Miller had stuck his head in the doorway and beckoned to Lester. He froze and then glanced around at his near neighbors before pointing to himself—*who me*? Mr. Miller nodded and Lester shuffled to the door. "Your mother," he began, and Lester felt his legs go numb. *No way his ma could go so soon after his pops*. But the next words were, "she wants you to come home."

"What for?" Lester demanded.

Mr. Miller sighed. "Lester, I have no idea."

"Why can't I just go home later?"

Mr. Miller had started down the hall, but he stopped and gave Lester a weary stare. "Son, if a parent requests the child to be taken out of class, then we're gonna take that child out of class."

"All right," Lester grumbled. "I'm going."

He had gone outside and walked a couple blocks to a pay phone and called home, but Minnie didn't answer. That didn't surprise him—she could be sly as a cat. She was there, all right, but she wasn't going to let him get away with a phone call. When he came through the door, he heard her come to the stop of the stairs. "Lester! Lester!"

"What, ma?" he shouted. "You had to make me come home for no reason—"

But as she came down the stairs he saw that she was wearing her good suit, the grey worsted one with the piping at the wrists, and he knew. Before she even made it down the stairs, he asked, "Guilty?"

She nodded.

Lester felt his legs go numb again, and his spine seemed to be telescoping, elongating him, sending his head into the stratosphere. "Death?"

"That's a separate day—so far it's the one verdict." She took a seat on the divan and crossed her legs. "Lester, this is what we've been waiting for. Menuval—scoundrel! He should live when your father should not?"

Lester stood dumbly in the doorway—he didn't seem to be able to will his legs to move. "Ma . . ."

"You wait, tomorrow you'll rejoice, you'll celebrate that justice is done."

"But—"

"You're a good boy, and you did the right thing, giving your statement, you've got nothing to worry about."

Lester forced himself over to the armchair and collapsed into it. "Was she there?"

Minnie rolled her eyes. "The sister? What difference is it if she was?"

"Just tell me."

Minnie shook her head, the trace of a smile playing on her lips. "Such tears, I never thought I would see."

Lester reared up from the chair. "Ma! What are you saying?" He flung his arms in the air. "I can't hear this. You're saying she was . . . distraught . . ."

"No, no. no. If it upsets you, don't think about it."

Lester went over to the couch and stood over her, his hands on his hips. "Tell . . . me . . . the . . . truth."

Minnie stuck out her bottom lip. "There was some sniffling—"

"Who was sniffling—"

"—the daughter and the mother—"

"—sniffling, or wailing?"

"Maybe some wailing."

"Godammit, Ma! For what do I—"

Minnie gasped. "—This is how you speak to your mother!" She stood up, all 4' 10" of her, and advanced on him. "Your father would never—"

"—what, Ma? He would never *what*? It doesn't matter anymore what he would do because he'd dead and he's never coming back."

She clapped her hands over her ears and marched to the stairs. "Such disrespectful language from his only son!"

Lester stood there and watched her until she disappeared at the top step. Then he shook his head and headed out the door.

That was the day: it was over for Salim and it was over for him. His sophomore year, and then his junior year, he had willed himself to believe that Salim would be found innocent, that he would walk free, and someday, after a reasonable and civil interval, Naima would smile at him again. They would begin a series of earnest high-stakes conversations in which he would display the kind of courage and valor he had demonstrated that day at the lake. He would bring her round to an understanding of his position: he had never meant to cast suspicion on Salim, and the whole thing had been a terrible mistake.

There was no one moment—but he had felt her slipping away. All the letters he had written to her, he decided to burn them in the backyard. Back then, he had resolved to quit school, maybe even leave town. All because he knew she would never look him in the eye again. He would be known as the boy who had pointed a finger at Naima's brother, the one who had sent a man to prison, maybe even for life—or worse.

Lester shook his head hard and jammed his hands into his pockets. *Focus*, he told himself, as he looked up at Amos Sullivan.

He had come home to Trenton to accomplish his longtime goal: force the powers that be, the Randolphs, the Bernsteins, to give Salim a new trial. And maybe, just maybe, he could join the fight against the Death Penalty and exonerate himself, so that Naima would see, or she would know—somehow. He smiled to himself as he added the words Salim had spoken to him that day at Uhuru: *by any means necessary*.

Sullivan gave Lester a quizzical look. "Well, it's gonna take a lot more patience than you've got 'cause you're dealing with the syndicate—you know, the grifters who've been greasing palms since J. Edgar Hoover and the like."

Lester leaned forward in his seat, nodding. "I'm looking to make the comfortable uncomfortable."

"Well. It's more than just politicians and socialites. You've also got the riffraff, the scum." Sullivan seemed to be enjoying himself now. "Bad news makes for good business," he said, and then paused for effect. "You work here, you'll begin with a beat at the Mercer County Court House, reporting on trials, that sort of thing."

Lester glanced up at Sullivan.

"Anything I should know—like, why you don't seem to want it all that much?"

Lester tried to recover. "I'm all about righting wrongs, you see, and I'm not sure this job will give me a chance to do that."

Sullivan yanked on his tie, and glanced guiltily at the bank of blinking lights in front of him. "See, I was gonna spare you any personal hoo-hah. You're not the type to go all March of Dimes on me, are ya? Crying over the crippled kids?"

Lester had started to get up, but he sat back down, mystified as to what Sullivan meant. "I guess."

Sullivan leaned back in his chair and crossed his arms. "The murder of your father. That by any chance the reason you're back here?"

"No!" Lester jumped up, and then realized that he spoken much too loudly, and so he sat down again, yanking on his own tie, and taking a deep breath. "I mean, yes, my mother, she still lives here, you know. And she's put a lot of pressure—"

"—typical Jewish mother—"

"—you got that right."

"Am I correct in assuming you weren't satisfied with the outcome of the trial? Hell, scratch that—everybody who ever took a shit in Trenton knows the case was flimsy."

"Right," Lester said, feeling like he could finally take a deep breath. "Salim—uh, Mr. Johnson, I believe he was railroaded, and I—"

"Malarky!" Sullivan leaned on his elbows, running his hands through his windswept hair. "You 'believe.' I say, you *know*. And now, you finally grew a pair, am I right?"

Lester stared at Sullivan.

"I was in the courtroom, you know. You should kiss Ross Bernstein's ass."

"He lied to me," Lester sputtered. "He tricked me,"

"That's right. Bernstein asked you if you signed a statement, right?"

"Uh huh."

"And then he read it out word for word?"

Lester nodded, as he clenched his right hand into a fist.

Sullivan took a dramatic pause and then advanced on Lester. "But he never asked you if what he read to you was *true*. Clever, that one."

Lester stood up. He could feel his legs trembling and he wasn't sure he could walk to the door, but he had to give it a try. "I just—"

Sullivan waved a hand at Lester. "Relax. Relax! I'm on your side. Ross Bernstein, Bertrand Randolph—they never had a case. But you know and I know that all a black radical's got to do to end up in the slammer is sneeze in the wrong direction."

Lester clutched the doorjamb. Why hadn't anyone ever said these words before? All this time he'd been under the impression that he was the only one who knew Salim was innocent. Well, except for Naima. She had never stopped working to get her brother released. "I—I'm grateful. To you. I just . . . a man was sentenced to death because of me." He staggered back to the chair and flung himself into it.

Sullivan shrugged. "Been commuted, though."

He looked up at Sullivan, his mouth trembling. "Yeah, but Gregg v. Georgia last month—"

"That doesn't affect your Mr. Johnson—"

"Right," Lester said, sighing heavily. "But I haven't had a night's sleep. I just—"

Sullivan stood up. "Look, if I don't take some of these calls, the ceiling's gonna come crashing down on both of us." He reached a hand toward Lester and they shook. "You're someone who dots all the 'i's,' crosses all the 't's'—am I right?"

Lester nodded wearily.

"Well, you'd better think long and hard about beginning your crusade. Go home, get some rest, have a beer. It's a free world out there, two hundred years of freedom, and we've already got a few weeks of the next century under our belt."

Lester left the building and headed down Perry Street, walking at first, and then running. He wasn't sure he wanted the job, even if it were offered, but there was something much more than that: he had—or seemed to have—permission to investigate Salim's case, maybe clear his name. His mind was a whirl of possibilities—he needed to talk to Mrs. Cala again, find out what she knew. He passed a phone booth and slowed down, intending to call Santo. But then he remembered—he was on shift and there was no way to reach him. Unless it was an emergency—and then Pops had some way of getting word to him. But this wasn't an emergency.

He headed over to the old "Siamese," in Hermitage, where Minnie still lived. He had spent a week there with her as he searched for an apartment he could afford. When he found a place, she had pushed all kind of things on him: a sofa, a cedar chest, a fondue pot, but he declined it all, accepting only a lamp and his father's shoe shine kit.

Minnie no longer worked at the factory—she had the insurance money now, and so she devoted herself to preparing Lester's favorite meals, which meant that she expected him for dinner every night. One thing about the *Trentonian* job that appealed to him: he would be working evenings and nights, as much as he would be days.

"Ma!" Lester called as he came in the door.

Minnie came out of the kitchen, a cigarette in her hand. "My son, the macher. Your father would be proud."

Daily now he heard the "your father's." *Your father, God rest his soul, he would be so proud of the first Gold to go to college. Your father, God rest his soul, he wanted you to marry Jewish and give us grandchildren.*

"Ma, I didn't take it."

Minnie frowned at him. "Why not? It's a good job, yes?"

Lester nodded and sunk into the overstuffed chair. "I just, I want to see if I can get a shot at a paper that's a little more prestigious. My stories will have more clout."

Minnie waited a beat and Lester knew what coming. "So. You go talk to the Havesons, they'll give you a job, they respect your father."

"Are you *crazy*?" He smacked his forehead with his hand. "You know what Ross Bernstein says? He says I got shell shock from that day. I'm never going back there. *Never.*"

Minnie sighed. "What, like the soldiers?"

"Yeah, like I been in a war."

"Forget the cooking—I'll order from Wenarski's."

Lester stretched out his trembling legs and took a deep breath. Minnie had been grilling him for months during his job search. He had been forced to inform her as the daily rejections rolled in from the major papers: the *Philadelphia Inquirer*, the *Denver Post*.

*"Schlemiels!" Minnie would shout, but then she would add, "May*be you should have gone into business like your father so you could be

in charge of your own destiny and get rich."

And Lester would groan and sink deeper into the old chair.

Minnie picked up the receiver, but she was too distracted to dial. "Just think—you say yes to Mr. Sullivan and all the mishegoss is over."

"Ma," Lester said. "C'mere. Sit down." It had taken years, but Lester had worn her down, made her see that his confession had been coerced. He was never sure, though, just what she believed. Sometimes she seemed to accept his view, and other times she seemed to revert to her old rants and prejudices—that the Hasidim had killed Yussel. Because he had good business sense. Or because they resented his success.

Minnie came over and took a seat on a low chair.

Lester leaned toward her. "Here's the main thing, ma. Sullivan, he . . . he knows. He understands what I've got to do."

He could see the tears shining in her eyes. "My son is going to win the Pulitzer Prize. He is going to call that Mr. Sullivan."

Lester smiled and shook his head. "If I took it, I'd be sitting around in court, or talking to beat cops. Like Santo—he'd be a source."

Minnie rolled her eyes. "That boy don't know from his tuchas. Always getting you in trouble, he was." She got up and headed back to the phone. "Maybe you should call Flora—she knows the big shots."

"Ma," Lester groaned. "How many times do I have to tell you? She *broke up* with me."

"But now you'll get a good job, and if she's a smart girl, she'll see that she's got a good future with you."

At Columbia, Lester had fulfilled Minnie's dream and gotten engaged to Flora Klein, a nice Jewish girl, and, more importantly, an activist. She had been a senior when he was a freshman, but she set her thesis aside to spend long nights with him in the common room or the library, discussing Frantz Fanon and James Baldwin and W.E.B DuBois. She was as strongly against the death penalty as he was, and she didn't ask him to explain his views. She simply accepted that all right-thinking people were activists against the war, or against the death penalty. Still, he had spent many hours in front of the mirror, practicing. *My father is dead. My father's dead. My father died.* He tried out the phrases over and over. Short and sweet, and delivered in the most neutral way possible. And when at last he gave it she had accepted his mumbled explanation and not asked anything more.

It didn't take Lester long to discover the one thing that was more important to Flora than anything else: She had been a Freedom Rider in 1964, flocking to Mississippi along with thousands of other earnest Jewish boys and girls. At Columbia she spent way more time on the streets manning barricades and carrying placards than she did in the classroom. Right after Martin Luther King was assassinated, when Lester had been sitting shiva, Flora had been occupying the university buildings with other SDSers and clashing with police in Morningside Park.

Minnie picked up the receiver. "You let me call the shadkhen."

Lester leapt to his feet. "Ma, no!" He turned away from her and thrust his fists over his head, a beseeching gesture that he only resorted to with her.

She frowned and shook her head. "This I deserve? A son stomping around the house? Your father never raised his voice to me."

Lester sighed heavily and collapsed into the chair. "Last time you set me up it was a disaster. Remember?"

"Esther Bettelheim? A lovely girl. You're so picky picky."

"She blew her nose all through the matinee! And you know what she ordered for dinner? Cottage cheese. That's it—nothing else! And then she doesn't even speak to me at school the next day."

"My son, the macher. Ivy League is all he knows. You turn up your nose at the old neighborhood?"

Lester got up and went over to where she was standing, bending down to embrace her. "Ma. I'm here, aren't I?"

She reached up and patted his cheek. "Bubele, all I ask is that you don't bring home a goy—I've only got a few good years left. A matchmaker, she knows her trade. Mrs. Applebaum. She's the best."

Once Lester had gotten to know Flora, he had come to see that she protested for the sake of it: she had wanted to right every wrong, rail at anything she considered inhumane. But Lester had been fighting for one man and one only. Samuel Salim Johnson. For a while, he had been able to deny the reality of Salim's situation: long enough for him to get his undergraduate degree at Rutgers and his masters at Columbia—he was an excellent student, focused and organized.

But now with Gregg v Georgia, he had lost all sense of contentment, even safety. It didn't matter that, as Sullivan had said, Salim's situation didn't change: once his sentence had been commuted, it could not be changed back. But only one thing mattered to Lester: his *mitzvah*. During those long hours in the Trenton Library, he had felt more alive than he had the whole time he was at Columbia. He had found her again—sure, it was only a few articles—buried in the Local section. The New Jersey Activists Against the Death Penalty, led by one Frieda Naima Johnson. They protested at Columbus Square and at the Trenton State Prison, where Salim was held. He had no doubt that she hated his guts, that if he were to go to her and stand before her to beg her forgiveness, she would probably spit in his face, but he also knew that they were fighting the same fight, and that that fight meant everything to both of them. And so there was hope.

He was glad, in a perverse sort of way, that Flora had left him—for all her marching and chanting and door-to-door canvassing, she could never understand. He, Lester, was responsible for another man's life. Yussel's life had been snuffed out and there was nothing he could do about it—he couldn't bring him back, or intervene to stop the bullet—but he could make sure that Salim's life was not similarly wasted. At the very least, he could spend every ounce of time and strength and wisdom he had, trying.

He got up and went over to the table by the phone, opened the drawer, and took out the Wenarski's menu. "Ma, trust me. I know what you want."

She smiled. "The pastrami?" She beckoned to him and he handed her the menu. "Not just the wedding! I can't die until you give me grandchildren."

"I know, I know. But there's time. I'm still young."

She frowned, pursing her lips. "Not so young."

"It'll happen, you gotta have patience. Give me until you're seventy-five."

"Oy—so old!"

Lester grinned and wagged a finger at her. "Not so old."

She sat down hard on one of the dining room chairs. "The insurance money—I saved it all, for your wedding. A real nice wedding."

Lester and Flora had met with Rabbi Greenberg to prepare for the wedding, and the rabbi had grilled him about Yussel's death. How did he die? How old were you? Where were you when he was killed? And Lester had haltingly, bashfully, spat out the words, all the way up to the part where he always choked. *I didn't see. I couldn't see. I don't know.* Later that night, Flora had interrogated him further, sniffing out his recalcitrance, demanding a fuller explanation. He begged off, telling her he had a migraine, but then she called and left a message with his roommate. She had to see him—it couldn't wait. Could he meet her on campus? He met her at the Rathskeller, where he downed four shots of Jack Daniels, and then rambled through the entire Salim fiasco, even the visit to the head shop, buying the flute, how he had had a crush on the sister. All of it. The longer he talked, the quieter she became. At the end, she had taken his hand, and sat there in silence, trembling, as fat tears trickled down her cheeks.

A few months ago he had read in the alumni bulletin that she had married somebody named Ebenezer Abernathy at the Mother Bethel African Methodist Church in Philadelphia.

"She married Scrooge!" Santo had crowed, but Lester could barely chuckle. Mostly, he just thought about how Flora would be a lot happier with Ebenezer Abernathy than she would have been with him. Lester, a privileged white man, had sent a black man to jail, and Flora could not abide that fact. It killed her love for him, it zapped it right out of her, there in the Rathskeller on the Columbia University campus, when the summer of 1964 was many years gone.

12

Bearing Witness

At 7:52 the next morning Lester was standing in the hallway outside Courtroom 2012B, trying to peer through the pebbled glass. But he could see nothing—not the jury members, or the attorneys, or Ross Bernstein in his robes, presiding at the bench. He decided to go over to the Clerk's Office and see if he could make an appointment. Then he sat on one of the long benches in the hallway, waiting for 12:30, when he was told Bernstein could give him five minutes.

He wanted to see the documents pertaining to Mrs. Lillian Cala as a witness. Supposedly, she had given a statement. What did it say? Bernstein had not called Lillian to the witness stand, claiming that Lester's testimony and Officer Randolph's testimony was sufficient to convict.

Once, when Lester had been studying in his dorm room at Columbia, he had been called to the phone. Minnie had chatted with him as usual, and then towards the end of the call, muttered, "Lillian regrets what she said." Try as he might, he could get nothing more out of her, and before she hung up, Minnie had denied ever saying the words.

On a different night, Lester had received a call at 2:00 a.m. and stood shivering in the hallway of the dorm in his boxers as Santo's voice raged through the receiver: Carol Cala had married Charles Hart Underwood, the boy from Lawrenceville who had cheated him that day on the court.

"So what?" Lester had replied. "She's a free agent. I mean, she was."

"You don't understand," Santo wailed. "Dino moved out." Dino, who Lester remembered only from the night of the shiva, but who had dominated his childhood nonetheless, manifest as a protective force—the one who would beat you down if you looked at his daughter the wrong way, the man Santo had always hated and feared.

Lester thought back to the night in the basement with Carol, when they had read Cicero, and she had let him get on top of her, and stick his tongue in her mouth, when he had pawed her breasts, a blind, breathless 15-year-old. Now Dino was gone, and Carol had married Charles, the prig who had cheated Lester out of a win at the Green Meadows Country Club.

And he, Lester, was back in Trenton, and back at the courthouse, where on the steps five years earlier Ross Bernstein had been lauded for bringing a dangerous criminal to justice and had congratulated Lester for his bravery. He stood up, went over to the pay phone, and dialed Amos Sullivan, telling him he would take the job. Sullivan was curt and jovial, saying that he should report for "morgue duty" the next day, but Lester had a lot more on his mind than the morgue. He knew what his first story would be.

Bernstein's secretary, Cynthia, poked her head out of the door that said Clerk of Courts, and beckoned to him: Bernstein was ready.

"Mr. Bernstein," Lester said, as he came through the door to the judge's office.

"It's *Judge* Bernstein in my chambers," he said, winking at Lester.

He didn't look any different than he had the day he had congratulated Lester on the courthouse steps: big head, curly waves of red hair that lifted from his scalp in a bouffant style, and an incongruous sprinkling of freckles across the bridge of his nose. Just like Naima, Lester thought. Only Naima's freckles were a lot more charming.

Naima: she was the reason he was here, the reason he had taken the second-rate *Trentonian* job.

"Seriously, five minutes," Bernstein said, glancing at his watch. "Four and a half. How's your mother?"

"Fine, she's fine." Lester winced. "I, uh, I want to see if . . . ." He stopped himself. It didn't make sense to lead with the idea of a new trial. He needed to keep it simple, and then build to bigger possibilities. "You said . . . that Mrs. Cala, she was one of the witnesses."

Bernstein broke into a wide grin. "Whoa. Time machine! Are we talkin'—what? 1970, 1971 here? I don't even know where that file might be. You know, we destroy a file after four years or send them to storage. Budgets are tight." He paused and then put a hand on Lester's shoulder. "Bygones, Lester. Let him rest in peace."

Lester shrugged off Bernstein's hand and pushed ahead. "Remember, you said 'Lillian Somebody.' On the courthouse steps, you told me. I think she may have seen something, and I don't believe her testimony was included in the—"

"—She didn't see anything," Bernstein snapped.

"So you *do* remember," Lester said.

Bernstein eased onto the edge of his desk and folded his hands. "You hear a shot. You come running from the back, but—correct me if I'm wrong—you hit your head on the counter. And you break your glasses, right?"

Lester took a couple steps toward Bernstein, narrowing his eyes. "See, here's the thing. I know what I *didn't* see. And I *didn't* see Salim Johnson in my father's store, on that day or ever."

Bernstein leaned back and crossed his arms. "Lester, have you heard of something called retrograde amnesia? This is a medical condition, which can occur from hitting your head. And in these instances, the victim, the sufferer, he doesn't have good recall."

Lester shoved his hands in his pockets and rocked up on his toes. "As a matter of fact, I recently interviewed Mrs. Cala." He looked Bernstein dead in the eye and proceeded with his fabrication. "She was passing by the store. And she says now she might have some new information. New recall."

Bernstein opened his heavy lidded eyes a bit wider. "Now you're trying to tell me that there's new evidence and that is not something I'm going to entertain."

Lester put his hands on his hips and faced Bernstein. "Look. I got to make this right."

Bernstein nodded and then smiled. It was clear he thought the standoff was over. "Young man, your conscience can rest easy. You are doing society a favor. We all sleep a little better at night knowing that Sa—uh, Mr. Johnson—knowing that his kind is in jail. I myself, I have daughters, and I would be truly horrified if I thought they could be fraternizing with that sort of individual."

Lester shook his head. "Here's the thing. He's one of my people, you see?"

Bernstein's bushy red eyebrows shot up. "Sa—Mr. Johnson?

"Yeah. He's Jewish."

Bernstein frowned for a moment, and then glanced up, recovering. "Yes, the mother. Hadassah Ruth Johnson, nee Graverstein. We interviewed her at length." He stood up, walked around behind his desk, and began to shuffle papers, as if to say, this matter is closed. But then he stopped and narrowed his eyes at Lester. "You seem to think I haven't done my homework here, Lester. I know all about Mr. Johnson, his travels. A good deal of foreign travel. Where he buys his undershorts. He doesn't take a shit I don't know about it. You see?"

"You mean *bought*," Lester began, "because I think in prison—"

"—he traded his yarmulke for a fez. International travel to

Morocco. Did you know that he flies the Hammer and Sickle from the balcony of his apartment?"

"You mean *flew*. Don't think you can fly any flags in—"

"—you've heard of the Red Menace, I assume," Bernstein said, nodding. "And his so-called bookshop—a front for selling marijuana. One of these louche left-wing types. He was known to consort with radicals."

"Like, what sort of radical—"

"—your Charles Mansons—!"

"—no way."

Bernstein wagged an index finger at Lester. "Make no mistake. Charles Manson has plenty of compatriots—a whole band of them. SDS, the Weathermen, the Black Panthers."

Lester rolled his eyes, and Bernstein came around from behind the desk. He frowned at Lester and spoke in a measured deliberate tone. "The only difference between Mr. Manson and Mr. Johnson is one of race. Both of these . . . uh . . . *gentlemen* have the bonny luck to be living in the U S of A, where their death penalty sentences have been commuted to life. So you see, Lester, your Mr. Johnson is going to live out his existence on the state dime."

"You've got to understand," Lester blurted, "that since Gregg v Georgia, I. . . ." He paused and lowered his voice. "I don't sleep at night. Just the idea that it could be reinstated, it's terrifying. And New Jersey is moving in that direction."

"Do you remember the last execution in Jersey?" Bernstein asked.

Lester glumly shook his head, as the image of Old Sparky from the school library blazed into his brain.

Cynthia stuck her head into the doorway. "Mr. Bernstein, you're late for—"

"Right-o!" Bernstein crowed, bolting for the door. "Walk with me, Lester," he said, beckoning, as they started down the hall. "Ralph Hudson, 1963."

"I was ten," Lester said softly.

"My point is—even with the new capital cases, with the appeals, it could be years before they're executed, if ever. In this state, there haven't been any executions since then, and who knows when the next one will be. Your Mr. Johnson isn't in any serious danger."

Ross Bernstein waved as he peeled off, scuffing his loafers down the polished floors of the courthouse toward Courtroom 2012B, where for the next few hours, Lester presumed, he would sit quietly behind the huge dais of the bench, leaving it to the attorneys to raise their index fingers, rail at the jurors, in thrall to monsters of their own.

Lester made another phone call, drove to Colonial Avenue, and rang the bell at the Cala home. Lillian came to the door and then ushered him into a large living room. He barely remembered the place, but he was certain it was profoundly changed. Now that Dino was gone, it was all beige wall-to-wall carpeting, spider plants, and macramé, with Joni Mitchell on the stereo.

Mrs. Cala moved languidly to the sofa and looked up at Lester. Her face was full of lines, new lines, ones he didn't remember being there.

"This is a Peter Max design," she said, indicating the flowing sleeves of her caftan, the long swooping strokes of rose and gold.

She saw him staring at her canvas deck shoes. "I go to the beach now, every day, and just walk."

Lester nodded as he looked around for a chair. The one nearest to him was a dramatic curve with a yellow and gold pattern. He lowered himself gingerly into it, fingering the scratchy fabric.

"My Carol, she's married, you know."

"Santo told me."

"She's got a charge account at Bergdorf's. And they're members at Green Meadows."

Lester nodded. "I was engaged, you know. She did Freedom Summer."

"Your mother told me—she was so pleased."

"She broke up with me," Lester blurted. "She thought I was a sellout." He found himself smiling idiotically. "Only I'm not. See. That's why I'm here. I told Ross—Mr. Bernstein. I have to undo this thing."

Lillian sighed and looked over at him, her mouth turning down, as if to say, *Oh well. Why bother?* Lester remembered Carol saying that her mother was as lax as her father was strict. "What if you just refused to do your homework?" he had asked her back in high school.

"She'd implore me," Carol had said with an indulgent smile. He feared that, like her daughter, Lillian was too easy.

"Ross Bernstein," she said, smiling. "He tell you about me?"

"No," Lester said, reflexively. "Well, I said you were a witness." He omitted the lie he had told about Lillian confessing to having new information.

"That we're an item?" She leaned back and crossed her legs, Indian-style, settling on the couch.

"You mean—"

"—he didn't say? It's not a secret. Carol's not happy about it." Lillian smiled for the first time and he saw that her teeth were stained from smoking. "But what can you do?"

He couldn't tune out the music—Joni Mitchell was singing, "he got the urge for going." It seemed a little obvious. He checked Lillian's face, but she seemed unaware, even blithe. *The urge for going.* Had Dino left her? To hear Lillian tell it, Ross was the one who had moved into Dino's territory, and it was Dino who had to scram.

She brightened up when she mentioned Bernstein, as if coming out of a fog. "The sister—what was her name?" She stared at him, perplexed. "Funny name."

"Naima."

"Yes, she's one of the anti-death penalty picketers at the Statehouse. They're always in the papers. I've driven past the prison for years, you know. It's right by the doll factory." She leaned forward, and Lester could see the vertical lines on her upper lip, smoker's tracks.

"How is Minnie? Are you sure she's okay? You know she was always so proud of you."

"I know."

"Yes, of course you do. Such a good son."

He nodded absently and thought about asking her to turn down the music.

I've looked at clouds from both sides now
From up and down, and still somehow
It's cloud illusions I recall
I really don't know clouds at all.

"You want me to be a witness," Lillian was saying. "*Witness*. But that was you, yes? You were very brave, Lester, stepping up and pointing the finger that way."

"But I didn't!" he cried. He jumped up from his chair and began to pace. "I—that's why I came back here. I just took a job, at the Trentonian, and, really, I could do so much better, but I . . . ." He stopped and slumped back into the armchair, trembling and dizzy. He could feel the earth turning, another day, another night, and Salim was still behind bars.

She looked up at him, dazed. "I was on my way to the bank to deposit my paycheck. I have the deposit slip—time and date. 4:28 p.m."

He gripped the arms of the chair. "The murder was at 4:19."

"I was just walking by."

"So you might have seen something."

"What time was it?" She looked up at him blearily. "I don't remember."

"Whatever you told them." He held his breath, waiting. "The

shooting was at 4:19."

She gave him a helpless shrug.

"You probably saw the killer!"

"But I was just walking by."

"I know, but there's a big plate-glass window. Didn't you look in? Wouldn't you have maybe seen him and waved?"

"Saw who?"

"My dad."

"Maybe. I did sometimes wave to him. But the sun was strong that day—that's my impression—and there may have been glare."

Lester covered his ears. "The music?" he said, and he almost laughed: now he was the one who was imploring.

Moons and Junes and Ferris wheels
The dizzy dancing way you feel
As every fairy tale comes real
I've looked at love that way.

Lillian got up and walked over to the stereo, but then she seemed to change her mind, and she came back, flopped onto the couch and covered her eyes with her hand. "Charles, what an odious little shit."

"Charles?"

She opened her eyes and turned to him. "My daughter, she's lost to me." She sat up and arched her body toward him, her mouth tight. "Why don't you give up this charade? You're not a child anymore. This isn't make-believe."

Lester actually gasped, he was so stunned by her words. "Who ever said it was? This is real-life shit! A man was on death row because of me!"

She stared up at him, unruffled, maybe even a little fascinated. Her eyes were hard now, glinting with flecks of light. "What I saw was a young man. A young man."

"Black or white?"

"White."

She got up and went over to the coffee table, where she opened a ceramic box. "Lester, do you turn on?"

"You mean, grass?"

She nodded. "There's . . . something I've been intrigued by. Have you heard of LSD?"

"Sure," Lester said, afraid of being caught out as the child she had just accused him of being. "What Timothy Leary puts on his sugar cubes."

Mrs. Cala didn't even seem to know he was there, and she seemed oblivious to Joni Mitchell blaring *as every fairy tale comes real.* Maybe that was the point? If you lived in your own fairy-tale world, nothing else mattered.

Lillian casually lit a marijuana cigarette and settled back on the couch, taking a long toke. "My therapist, Gil Whiteside Whitcomb, he is a pioneer of sorts in the therapeutic use of LSD. They use it in Psychotherapy to promote healing." She took another long draw on the joint. "Have you heard of Gurdieff, Lester?" She didn't wait for him to answer, but continued in a melodious singsong. "He established the Institute for the Harmonious Development of Man at Fontainebleau. He believed that we need to get to a higher state of consciousness, a balance of body, mind and emotions, what he called a Fourth Way. We're all just walking around in a waking sleep, like automatons." She glanced up at him. "And so I left my husband. Ross was a part of my awakening. I began to study with Madame de Salzmann. Encounter groups at the Square Peg up in the West Village."

A long curlicue of smoke wreathed her dark hair and her voice seemed to emanate from inside the cloud. "We Westerners, we've missed the boat. A regimen of psychedelics can be psycho-therapeutic, you see. To dismantle the rational mind, or change your value structure. Allow us to see the universe the way the early shamans did. A kind of mysticism." She reached for a pale blue pamphlet with dog-eared edges. "I'd like you to listen. Just listen. So much we don't let in. You know?"

She was lost in her own dreamy world. As she began to read in a smoky contralto, Lester realized that she wouldn't be any help at all.

"In our society, mainly concerned with production and efficiency, the drama is that our capacity for questioning, still so vivid in early childhood, is very quickly eradicated or pushed aside for the benefit of our capacity for answering. When a child has a real question, most of the time he is immediately given a stupid answer. In the best cases the educator goes to the dictionary to be sure his answer is accurate. But anyhow unconsciously, if not proudly, he closes the question. From school to the end of our life it is always necessary to answer. We are compelled to learn how to answer. If we don't know how to answer, we are just no good."

Lillian kept on reading, but Lester got up, walked to the door, and out onto the streets. She knew—somehow Lillian knew. *To answer.* Naima's charge. He felt himself rocketing back to Mt. Calvary and to the side street, parked in the Valiant, Naima behind the wheel and he in the passenger seat. *Je responderay*. The beauty of those words on her lips. She had spoken to him of his *mitzvah* as if she were inside his head. He had followed every article about her—or rather, her group, the New Jersey Activists Against the Death Penalty. He would find her, he would wait as long as she deemed necessary, he would ask all the right questions, and he would be open to the answers, like Madame Somebody and the Square Pegs. *Je responderay.* The answers would come rolling down from the mountaintop, the way Martin said they would. Naima's hero. He could still see her, eyes shining. *Lester, they killed the finest human being on this planet. How can I stand by and just let that happen? How can you?*

The answer was easy. He couldn't.

In his waking hours he never let himself think about the sleepless ones. And in the sleepless hours, he thought of her. He dreamed that she could love him. And then—he usually stopped himself there, shut the fantasy down. But now, with the pot smoke still clinging to his nostrils, it was as if a pathway was opening to him: he was ready to go spelunking into the recesses of his brain, to bat away the cobwebs of rational thinking, and step into a glorious Heaven, designed by Peter Max in glorious swoops of rose and gold, Naima at his side. *As every fairy tale comes real.*

He stopped beneath a lamppost and stood staring at its intricate scrolls, as if he were stoned on the LSD that Mrs. Cala had spoken of. Now, in this very moment, he could acknowledge those nights right after the trial, the endless fretful shredding of his dreams, the half-lucid nighttime pageants in which he tortured himself with the most horrific possibilities—Salim electrocuted, and Naima so distraught that she threw herself off the Delaware Bridge, or leapt from the nave of Mt. Calvary Baptist as the giant organ shrieked and bellowed. In his sleepless hours, he composed his answers to her, sometimes epic speeches, other times funny self-deprecating asides, or long florid apologias, but in every single one, she responded. She saw how truly he had reformed himself, she knew how singular was his obsession. Yes, he would always say, I will find a way to set your brother free.

13

Truth or Consequences

Lester stood in the alley, pinging stones at Santo's window. It was ridiculous—Santo had a good job now, and still they didn't get a phone. Santo liked to make his calls from the pay phone on Whitaker in front of Romeo and Juliet's, a block from the rowhouse.

Finally, Lester went around to the front porch and knocked. After a few minutes, Pops came shuffling to the door and let him in.

"He up there?" Lester asked.

Pops nodded. "He worked a double shift."

Pops had aged rapidly in the time Lester had been away; he'd been okay until about a year ago, when he had a small stroke. Now he moved slowly, and he had coughing fits.

Lester followed Pops into the living room and took a seat on the couch—the same musty couch they'd had when he and Santo were in high school. Pops always kept the drapes drawn so you never knew whether it was night or day when you were inside.

Pops settled into his recliner. "How's your mother? I heard she lost her job."

"Yeah."

"But she's doin' okay?"

Lester shrugged. "She still thinks the Gestapo's gonna come pounding on the door. Yeah. I just left her—she was watching Milton

Berle." He turned to Pops. "Guess what? I got a job. The Trentonian. Just last week. Mostly the morgue." But he knew what his first story would be, and it wouldn't be anything Amos assigned. He decided to take a risk, speak it out loud. "I'm doing a story on the prison."

"That so?" Pops said, without turning toward him. He pointed at the set. "That lady's about to be reunited with her son. He just got back from Vietnam."

A young man in a military uniform stood behind a curtain, and then was ushered onto the stage, where a woman in a blue dress sat primly blindfolded.

Lester got up and went into the kitchen to get a soda. "My ma, she likes Kojak. The lollipops," he said as he resumed his seat. The woman was now frantically hugging the young man. Then Bob Barker strode onto the stage, grinning. "Hoping all your consequences are happy ones," he said, as the theme music played.

"Now that Bob Barker, he's a straight up guy," Pops said. "But I'll tell you the one who I don't like. Gene Rayburn. Always slobbering over the women."

Santo came downstairs, in jeans and a t-shirt, scratching his armpit.

Pops nodded in his direction. "Trenton's finest."

Santo flashed the devil salute with his left hand. "Dago pride."

"You're saying dago pride to a Jew, for chrissakes," Pops said, and then gestured toward Lester. "This kid is gonna interview the big shots."

"You took the job?"

"Affirmative."

"He's gonna clean up Trenton."

"That ain't possible, I hate to rain on your parade."

Pops shook a finger at Lester. "You go interview Mayor Holland. Now there's a mayor for you. Second time around. He was mayor back when you boys were just rugrats. And a Roman Catholic, he is.

Was gonna be a priest before he chose public service."

Santo disappeared into the kitchen and Lester nodded politely as Pops started one of his rants. "Fiorello LaGuardia, now *that* was a mayor. He knew how to run a city."

Santo reappeared and leaned against the chifforobe in the dining room, smiling as he wolfed down slices of cappicola. "Pops is only tuned to the dago channel."

"These dumbasses think we're all a bunch of Luigis who stuff ourselves on pasta. The Poles, the Greeks, they ain't contributed nothin' compared to us! Sgt. John Basilone, a Marine, received the Medal of Honor. Served in WWII. What about Chef Boyardee, huh?"

"Here we go," Santo said, grinning at Lester.

"They was the largest provider of rations to US forces in WW II. Henry Mancini, one of the greats. Tony Bennett, we knew him as Benedetto. Rocky Marciano, undefeated heavyweight champion. Concetta Ingoglia, you know her? That is Connie Stevens."

Lester laughed. "And how 'bout Lawrence Ferlinghetti, Pops? He's Italian."

Pops waved his hand. "Garr-bage!"

Just then Anthony appeared, coming up the stairs from the basement, and hurriedly crossed to the kitchen, his eyes cast down. Lester barely recognized him—he was lean and angular, and his head was shaved.

"Hey, how's it going?" Lester asked, but Anthony didn't even say hello.

"My nephew, the drug addict," Pops muttered.

Santo beckoned to Lester and they moved toward the door. Once they were on the street they climbed into Santo's Ford LTD.

"This is one righteous ride," Lester said as looked around at the pale green interior and the big reclining seats. "When you get this?"

"352 pounds of torque. Wood trim. Power windows."

They headed past Columbus Park, where each had made himself known to the other more than a decade earlier. Santo made a left on Chambers and then another left on Greenwood. Lester stared out the window at the cinder block one-story offices—a real estate company, a mom and pop grocery, a pawn shop, a barber shop. Farther down the block were old Tudors, the former homes of Trenton's elite, now rehabbed into storefronts and apartments.

Santo looked over at Lester. "I got a reporter with me, doing a big story."

"Actually, know what my first story is? They're feeding pork to the Muslims up at the prison."

"Serious?"

"Yeah, Elijah Muhammad, he says pork is the devil's meat, something like that. Pigs are nasty."

"Elijah who?"

"Muslim Brotherhood."

"You're mixin' with the wrong crowd."

"The guys with the bow ties, on the street corners."

"Yeah, that's some crazy shit. They need to let the good citizens of Trenton walk around in peace, unmolested. I make sure I get a regular dose of pork, keeps me bright-eyed and bushy-tailed. Over at Tony Mastranni's I'll get two, three, of his pork sandwiches. With bacon, if he's got it."

"I think it's from the Bible—pork is unclean."

"Hey, if the blacks don't want it, then it's more for us."

"Well, Amos hasn't exactly green-lighted the story. But I got a lead. Remember Harlan Buford, that friend of my dad's? He's been a guard up there for years. Called him, asked him to meet me out at Mastoris's tomorrow."

"Here's a thing. You ask him if they ain't got some radio show up there."

"What, at the prison?"

"Tellin' you. Salim is on the air. On the jigaboo frequency, like maybe 250 watts."

"You heard it?"

"Nah. Ain't nobody outside the prison can hear it. That blind cat, plays the saxophone?"

"Rahsaan Roland Kirk?"

"Yeah, rah-something. Some Rasta-farian bullshit, yeah. He bankrolls it. Randolph is investigating it, I believe. Gonna shut it down."

"Damn, I'd love to do a story on that—you're saying Salim's the DJ?"

Santo shrugged. "You gotta get yourself a juicy story—like that girl who was murdered. Kristen Huggins, over at the Capitol Club."

"Nah. See, one of the pork protesters is none other than Salim Johnson. I'm gonna try to interview him."

"You gotta change the channel on that shit, man. It's old news." Santo made a right on Broad, and then hit the gas. "I'm taking you over to Lorenzo's so you can start making contacts."

"I been there—last week. I had a beer with Harvey Samuels."

"I drop in there after my shift sometimes, order a steak at the bar."

"Joe said Dean Martin was in there last week."

"Lemme set you up. Who you wanna see? How 'bout that tall girl, the pediatric nurse?"

Lester sighed. "I dated her, maybe twice, back . . . I don't know, after we graduated? Shit, get out your little black book. Anything to get my ma off my back. She's threatening to call Mrs. Applebaum."

"Code fucking red. That's heavy."

"I thought you were boffing Angela."

"Nah. She moved out to the wilderness, Idaho or something."

Lester opened the glove compartment. "You got a gun in here? Handcuffs?"

"Keep that shit in the cruiser."

"You know who I ran into. Carl Garfinkle. I always thought he'd end up on Wall Street."

"That dick works for the Havesons."

"Seriously? He didn't say anything."

"Just started there. You know they made it a pharmacy now."

"Yeah, Ma told me. I haven't even been by, it's too weird." Lester turned to Santo. "You know I haven't dated anyone serious since Flora."

Santo rolled his eyes. "You mean 'Flora I Did Freedom Summer Klein?' Fuck them longhairs. They just want to bring this country down. Flora and Amos Sullivan, they're the same—think they're some big champion of the Negro cause."

"*Black*. You gotta say black now."

"They's no more black than I am white." He thrust an elbow toward Lester. "What color am I, huh?"

Lester grinned. "Uh . . . maybe olive?"

Santo nodded and Lester stuck his own arm out. "So what color am I?"

Santo glanced down at Lester's arm and grinned. "You're *gold*, man."

Lester laughed. "Amos is a good guy. And Flora, well . . . she was intense, I'll give you that." He turned to Santo. "But I can't believe you're okay with what we did in Vietnam."

"Hey, Anthony was over there. I mean, he served his country, but I don't even recognize the kid anymore. He got a monkey on his back over there, and he ain't shook it yet."

"He stays with you now?"

Santo nodded. "I expected that kid to come home in a body bag. What a dumbshit—the fucker *enlisted*."

"What for?"

Santo shrugged. “Maybe he wanted to fuck them Chinese chicks.”

“Vietnamese.”

“Same difference.”

Lester frowned. “Actually, China invaded Vietnam, so did the French—”

“—All I know is, in the daytime, you wade through rice paddies killing gooks, in the nighttime you turn on. Horse was everywhere.”

“I would of thought it’d be you, and not him.”

“What, *strung out*?”

“Nah. Just . . . maybe locked up or something. All that shit you were doin’ back in the Columbus Park days.” Lester laughed. “And now you’re hanging out with Randolph—”

“—Hardly. He’s some big fuckin *detective* and I’m just out here walkin’ a beat. Louie got me on the force—he’s got connections. Now that Pops is sick I got to have regular work. Shit, I’m bulletproof. My uncle pays the cops to look the other way.”

“Since when?”

“Since forever.”

“When we were working there?”

“Fuck yeah, you dumb heeb.”

“Don’t tell me ol’ Randolph was on the take. Back in the day.”

“Hell yes.”

“Well. You’ve got your beat, and I’ve got mine now. Don’t you get it? I’m going to cover Salim’s case, as a reporter. I’ll have access to stuff I wouldn’t otherwise have. I might even be able to interview Naima.”

“You’re hot shit now. Gonna get published in the Partisan Review.”

“You know Mrs. Cala is listed as a witness.”

Santo struck the steering wheel with the heel of his hand. “Listen, man, you *gotta* let that shit go.”

"Seriously, I was smokin' pot with her last week. You don't think I'd rather be working for the Philadelphia Inquirer or something? I came back so I could investigate—"

"But it was *eight years* ago. Seriously, you're seein' ghosts, and that's gonna hold you back from the future you got planned. You're stuck in the past." Santo glanced over at Lester. "I wasn't gonna tell you this, but you'll find out anyway. You know there's been letters to the editor in the Trentonian."

"About what?"

"I mean letters from *her*."

"You mean—"

"—None other." Santo angled his chin toward the back seat. "Yesterday's is probably back there. Pops always reads it when I'm taking him to the doctor."

Lester rummaged around in the back seat and came up with the grease-stained front page section. "Shit, I've been pouring over the microfiche from years ago, and I didn't think to be reading it now." He turned to the editorial page. "Oh, wow. I see it. Frieda Naima Johnson." Lester said the three words of her name slowly, as if it were an incantation. "And I see here, their group, they're calling it 'Friends of Salim.' Listen to this. 'We will not rest until those who are unjustly incarcerated are given a fair trial. Salim Samuel Johnson, an innocent man, has spent nearly six years in Trenton State Prison, and now, in October 1976, he is in greater danger than ever.'"

Lester felt his stomach drop, and he turned to Santo. "What's that mean?"

"It's just spin, you know? She's trying to make it seem worse than it is."

"Wait. 'Community leader, friend to all, patriot'—"

Santo snorted. "Patriot! My dick is more patriotic than he is. My dick salutes, and that's more than he does."

"Just listen. 'The great peace we feel in knowing that our brothers and sisters of Mother Africa are with us and that our people here at home are marching with us, at Trenton State, and all over this nation, marching up the wide boulevards, arm in arm, in the great cities of this motherland. To all right-thinking people, the time has come to cast off your slave consciousness. No longer will we be the wretched of this earth. Love, Naima."

Santo rolled his eyes. "Amos Sullivan is a putz for publishing that dreck."

"How many of these letters are there?"

"How the fuck would I know? Pops just started reading that to me, I think it was yesterday morning."

"Well, you know she goes up there and visits him, at least I imagine she does. And it sounds like she knows something. Some kind of danger."

"She's probably making that shit up."

"No way. Nobody has more integrity than that girl."

"She's just trying to get him out."

"Seriously. Wouldn't you? If your brother was in there—"

"Don't have a brother—"

"Anthony, then. If he was in there."

"Let sleeping dogs lie."

Lester leaned forward, trying to catch Santo's eye. "Now you see, it's just the opposite. I'm waking up the dogs. By the time I'm done they're gonna be howling in the streets. The pork story is just my entrée. Now that I've got a beat, I can get in there, interview all kinds of people."

"That's just nuts. Make your mark with something people give a shit about."

"Look, you got your ducks in a row. A good job. Taking care of Pops. This thing, this is my way of making things right. If he's really in danger in there, what if he's killed? Then that's on me. One life gone, and now it's all these years later and I ain't stepped up yet. I know he didn't do it. And if I can find out who did, well . . . . Truth or consequences, that's all I'm saying."

"You watch too much boob tube."

"I'm gonna investigate this thing, so we can get him a new trial. And Lillian, if I can get her to be definitive, we can put her on the stand. She was walking past like a minute before the murder. If she could remember . . . she says LSD would . . . ."

"Yeah, that'll go over like a lead balloon. She gets up there on the stand and babbles about some acid trip. Besides, she's a crappy witness—she's the judge's mistress."

"Shit, are there no secrets in this town?" Lester shook his head. "You should see her, man. You know how people get stoned and they're having fun? Well, she looks like she's getting ready for a trip to hell. Some weird people she hangs out with. Square Pegs?"

"Never heard of 'em. I guess it's not as weird as the Strawberry Alarm Clocks."

"You're right. It'd be like putting Maude on the stand."

Santo started singing, keeping the beat by banging on the steering wheel. "'Lady Godiva was a freedom rider!' Yeah, popping Miltowns and getting an abortion, that would really make a great witness."

Lester grinned. "Yeah, she's flaky like Maude."

Santo pulled into the parking lot, put the car in park, and shut off the engine.

Lester looked over at the black awning that spelled out Lorenzo's in fancy white script. He had been here a couple times with Samuels and Joe Earl, and he was starting to feel like a regular.

"That bitch Carol. I tole her, you know, if she wants kids . . . ."

Lester stared at Santo. "That is so far out I can't believe what I'm hearing. *If she wants kids*. What does that have to do with you?"

"It ain't so far out as you think."

"What's that supposed to mean?"

Santo sighed and shook his head. "I could of given her security. A real family."

"That's hardly much security—that maybe someday, if she begged you, you'd make an honest woman out of her, and buy her a house in the suburbs."

"Oh, she's got the house. Big fuckin' Tudor out in Pennington. It ain't my fault that she married the world's biggest dipshit."

"And liar. Don't forget Green Meadows. I can't say it surprised me. What else was she gonna do?"

"She don't love him, I can guarantee you that. Listen to this crazy shit. They met at Career Day—you believe that? That bitch grew up south of Battle Monument, just like the rest of us dagos. Lillian and Dino—they ain't nothin' but middle-class strivers, dumb Catlicks, go to St. Mary's every Sunday. She thinks she's gonna be Anne Bancroft or something. She's eating caviar and he's in a smoking jacket, smoking Monte Cristos. Tell you what. They took a flight on the Concorde. I seen her crossin' the street the other day, on my shift. She's got this getup on—the mod look, with the frosted lipstick and the boots. She's a street-rat dago like me." He rolled his eyes. "I'm gonna smack that hoity-toity smile right off her face."

"You don't mean that." Lester turned to his friend. "Promise me you won't do anything stupid."

"I ain't in the mood for promises."

Lester leaned back in his seat. There was a brooding sour note in Santo's voice, as if he had walled off the sentimental parts of himself.

"She thinks she's all goody two shoes now 'cause she works with the retard kids. Big fuckin' deal—what you gotta tell 'em? Get your hands outta your pants, stop picking your nose, say excuse me. Know what she told me? She's takes a sleeping pill every night, like outta Valley of the Dolls or some shit."

"Wait. So you saw her?"

Santo continued in a mocking tone. "She shops at Bergdorf's.

She got Audrey Hepburn's autograph. He took her to Cabo." He turned to Lester and grimly shook his head. "It's like her mind is tuned to the bullshit channel."

"How do you know all this crap?" Lester asked, frowning at Santo. "Don't tell me."

"So what?"

Lester opened the passenger door and got out, and then began to pace. "That's why we're here. Right? Are they in there?"

"How would I know?" Santo snapped, as he opened his door and stepped out into the parking lot.

Once inside they took seats at the bar. Lester was wearing a dress shirt and a light jacket, with chinos, and loafers, but Santo wasn't really dressed for Lorenzo's—he had a black leather jacket over his t-shirt, and he was wearing jeans. Santo ordered two Jameson's, neat, and when they came, he pushed one over to Lester.

Lester knocked it back in one gulp, and then sat there, a dim heat spreading through him, a righteous I-told-you-so speech fomenting in his brain. Santo was a fool for carrying on this way about Carol, and Lester was the only one who would step up and be the good friend, tell it to him straight.

"Get this," Santo said, leaning in. "Suppose Carol gets knocked up. How do you know Charles is the real father?"

Lester searched Santo's face, his dark troubled eyes, the rigid line of his jaw. "Just so you know—I have no idea what you're talking about."

"The father doesn't always know. I mean, look at Dino, he took off for the South Seas, or some shit. He's a sailor now."

Lester thought about Lillian in her deck shoes—she wanted to be seen as a free-spirit, the carefree vagabond and beachcomber. But she had seemed like a wraith, a woman who was lost to herself, flitting around to encounter sessions and gurus, as if her life depended on it.

"Lillian can't stand Charles, if that makes you feel any better."

Santo shrugged, and then sighed heavily. "Maybe Dino isn't even her real father."

Lester laughed. "Right, I'll bet it's Ross."

"Nah. She don't have that carrot-red hair."

"That's a recessive allele."

"Gee, I love it when you talk dirty."

And then Carol and Charles were stepping into the foyer, Carol in a long crushed velvet jacket and a mini skirt, and Charles in a tux.

Lester jumped up and headed toward them. "Join us for a drink?"

Carol hesitated, glancing toward Santo, who sat glowering at the bar. Her smile was reserved and there was a new sophisticated lilt in her voice. "Lester, so good to see you."

Charles pumped Lester's hand. "Old man. I heard you're at the Trentonian now."

Lester nodded.

"I've just been sailing down in the Gulf. The Keys."

Lester looked down to see that Charles was wearing deck shoes with his tux, and he thought of Lillian, sitting on the couch, her feet tucked up under her, the deck shoes on the rug.

Santo walked past without looking at them and muttered to Lester, "I'm gonna hit the head."

Lester followed Carol and Charles out to the dining room. They seemed to already have a table there, a bottle of champagne chilling in the ice bucket. Charles took a seat, and Carol excused herself, heading back toward the bar.

Charles beckoned to Lester. "I always get the Herbie Gross salad. Best salad on the East Coast—no lie. Three kinds of lettuce, bleu cheese, anchovies—"

"—You do that," Lester snapped, as he stepped into the adjoining dining room. Harvey Samuels was there, chatting with several men at a back table, and Lester approached him with a hearty handshake.

“Sit with us,” Samuels commanded, but Lester shook his head, pointing back to the bar. He headed through the dining rooms, feeling embraced by the soft yellow walls and the flickering candles. Someone was playing “Stardust” on a piano in one of the back rooms. He resumed his seat at the bar. Santo wasn’t there, and so Lester downed his friend’s shot, letting the warm whiskey swirl down into his limbs. He just wanted to feel like himself again, like someone who had a good job and a nice warm place to lay his head. *A future.* That’s what Minnie would call it.

Carol walked past him, coming from the coatroom. A minute later, Santo appeared at the bar. “Let’s go.”

“We only just got here.”

Santo turned and walked out, and Lester followed him into the parking lot, waited for Santo to open the passenger door, and then got in. “Did you see that he was wearing deck shoes with a tux? What a pompous ass.”

Santo said nothing. His face was grave and he was sitting ramrod straight in the driver’s seat.

“Here’s the thing,” Lester said eagerly. “I was thinking. Charles and the law firm, we approach him. What if I could get him to represent Salim pro bono? A new trial.”

“That’s ridiculous, and it’s waste of time.”

“But he—”

“—Fuck that noise. No regrets. That’s my motto.” His voice was cold, almost robotic.

“You seriously want me to act like Salim’s not sitting up there in a cell for years now?”

“That dude’s trouble, man,” Santo said, as he pulled out onto the highway. “If he weren’t locked up for this he’d be in there for something else. He’s the criminal element.”

“Where are we going?”

"Don't ask me 'cause I don't know. We're just driving. I gotta drive."

They sat in silence for a while, and Lester stared glumly out at the hulking shapes and twinkling lights of Route 29. He could see the State House with its Golden Dome, and as Santo headed north along the Delaware River, he realized that they were at the Washington Crossing Bridge. Santo made a right onto Pennington Road, a left onto Route 31, and took the right fork at the Wayside Inn. The streets got wider, the grand driveways lined with stands of stately old growth trees—maples, sycamores, chestnuts, oaks. They motored into cul-de-sacs, the backyards lit by the moon, until Santo finally pulled up across from a Tudor with electric candles burning in the downstairs windows, and turned off the engine. After the half-lit coziness of the bar, the electric light seemed harsh.

"Who's house is this?" Lester asked.

"Nobody."

"Hell if it is."

"They're not the type to close the drapes, you know. I seen 'em."

"You're not worried about getting caught?"

"I ain't doin' it on my shift. Well, most of the time."

"You are so seriously fucked," Lester said loudly. He opened the door and stepped out into the street. "I gotta take a leak something serious. You hustled me out of there so fast."

"So go. Dark as shit out here—nobody'll see you."

Lester stood shivering at the edge of the cul-de-sac. He could just make out the spiky branches of trees across the frozen hillocks. When he returned to the car and opened the door, the dome light didn't go on. As he lowered himself into the seat, he heard muffled coughing. It took him a minute to realize that Santo, crouched near the window, was crying. Lester had never seen him cry before, and he sat there, helpless, staring at the dumb candles in the window. *They look like menorahs*, he thought. That's why they bothered him so much. Carol was Catholic, Charles was Presbyterian or Episcopalian, or Methodist, some rich white people sect.

Santo's sobbing had compelled Lester to silence. The wretched moans told him that Santo was a man foundering on the shoals of what he had lost. And Lester knew how it felt to be off-course like that. The night with Naima, when they had rushed out of Calvary Baptist, the sky was streaked with mauve and violet and he could just make out the first glints of stars. Just walking next to her had made him breathless. Just hearing her speak his name, and the beauty of her, it had struck him so hard, made him founder, go way off course. The next day he had gone out and cashed his paycheck, all $22.57 of it, and taken it to the Sunday service at Calvary, put it all in the collection basket. *An offering*. He told no one he was going, and afterward he wandered, dazed, among the regal women in hats and gentleman in elegant suits, but he didn't spot her, and he had gone home feeling lost. He understood it now: The business of offering up everything he had—it was about providing a rationale for why he felt so bereft.

Santo coughed and cleared his throat. "It's like all this time her old man, he hates me, he won't let me near her, and now . . . I wanted to be the one, you know, to father her kids."

He looked over at Lester, and in the darkness all Lester could see was a shadow where his eyes should be.

"I even had the names picked out. If it was a boy, Dante. And if it was a girl, Samantha. After that lady on Bewitched."

"It doesn't have to be her. Why don't you just have kids with some other girl?"

"Fuck knows." Santo stopped and blew his nose. "Back at Lorenzo's I followed her into the ladies, felt her up, fingered her, in the stall."

"And she *let* you?"

"She never says no to me." Santo took a deep breath and then turned sideways in his seat so he was facing Lester. "Look, I need you to do me a solid."

"Okay." Lester knew he couldn't hesitate. He had to seem as though he was all in with Santo, whatever the plan.

"Hands off the Salim case. Okay?"

Lester hesitated. "But why?"

"Why? Cause it's upsetting to Minnie, that's why. And it pisses off Pops, and then I gotta hear about it all day and all night."

"Why should he care?"

"He's sick now—the big 'C,' he calls it—he hardly goes anywhere. He's just an old busybody, and stupid shit sets him off." Santo shifted a little more toward Lester. "Just let it go, okay? Look. Look, I got an idea, I got a good idea. Something might change the whole game. What you need is new evidence, right? Well, we go back to the scene of the crime. We reenact it."

Lester turned away, out toward the dark houses on the eastern edge of the cul-de-sac and beyond to a twinkle in the distance, a tiny dot of light. "You're bat-shit crazy."

"We go back to the Havesons."

Lester turned and stared at Santo. "What, you're saying break in? That's lunacy."

"Not at all, my friend. I'm on the force now, and I got to protect the local businesses, make sure no prowlers are on the property, that sort of thing."

"It ain't even the same shop—it's a pharmacy now."

Santo shook his head. "So I heard, you dumb putz. That don't matter." He put his hand on Lester's arm and moved in close. "See, I got it all figured out. It's like that Hitchcock movie—Pops watches all of them. The lady who's the klepto. She steals from the safe at her job, can't help herself, but then when Sean Connery makes her reenact it, she remembers everything and she's cured."

Lester turned back to the window, searching for the pinpoint of light. "Are you in cahoots with Mrs. Cala or something? She was giving me a bunch of psychobabble and now you are too. Everybody's a nut case."

"Look, I'm saying, it works. The klepto, she don't steal no more."

"I don't see what that has to do with me."

"Look, dipshit. You go back to where it happened, and you see the whole thing again, just like a movie, and then it's like it never happened."

"I don't—"

"Promise me you'll think about it. You'll consider it."

Lester stared out to the street, focusing on the fake candles, the ones that looked like menorahs, in the window. Something was happening to Santo. He had been so cold and distant when he was talking about Carol and Charles, but now he seemed to be softening. He was almost begging Lester to wise up and deal with the murder. Lester didn't believe in the idea that someone could be "cured," but he could see that the whole business mattered to Santo, and he couldn't turn away from that. His friend was a changed man, he was no longer the same kid he had known in high school, and all the way back to the playground. Maybe Santo had a *mitzvah* of his own, and maybe it had something to do with Lester healing the pain of Yussel's death. "I guess so," Lester said. "I'll think about it."

14
Cat and Mouse

Mastoris's Diner was out in Bordentown, near where Harlan lived, so Lester suggested they meet there—he was asking a favor, after all, and he wanted Harlan to be well disposed toward him, so he made the drive. Besides, Mastoris's was a great place for a reporter just starting out to get what Sullivan termed the "juicy" stories. The place was filled with night shift workers, bar closers, drunks, daters, taxi drivers and insomniacs. Besides, the cops were always in there and Lester figured he'd need to start familiarizing himself with the new Trenton force, Santo's brotherhood, in case he needed favors.

"So you're working at the Trentonian, are you?" Harlan asked as he took a seat in the booth across from Lester.

Lester smiled. "Yeah, so far Amos has been making sure I familiarize myself with the morgue. He doesn't want my Columbia sheepskin to go to waste, after all."

Harlan chuckled. "Hell, your dad would have been so proud of you."

Lester ducked his chin, and then grabbed one of the big plastic menus for cover. He cleared his throat and then announced loudly, "I'm gonna have a ham sandwich. Pork. I'm in the mood for pork."

Harlan studied the menu for a minute and then leaned toward

Lester. "I'd drive near an hour over to Gold's to get my meat. Your dad only offered the best. The customer was always right." He put the menu aside and winked at Lester. "You were just a little tyke running around, playing on the floor."

"Sawdust."

"He used to let you punch the key on the register to open the drawer, just to hear the bell ring."

A middle-aged woman hustled over to the table, greeted Harlan and Lester, and flipped open her notepad.

"Cheeseburger and fries," Harlan said, "and my friend here, ham on rye." He grinned at Lester. "Should I assume rye?"

Lester nodded. "You should assume rye."

"That's Margie," Harlan said, as the woman headed back toward the kitchen. "She was . . . class of forty-nine, I believe. My sister and her was buddies maybe in middle school. Nice lady, but she's getting long in the tooth, wouldn't you say. Hard worker, though, nobody can say otherwise."

Harlan was what you would call a hard worker, too. Lester guessed that he was in his sixties: he was big, shambling man with thinning hair, a sunken face, and sagging jowls. He'd been working up at the prison ever since Lester could remember. He looked awfully fragile to be a guard, though: weren't they supposed to be intimidating, the overseer jangling his keys?

Harlan launched into an explanation, almost as if he could read Lester's mind. "I got ticker problems—had to have surgery last year, and I ain't been fully myself since. My doctor says to stay away from eggs, why, I couldn't tell you, but he don't say nothing against protein. My wife, she eats the cottage cheese plate, but that ain't for me." He patted his gut and grinned.

Lester pushed the menu aside and leaned forward. "I heard that they've been serving pork up there, something about a tight budget? And the Muslims went on a hunger strike?"

Harlan leaned back in the booth and crossed his arms. "I can tell you one thing, none of them was Muslim before they got to prison. A lot of these blacks we got up there—they're godless people. Al-lah, Al-lah, that's all you hear up and down the block, but they don't even know what they're saying. Buncha mumbo-jumbo so they can get kosher meals is all it is. And grow their beards. You ask me any religion that says you can't cut your hair might as well be voodoo. Next thing you know they're gonna be sayin' they can't cut their fingernails. Or what if their God tells them they can't flush shit down the toilet? Well, then we're all up shit creek!" He slapped his big hand on the table and guffawed.

"Thing is," Lester said. "I'm hoping to interview one particular guy up there. Salim—"

Harlan shook his head and then put his hand over Lester's. "—You don't have to tell me. We all got a strong dose of Mr. Johnson up at Trenton, and I can tell you he's treated very good." He pulled his hand back and gripped the lip of the table. "Now this is something between you me and God, but I look out for that fellow, on account of . . . *you know*. What you been through and all."

Lester leaned back against the booth and shut his eyes. How could it be? This old codger, from the Class of '56—Yussel always used to say that they went back that far—he'd never paid any attention to the Sixties, or the Great Society, the Civil Rights Movement, any of it, and yet he was looking out for a black man, one who all of white Trenton feared, in the name of a beloved old Jew.

Lester opened his mouth but the words caught in his throat, and before he could speak, Harlan was pushing on.

"Salim Johnson. I've been up there for—what—twenty-three years now, and I can't say I've seen many like him. Highly intelligent, for one thing. Now they've all got their . . . *affiliations*, shall we way? Most of them, they care more about an insignia or a tattoo then they do about a human life. They'll stick you soon as look at you. They come out of the underbelly and they stay right there, don't like to move up or down, just hold right there where they got their teeth on the teat." He glanced over at Lester and nodded. "But that fellow, you'd think he'd be one angry sonabitch. And yet . . . ." He shook his head, marveling. "First time they brought him onto death row, back before they commuted the sentences, he was grinning like he was gonna shuffle off to Buffalo. He's doing a two-step down the range, up in the third tier. That Negro is crazy like a fox. Been up in solitary almost since the first day he got there. Won't follow no rules without you have to beat him into it."

Margie brought their plates of food, but Lester barely noticed. "What, you mean, he's getting beat up in there?"

Harlan lowered his voice and leaned toward Lester. "I'm saying, he's given to sacrifice. He looks out for the young lions, you follow? The old heads runnin' drugs up in there—not that it ever happens, mind you," he said, winking at Lester. "And he counsels the newbies, I guess you'd say, tries to keep 'em on the straight and narrow. So we have to put him in the hole for his own safety, you understand."

"You mean the gangs are out to get him, for interfering?"

Harlan frowned. "Most folks don't have a dad-blamed clue about what our job is up there. We're not the judge and jury, we don't make the rules, and we don't antagonize. Our job is to keep the guys safe from each other. Heck, sometime it's safe from *themselves*, you hear? There's some hard heads up in your correctional facilities, specially nowadays. Once you had your Attica, for example, we had to re-think safety, understand? I mean, look at how they went at *each other*. What they did was way worse than anything Old Sparky could do."

The chair materialized, black straps dangling, and Lester found his voice. "I read about Old Sparky, back in tenth grade or something, and it terrified me. Gave me nightmares!" Lester began to cough, and he took a slug of coffee, relishing the acid burn in the back of his throat. "I . . . I read about what happens when they throw the switch. The condemned shakes from the torture. His skin stretches. He defecates, he urinates, his tongue swells, and his eyes pop out."

"Bull pucky. That's a lotta hype. Nowadays they give 'em the needle. And nobody's been executed in Jersey in ages anyway. They all got a million appeals, takes forever before they ever get to lights out. Now they got it more humane—they go to sleep real peaceful-like. All you liberals, you'd change your tune in two shakes if you'd spend a week up there." He shook his head. "Makes you question why God ever created Adam and Eve." He gave Lester a wry smile. "Capital punishment serves a necessary function. Like I said, sometimes you just gotta flush the turds, you know?"

"But—I'm all about trying to get him a new trial. Don't want anything bad to happen to him on my watch, you see?" Lester took a breath. "If I could just talk to him—"

"—Won't do you any good—"

"—But, see . . . I know he's innocent." He stopped and regarded Harlan, waiting to see if he would believe him.

Harlan shook his head. "They're *all* innocent, to hear them tell it."

Lester paused and then reached in his back pocket for his wallet. He had just cashed his first paycheck yesterday, and he took out $96.00 and spread it on the table in front of Harlan "We both know that my dad trusted you with his life—" He stopped and stared down at the placemat. "I didn't mean it like that—"

Harlan gave him an avuncular nod. "No, of course not."

Lester smiled weakly. "What I mean is, they all say they're innocent, but I'm gonna bet my paycheck right here that Salim has never once said that. If I'm wrong, then you take all my money, and I'll give up right now. I won't investigate." He looked into Harlan's eyes and held his gaze. "Am I right? In all the years, he's never once said—"

He stopped and smiled at Harlan. When he had first reached for his wallet, he could feel his palms starting to sweat, and his heart rate ramping up, but now that he had made the wager, he felt better than he had in weeks.

Harlan grinned. "You're a smart kid, you know that?"

Lester grabbed the cash and stuffed it back into his wallet.

Harlan signaled to Margie for the check. "Okay, here's what I'm gonna do," he said, sighing heavily. "Besides buy you lunch. First, they process them down in the basement of the courthouse. And it just so happens that your Mr. Johnson's got a court date two weeks from Thursday. Depending on who's on the bench that day, he could be sitting down there a good while."

Lester slapped the table with his palm. "Far freaking out! She must have got him some kind of appeal or something!"

"Who did?"

"His sister. Naima."

Harlan shrugged. "No idea. But give me a day or two and I'll get you the time of the hearing. You know, he's got hisself a good lawyer, that's for sure. You heard of Racehorse Hafferty? Real name is Frederick. His father was mayor number of years back. Died when he tried to save an old man who had fallen into the Delaware River. A real hero type."

Lester reached over and pumped Harlan's hand. "Right *on*. I promise I'll be discreet. You won't even know I'm there."

Harlan stood up and he and Lester walked to the door. Lester walked to his car and Harlan followed him, standing there shielding his eyes from the sun.

"I'll bet you don't remember the old McGuffey's Reader. That was back in the day when your dad and me were just schoolboys." Without waiting for a response, Harlan continued. "They had this one story I always remembered. A mouse keeps trying to climb out of a box. He tries and tries, but it's no use. But he sees this bowl of milk in the corner, and he jumps in and runs in circles, just around and around, until he churns that milk right into butter. So he can slide over the edge of the box." Harlan tossed his head back and laughed. "He's free. Now you see, that mouse, he had perseverance. And your Mr. Johnson, he's just like that mouse."

A few days later, on a cloudy Thursday, Lester jogged up the steps of the courthouse, past the Doric columns and the marble statue of Justice with her long flowing robes and the blindfold over her eyes. He entered the lobby and hustled past the imposing portraits of governors and statesmen long dead. He then took flight after flight down into the dim heart of the building, where he made his way through double doors into a low-ceilinged room with beige walls. Harlan was there, in his uniform—gray shirt and black trousers.

Lester saw Salim instantly: he was sitting on a low bench with his back to him, wearing a khaki-colored prison shirt and pants. At a small table on the other side of the room, two prisoners were seated, talking with what Lester assumed were their public defenders. Both inmates wore leather belts around their waists and had their hands cuffed to the belt in front of them. But Lester could see that Salim's hands appeared to be free: he had one arm up along the back of the bench.

Lester gave Harlan a polite nod and angled his chin toward the bench.

"Is he . . .?"

Harlan raised one wrist, indicating, *He's shackled.* He put a gentle hand on Lester's shoulder and spoke softly. "Remember. McGuffey's mouse. You just keep running in a circle, you're gonna float to the top, get what you need out of him."

Lester smiled and nodded, but he knew his attitude was all wrong. He had come down here, he had arranged this whole thing, because he wanted to do anything he could to help free Salim, and now here he was almost giddy with relief at the news that the man was shackled.

He was here as a reporter and that meant he had to be impartial. He would interview Salim, politely ask questions, extract information, and then when he could get back to the newsroom, he would formulate a powerful and effective story about justice maligned.

He stood there, his legs trembling, pinpricks of sweat stinging his palms. Salim was facing a long counter and Lester could see a big woman with thin eyebrows and dark hair teased high sitting at the counter. A line snaked toward the window where people stepped up to hand her papers. He could hear the distant clacking of a typewriter.

To the right of Salim's bench, there was a long corridor, and Lester figured it probably led to the bathrooms. He turned to Harlan, took a deep breath, and nodded. He didn't want to shake hands just in case it could appear that they had settled on some sort of agreement. He moved stealthily toward the counter, almost tiptoeing, past a sign with an arrow that pointed to the "Community Room." Salim didn't turn around and Lester walked quickly to the end of the hall. He stood in front of a door marked "Records," preparing himself to return to the room that Harlan had called "Holding" and face Samuel Salim Johnson. He plotted his strategy: He would enter in such a way that he would be facing the prisoner, and Salim would have a chance to recognize him. The last thing he wanted was to come up on Salim from behind, as if he were ambushing him.

He moved back down the hall, his palms sweating freely now, and approached Salim, who had one wrist shackled to the railing that ran alongside the bench. His other hand, the left, lay passively in his lap. His freckled face was ruddy, his eyes the same feline green-gold that Lester remembered from the encounter at the shop. He looked up and saw Lester, and after a moment he smiled.

"Well, if it ain't young Lester Gold stepping up on my front porch."

Lester almost bowed to Salim, and then hated himself for

performing such an ingratiating gesture. He nodded and took a seat at the other end of the bench.

Salim grinned. "Why so far away? You got nothin' to be afraid of—looky here," he said, holding up his shackled wrist. "I couldn't hurt you even if I tried."

Lester nodded as his stomach plunged and his guts seemed to swirl in place.

"You here to keep me company in the Green Room?" Salim asked earnestly. "While I wait to go up before the big bad Mag-is-*strate*. You wanna come up and watch me be a-JOO-di-cated? Oh, right, you already done that, old news, am I right?"

Lester was now trembling violently and he couldn't trust his voice. "Can I be honest?" he blurted. "I'm terrified, terrified that you hate me." He glanced miserably in Salim's direction.

Salim shook his head slowly, wearily. "Why I couldn't possibly hate you as much as you hate yourself."

It wasn't possible, Lester thought, that anyone could seem so satisfied, like a big cat lazing in the sun as he licked the bones of his prey. Here Salim was sitting in a dingy basement room with low ceilings under the buzzing fluorescent lights, handcuffed to a metal rail, and yet he seemed completely at ease. As Lester watched, Salim settled into his seat and stretched his legs out in front of him, as if he had come down to the holding room to meet Lester for a fireside chat. Lester glanced over at the other prisoners huddled miserably at the scarred wooden table, while Salim chatted amiably, his one-handed gestures expansive, the cold buzz of the lights somehow casting a warm glow about him. Just sitting near him brought back the day at Uhuru so many years ago. Lester hadn't been able to figure it out then, but now it was clear: Salim had an extraordinary inner balance, a compass that never wavered. He would be at home anywhere. And that was why the powers-that-be in Trenton loathed and feared him: he could not be brought down.

"I heard about your lawyer," Lester exclaimed. "Racehorse Somebody. He's excellent, am I right?

"Only ofay I can look in the eye."

Lester noticed a few fresh sprigs of gray in Salim's dark hair—but then he caught himself. *Fresh*. How could he know—maybe they'd been there all along, maybe he'd come out of the womb with gray hair for all Lester knew. He reminded himself that the only time he'd been face to face with Salim was the day at Uhuru.

A red fire extinguisher was mounted on the wall behind Salim and Lester focused on it, trying to right himself. Every time he glanced at Salim, the man seemed to morph, his face growing lighter, his hair darker, his eyes kaleidoscopes of light. He held some strange power—a shape-shifter, a shaman, a leader of men.

"I bet you're sorely disappointed," Salim said. "Here you was hoping I'd be back on Death Row."

"No," Lester said forcefully. "Just the opposite."

"Know who else got his sentence commuted to life? Charles Manson. Now he seems to think he's got it all figured out. He said that the only way to get Helter Skelter going was for him to go down and show the black man how to do it, by killing a whole bunch of fucking pigs." For the first time, Salim yanked on his handcuffed arm. "How ridiculous that that dumb cracker would have to show *us* how to do."

He smiled—or he seemed to smile, baring rows of small even teeth. "We showed him *how* up at Attica. Only thing that's gonna make it right is full-scale Armageddon. Louis Farrakhan, the Nation of Islam, he negotiated with the prisoners. Every one of them guards was white. Them crazy screws killed a bunch of hostages, and 29 inmates. The Weathermen retaliated, blew up their asses with a bomb. What were they on about? *White supremacy*," he said, making delicate air quotes with his free hand. "That's the rule of the land. And when the black man rises up, like he did at Attica, rest assured that they will try to be beat him down."

"I just . . . ," Lester began, shaking his head. He looked imploringly toward the prisoner. "Salim."

The chips of light in Salim's eyes went dark. "What you callin' me? You callin' me by my *name*? No, you little no-count peckerwood, you call me SIR."

Lester nodded miserably. "Okay. . . uh, *sir*. I . . . I wanted to tell you—"

"Now I think you owe me an explanation. What you doin' in my neighborhood? You come for a cup of tea? Cause I'm fresh out of Earl Grey." He smiled sweetly at Lester, and then made as if to lunge at him.

Lester jumped up, trembling.

Salim laughed. "Yeah, I didn't think you were afraid of me."

Lester realized that Salim's posture—relaxed, almost indolent—was a ruse: his panther energy coursed beneath the lean, coiled muscles. He glanced behind him at Harlan, who had taken a couple steps toward the bench. Lester waved. *I'm okay.*

"Maybe you're one of them commie pinkos? Come to set the *oh*-pressed black man free?"

Lester leaned toward Salim, trying to show that he wasn't afraid. "I want to make it right. Whatever it takes."

Salim nodded sagely. "Fred Hampton. Now he was a-*sass*-a-nated by the Chicago *po*-lice. Know what his crime was? *Sleeping.* That fine young brother was sound asleep when they gunned him down. He was guilty of feeding breakfast to children. He was guilty of promoting nonviolent activism. Guilty of being a community organizer. Now they killed George Jackson, one of the Panthers, up at San Quentin. Another innocent black man slain in cold blood. Where does it end? *You* don't right the wrongs. *I*—the black man—will right the wrongs. By any means necessary."

Lester inched a bit closer to the prisoner—if he could just get

Salim to listen for a moment. "You see, what I want—"

"—Bet you wish they kept us out there on a chain gang, that'd make you feel all righty-right knowing we *crim-i-nals* is making a *con-tri-bu-shun,* to this great country that your forefathers colonized."

Harlan had said that Salim had sacrificed himself for "the young lions," even spent time in the hole for his actions. Lester had never done anything like that, but now, if he could just get Salim to listen, he would prove that his true ventures were just beginning. He would prove that he was capable of greatness, the way Salim was. He took a deep breath and could feel his guts settling down. "I gotta tell ya, there weren't any Jews on the Mayflower. We were those people whose names got chopped off. Shimonsky, we'll call you Simon. Zapponik—we'll call you Simon too. The anti-Semites, they—"

"—Your father, was he in the camps?"

"No, but my grandparents—"

Salim leaned toward him and nodded. "Maybe those Aryans shoulda worked harder to round up you heebs. They only got six million and they shoulda got six million and *one*. Seems to me there's some errant kikes right here in our fair city of Trenton, ones who hatin' on the blacks so hard they got to get 'em all up in the jails so they can feel safe."

Salim beckoned to Lester with his free hand. "C'mere," he whispered.

Lester moved toward the middle of the bench, afraid to stay where he was. He wouldn't give Salim the ammunition he needed to call him a racist, a frightened white boy who shrank from a black man's touch.

Salim patted the bench seat next to him and whispered. "We *in*-mates, we ain't allowed to be touchin' on the guards. *Nev-ah*. No matter how no-count the fellow is. Ain't that right?" He beckoned to Lester to come closer, and Lester slid down next to him. He stared hard at the woman behind the glass so he wouldn't have to face Salim.

Salim reached out and gently picked up Lester's hand, placing it on Lester's chest over his heart. "You hear that?" he whispered. "Thumpa-thumpa, thumpa? That's the heart of a free man."

Lester yanked his hand away and slid back toward safety. "I just . . . I want to say I was wrong. About the testimony. And I'm going to make it right."

Salim nodded. "Little Jewboy come up in here to rescue me?"

"No, no," Lester said, raising his hands. He flashed on Naima, lit up by the moon, as she leaned on the steering wheel of her mother's Valiant. *You're not some white massa come along to set the Negro free.*

"Gonna save the black man from a life of slavery?" Salim taunted him, his voice rising. "Is that it? I bet you're a big admirer of Abe Lincoln, am I right? Cause he freed the—"

"No!" Lester shouted. "I knew that one! Naima told me. He didn't—"

In a second all the twinkle evaporated from Salim's yellow cat eyes, and his face went hard as concrete. The silence emanating from him was so powerful that Lester froze.

"You *dare* to speak her name? She is a *queen*, and you are a worm! A leech! A par-uh-site! Get away from me before I puke," he said, turning away. But it was another of his ruses and he turned back instantly, grabbing a handful of Lester's hair and yanking his head into his own lap. He spoke in a guttural whisper. "I will crush those two little pips in your trousers if you so much as speak her name."

As he let go of Lester's hair, shoving his head away, Harlan was standing over them. Lester jumped to his feet, shaking, as Salim spat the words at him. "Do. You. Understand. Me."

"Yes," Lester whispered, backing away. "I'm sorry!" he shouted as he raced down the corridor, blundering into the "Records" room where the big woman with the skinny brows was sitting in a metal folding chair, eating a ham sandwich. There was an exit back there, a red sign, and Lester pushed his way out the door and hustled up the crumbling concrete steps, where he faced a padlocked gate and a chain link fence. He sat down hard on the top step, and even though he was shaking uncontrollably, he was able to congratulate himself: better here than on the front steps, under the Doric columns, listening as Ross Bernstein lied to him. He thought of the statue at the top of those steps, the graceful woman with the blindfold over her eyes, and realized what had fallen away: Salim had nothing to do with his father's murder, and likely had never even set foot in Gold's, and Lillian Cala was a kook who probably didn't know anything more than what she had already told him. And now there was a new fact, a fact far more important than anything he had learned so far: There was a way into the seemingly impenetrable recesses of Samuel Salim Johnson's clever mind. *Naima.*

Lester scooted his butt across the gravel of the pitted step and put his head down between his knees, trying to breathe. He, Lester, was the mouse. He would persevere. Even Salim couldn't scare him into giving up.

15

North Star, Star of David

It was way past midnight and Lester was sitting behind the wheel of Yussel's 1962 Ford truck. It had been up on blocks for a few years, but recently he had decided to fix it up and get it running. It was Saturday night and he was in the parking lot of the Blue Note Tavern, an after-hours club out on Tyler Avenue. The lot was full, but he didn't recognize a single car. He had never been to the club, but he knew vaguely that it was frequented by men who worked in the nearby factories making floor tile or rubber hoses. Next door was Levin's Shoe Shop and a check-cashing place. He had called Pops, who said Santo was working the late shift, so Lester had driven out here alone, with one mission: to do what had been forbidden him. Naima waited tables at the Blue Note and she also performed there, according to Amos Sullivan, the man who faithfully printed her letters to the editor, as a sort of beatnik singer-poet.

Lester had had breakfast that morning with Minnie and she had casually handed him the op-ed page, sitting silently while he scanned Naima's latest letter. Once again he had failed to check, in his very own paper—at work, he couldn't allow precious thoughts of her, couldn't let them be sullied by the workaday world.

At the breakfast table he had read the letter with a thudding heart. *Humans beings, our brothers, are kept in cages.* And she had quoted Martin Luther King. *I am compelled to carry the gospel of justice beyond my own home town. Injustice anywhere is a threat to justice everywhere. Whatever affects one directly, affects all indirectly.* The last line especially—it was as if she were speaking to him. *All that I do affects you directly.* And it did. He had memorized those lines, they were a part of him now, just as she was.

The radio in the old Ford still worked, and at the moment it was blasting "Love Hurts" by Nazareth. He smiled to himself, thinking it was a bit too obvious. Love did hurt, but what he felt for Naima—could he really call it love? It was more like admiration. He hadn't seen or spoken to her in seven years, so it certainly wasn't love in any traditional sense. Would she speak to him? He doubted it, but he felt as if he no longer had a choice: he had to at least see her.

The song ended and he leaned back and closed his eyes, relishing the idea that he was about to disobey Salim's commandment. *Na-i-ma.* He loved to say her name, and he had been repeating it to himself ever since Salim's admonition. He would go into the club, he would say her name, she would come over, and smile at him, and they would embrace. He would say, *Don't cry, Naima*, and he would dry her tears. He would explain that he was devoting his life to saving her brother, that he had come to make things right. And he, Lester, was a man of his word. He was legit now, a reporter on a story.

He got out of the truck and stood on the running board. How he had loved jumping down from the cab when he was a boy and climbing the wooden steps of the two-story houses that backed up onto narrow alleys. Yussel would stop and Lester would carry the deliveries up the rear steps, put the bags in front of the kitchen door, ring the bell, and then race down and on to the next delivery. Every day after school, he headed straight to the store: the heady offal haze greeted him, his father packing a brisket in salt, or brining it in one of the big tubs. Sour pickles in a barrel.

He walked around the front of the cab, glancing at the silver letters spelled out across the big square grille: "F-O-R." The "D" was long gone, and tonight that seemed especially fitting.

He floated across the parking lot, imagining her smiling down on him, stepping off the glittering stage and taking his hand. But when he was inside and his eyes adjusted to the dim light, he could not believe who was beckoning to him from a corner table: Lillian Cala. Seated next to her was Ross Bernstein, looking groovy in a blue-striped button-down open at the neck. No tie. His red waves cresting high above his broad forehead. Ross's version of groovy, Lester thought, was what anyone else would view as hopelessly square.

Lillian was charcoal next to Ross's flame—her gray face and black hair shot through with gray, some dark metallic stones decorating her neck.

"Lester, I've been meaning to call you," she said, reaching toward him. "I've had a breakthrough. The therapy with my analyst that I told you about."

She reached out and clawed him closer. "Sit," she pleaded, and he did, taking a chair that was uncomfortably close, in the noisy crowded club. The skin around her eyes seemed frayed, almost as if she were burning from the inside out, and all that was left was ashes.

"I have been expanding my consciousness," she said, with great sincerity. "Never before have I felt so at peace. We are all one, Lester," she said, smiling beatifically. "I flow into you, you into me, and we two into Ross. No separation at all."

She was speaking in a normal tone of voice. Ross sat there as if she was talking about ordering a shrimp cocktail. Lester nodded, but he had no idea what to say. It was quite obvious that she was referring to taking hallucinogens.

"Now, Lillian, you don't want to fill this young man's head with that mumbo-jumbo," Ross said, giving Lester an avuncular smile. "He knows better."

"I'm here working on a big story," Lester said, standing up.

"Emma Jane Stockton. Murdered in my neighborhood, Mill Hill." He leaned against a pillar and crossed his arms—he had indulged himself in some new threads: a pair of Beatle boots like the ones Salim's compatriot had been wearing that night at Uhuru, and a corduroy blazer with leather patches on the elbows. He nodded sagely at Ross, as if to say, isn't it awful about that poor girl? The part about the story was a lie, but a harmless one. "I've got the best job in town. One thing we'll never run out of in Trenton—crime!"

Lillian gave him a mild stare. "You have my number?"

Lester backed away, giving her a wave. "So good to see you," he called as he headed toward the bar.

He sipped some Dewar's—it went with the elbow patches—as the sound of *her* voice snaked toward him. She was talking to someone from the stage, and the mic was picking up snatches of her conversation. The club was packed and there were maybe a hundred bodies between him and even a glimpse of her.

He grabbed a chair from one of the café tables and stood on it. She had her back to him, but it was unmistakably her—her slender elegance, her cloud of hair. A black man was seated at the rear of the stage, in front of some bongos. Lester jumped down and leaned against the bar, taking deep breaths. He had seen her, and now maybe that was enough, he thought. But then the bongos started a rat-a-tat-tat, stalking his heart, making it thrum harder, and then harder still, until it was more than he could bear.

He squeezed his eyes shut and the shop came back to him then—he thought he'd left it in the parking lot with the old Ford, but it came flooding in: the sweaty meaty fog that seemed to cloak everything, the little tray table in the back where he used to copy out sums, or dutifully scan his *Weekly Reader*, the ting! of the cash register. When the store got busy in the late afternoons, he stopped hearing the bell at all. The white aprons that hung on a peg in the back, stained brown with old blood, and then bleached by Minnie to a faded pink. He, Lester, was in charge of wrapping the orders in freezer paper and taping them, and then loading the shopping bags for the deliveries—a brisket for Mrs. Appelbaum, a shank and some corned beef for the Shelstein's.

He plunged into the crowd, straining for a glimpse of her, until he was able to position himself near enough to watch her. She was different, that much was clear right away. Not her hair—it was the same fiery halo it had always been—not her clothes, but her eyes. She had always had such calm, steady eyes, but now they were troubled, streaked by lucid flashes of rage. Maybe it was the spotlight playing tricks, and maybe she was just a different girl now, changed in ways that meant she would never come back to him.

Her dress was patterned in swirls of berry and black, with long bell sleeves. Her boots, laced up to the knee, were a deeper berry, dark as blood. *Na-i-ma.* There was something angular about her now, a new slant to her shoulders, a fiercer carriage, as if she'd spent the intervening years bearing aloft placards and signs.

She righted wrongs, she stood on higher ground—these truths he did not question. She seemed rooted up there on the stage, never to change her mind about him or the harm he had done.

He faded toward the far wall, crossing his arms and leaning back, eyes closed, as she began. She didn't introduce the song, or even say hello—she just began to sing in a warm hushed tone, which grew louder toward the end of the verse.

Whisper, listen, whisper, listen. Whispers say we're free.
Rumors flyin', must be lyin'. Can it really be?
Can't conceive it, can't believe it. But that's what they say.
Slave no longer, slave no longer, this is Freedom Day.

Lester smiled to himself, and then laughed—he *knew* the song. It was one that Flora had played—Abbey Lincoln, one of her favorites. The club-goers that surrounded him were both black and white, and everybody seemed to have turned out to groove. Naima was up there singing about slavery and freedom and the upturned white faces seemed as copacetic as the black ones. These were the Flora Kleins of the world, Lester thought. She had read Malcolm X and Marcus Garvey. Richard Wright, James Baldwin. And she discoursed fiercely on what she read; sometimes she seemed angrier than even the Black Studies majors. It hadn't sat well with him—not the writers themselves, he gave them every latitude—but her love for . . . whatever it could be called. The Black movement. Black power. Flora was a Jew. Abbey Lincoln, Nina Simone, these were Naima's songs, not Flora's. Then he laughed out loud: my God, they were *both* Jews—he had never thought of it that way before.

Naima's voice was louder now, richer, deeper, with an acid tinge to the notes. Her mouth was like a wide bowl filled with sound—basso moans and yelps and wails. Before she got up there people had been talking at the tables, eating and drinking, but now her strident vowels and chopped off consonants had silenced them, and they were glancing nervously toward the stage. With great deliberation, she placed her hands together, as if in prayer, her elbows pointing out, her head bowed. She began to chant. *Wah-ooh, wah—ooh.* Percussive and prayerful, strident, wild and loose—how could she contain it all?

She began to sway, eyes closed, chanting, groaning, bleating. He wondered if she were high, but then when she opened her eyes, it was clear she wasn't. Even from the far wall where he stood, her dark eyes seared into him.

The light enveloped her like a pale cloud. He swore he could smell her—soap or patchouli, a crystalline element. As he watched, the light changed, strobing across her, alternating bars bright and dark along her face and torso. She smiled, raising her arm in a fluid gesture, and then, shielding her eyes from the spotlight, she looked out to the audience. She pointed a toe, cocked a hip, all with the antic grace of a figure in a Jules Feiffer cartoon. She was Salim's sister all right.

And then he saw it: she held the *washint* in her right hand. The flute he had given her!

She raised the flute to her mouth and from it seemed to emanate birdsong. Lester found himself flowing back to Sunrise Lake and a sun-spangled girl sprawled on the bank, a crown of diamonds glittering in her hair.

I saved your black ass.

Nah, I saved myself.

Instantly his fantasy evaporated, and he could feel Salim's tense fingers on the back of his neck, his wiry strength forcing Lester's head down as he spat out rage.

Lester took a huge gulp of Dewar's: to muddle what needed muddling, to clear what needed clearing. No, he told himself, that wasn't Naima's way. It was wrong to think so. She might be angry—she had every right to be—but she would not allow herself to hate. He thought about it. She hated the system, she hated the white man, she hated users and phonies, and squares, but *him*—that was more than he could fathom.

She stood in a trembling cone of light, and as she swayed to the beat, she moved from light into darkness, and back into light. All that shone on her was one weak spotlight, but she didn't need even that—she was lit up with her own doing.

After a moment, she stood still, her eyes closed. He closed his eyes too, willing himself into her consciousness, joining her—now in darkness, now in darkness undone. He knew she hadn't seen him—he was a shadow shimmering in the back row. But nothing in the intervening years had prepared him for this: Naima, alive, free. He felt himself flowing out toward her, the way Mrs. Cala had described. He had never felt this with another girl, no matter how intimate they had been. Even Flora, who he had loved, to whom he had given his best self. It wasn't until this moment, standing in the

Blue Note's smoky shadows, as the bluesy vibrato of Naima's voice fell away and the spotlight dimmed, that he knew what it was to be separate. Loveless without her love.

The black man who accompanied her was now at the front of the stage, playing an upright bass. Naima was singing one of the songs from the church now, one of the songs from Calvary Baptist. *Woke up this morning with my mind, stayed on freedom.* He leaned against the wall and closed his eyes, letting the gospel vibe rattle him, making him bow down into the shadows, hammering him with a fierce longing. Why was this happening to him now? It was *her*—that's why. He had been so focused on Salim that he had gotten derailed: here, in front of him, was his original purpose, his north star. *Je responderay.* He took a deep breath and raised his head. He would not stand by. He would step up, he would make her see him for the man he truly was. Surely she understood that there was some special grace for a good man. Even a godly turn. How could it be that he had forgotten Shabbos, that he hadn't said any prayers since he had left home? Mama and papa—they came floating back to him now. Minnie with the shiny loaf of challah, Yussel with the prayer shawl. Yes, he would say an oath—no, he meant a prayer, what his father had said. *Barukh atah Adonai, Eloheinu, melekh ha'olam. Blessed are you, Lord, our God, sovereign of the universe* He muttered it to himself. But it didn't work. The words tracked through his brain like a freight train running empty back to the yard.

She made a Feiffer pirouette, the flute held aloft, strobing pinwheels of light, and then she raised it, its elegant body decorated with hummingbirds amid flowering vines—he knew the pattern as well as he knew the back of his own hand. The lilting birdsong of the flute zoomed toward him, swirling into his collar, his cuffs. And then the bird quieted and her rich contralto seized his blood. The notes of her disordered him; in her presence he was aslant. He could contain himself no longer, and he strode forcefully to the front, and then stood trembling at the lip of the stage, but she was gone.

What had lain buried between them began to rise up in him, to quicken, changing in ways there was no coming back from. When he was a boy—six or seven—his father used to come in at the end of the long day, and sit on his bed, to say goodnight. There was always a pencil behind his ear, and Lester would reach up and take it, smiling, showing his father what he had forgotten. A metallic tang clung to his clothes, his hands—the hands of a man who worked in blood, a gentle man who loved animals. Sometimes they had taken long walks in the state park or the Pine Barrens and Yussel would point out minnows, salamanders and frogs, water spiders, dragonflies, a wasp nest. One time they found a robin scuttling in the dirt, its wing broken.

That day, the day his father had been taken, was like any other day—he couldn't have known it would be the end.

Lester walked swiftly to Lillian's table. It seemed clear, now that he had witnessed the glory of a girl holding his gift aloft, now that he had seen her deeper burnished, shining brighter down through all the years that had separated them—it was quite clear that God would smite the one who had killed his father, he would make him small and useless, compacted by the enormity of his crime.

He crashed Lillian and Ross's table, unceremoniously inserting himself into a space so tiny that he was crammed up against their bodies.

Lillian turned to him, unsurprised, her eyes smoldering like banked coals. "Do you turn on, Lester?"

It was the same question she had asked him that day in her living room. This time he answered definitively: yes. He knew what she was asking: would he accompany her on her psychedelic journey, two witnesses, expanding the limits of the possible in a quest to solve a murder. *By any means necessary*—Salim's words.

"I'll do it," he said.

Lillian smiled. "Good boy."

"For sure," Lester said, and with a wave he strode out to the parking lot and got into his father's faded red truck, barreling down the highways, into the night, led by the three gleaming letters, the ones that remained: F-O-R.

Midnight came again and Lester was sitting in a different parking lot, in the passenger seat of Santo's cruiser. He was working the night shift and Lester had driven over in the Ford to meet him at Havesons Pharmacy.

When Lester told Santo about the night at the Blue Note, he glossed over the impression Naima had made on him, saying only that he was too far back in the club to get a good look at her. But the picture of her kept returning to him, every hour, every minute.

Santo homed in on the news of Lillian, which led him back to Dino. He seemed to be almost obsessed with him, and Lester wondered if his friend wasn't somehow identifying with the man who had got away.

"Carol says he's in Fiji."

"Where's that?"

"Polynesia, I think." Santo had turned off the ignition and he and Lester were slumped low in their seats. "How 'bout that? Just slip away. He's like the Invisible Man."

"God, I'd love to travel more—I've never been anywhere."

"Shit, I'm stuck here 'til Pops dies."

"He doin' okay these days?"

"Not too bad. And now Louie's sick too. He's got it bad—pancreatic."

"Man, what's happening to everybody?"

"Fuck knows. I heard you can get it from drinking coffee."

"*Coffee*? I never heard that."

"Live and learn."

"I bet Lillian's got it too. She looks real bad—kinda burnt up."

"She's takin' too many crazy pills."

"Yeah, I wouldn't be surprised if she turned up on the bus with the Merry Pranksters," Lester said, laughing. "But . . . I don't know, if it can make her remember, then . . . . Hell, if it could make *me* remember."

"Bullshit. It'll just give you a hangover."

There was one streetlight toward the front of the building, half-shaded by an elm. Santo's uniform was just a shade lighter than the dark interior of the cruiser.

"Yeah, but if she were convinced that she *did* remember? How about that?"

Santo banged the steering wheel. "You see these people trippin' out here. We pick 'em up all the time. They're bat-shit crazy, don't even know their own names."

"Yeah, but . . . I think she knows something. I think maybe she saw the killer."

Santo sat up suddenly. "Look, we goin' in there or not?"

Lester sighed and sat up. "Guess if I'm willing to drop acid, I'm willing to try anything."

Santo leaned forward and opened the car door. His belt creaked as he climbed out of the car, and Lester smiled to himself, remembering the sound, the way Randolph's uniform would strain against his body when he sat down. "Suppose we get busted—how's that gonna look? I got my reputation to think about," he said, grinning.

"Look, anything happens, you run. And I'll stick around—just one of the city's finest out here making sure the citizens are safe."

They moved quickly to the back door and Santo began jimmying the lock. In 30 seconds they were in.

"Damn, I'm good," Santo whispered as they stood in the dim hallway.

The place was all shadows but Lester could see down the hall that one light had been left burning—in the room that had been Yussel's office, a room no bigger than a bathroom stall.

"Okay," Santo said, glancing around. "We reenact it, see? I go out front by the window, and then you come from the back here, right? And run like you did before, then get down real close to the floor, like you was layin' down, so it's all the same."

Lester shook his head, unable to take a single step. The walk-in was gone, he could see that just standing there. And in its place was a high counter. His brain rebelled: the counter was supposed to be in the front, not the back. The whole place was permeated with a medicinal reek that was all wrong: cough syrup and rubber, bandages and menthol. He reached toward his Adam's apple, his tie-straightening gesture, only he wasn't wearing a tie. It was past 1:00 a.m. on a Saturday night and he wouldn't be back in the newsroom until Monday.

Santo grabbed his arm and Lester allowed himself to be dragged down the hallway, but when they reached the cubicle he stopped. They peered in to see a low Formica table and on it a lamp with a green shade, the bulb lit.

"What was this?" Santo asked.

"His office." The words seemed programmed to issue from him, as if they had been typed on a page and he was reading an actor's part.

Santo dragged him farther down the hall toward what had been the main retail space, the counters, the refrigerated cases, the windows that looked out on Market Street Lester saw that the place was all right angles now, weird rows, aisles, the floorboards canting, the doorframes hulking low. He found his legs as he turned back, heading toward the light. As he approached the office, he saw it: the mezuzah. It was at shoulder height, an oblong case about four inches long affixed to the right side of the doorframe. Bronze with a dark red stripe and a gold Star of David.

Santo was there beside him. "I remember when he placed this," Lester whispered. "It didn't save him." He turned to Santo. "There's a scroll in here inscribed with a Torah verse, in Hebrew. It's the name of God." He reached out and gently stroked the wood. "Blessed are You, Lord our God, King of the Universe, who sanctified us with His mitzvot, and commanded us to affix a mezuzah."

"It was his, right?" Santo asked. "You should take it."

Lester shook his head. "I can't. The blessing, it stays here, in this doorway."

Santo reached up and yanked the mezuzah off the wall, handing it to Lester.

Lester held it in his palm, staring down at it, and then his legs began to move, and this time he was programmed to run, to lurch toward the fire-exit door, to stumble out past the cruiser, and the Ford, and then step off the asphalt onto cold stony ground, moving past the briars tearing at his pants, and the cawing of a bird, stumbling toward a mighty oak whose branches made a soft rasp in the wind, and then tripping on the gnarled roots. He fell, and as he knelt there in a posture of prayer, he knew that was exactly right, it was what Yussel would have wanted him to do. He clutched the mezuzah to his chest, his fingers tracing the engraved letters, the raised star, as he bowed his head and whispered, "Adonai, Eloheinu, Adonai."

16

Climbing the Magic Mountain

The portrait of Naima kept returning to him for days afterward, but he knew to rein in those impulses, and habit aided him. For years he had refused to allow himself to believe that she'd smile in his direction ever again. Cautiously, he let himself add a few brush strokes—the light in her hair became a sort of halo, the laces on her boots became bindings that he would cut loose. He kept making these strokes bolder until he had almost convinced himself—maybe she *had* seen him, maybe she had smiled at him, maybe she was waiting for him to call. He couldn't explain it in a way that anybody would understand, but after that night, seeing her—he had begun to live again. All the newborn energy he had been gifted with after the encounter, he would channel into solving the murder and setting Salim free.

And then he conjured the girl. Not in the flesh, but close.

He had gone over to Minnie's for a late breakfast on Saturday. The phone rang and Minnie went into the kitchen to answer. Then she was standing in the kitchen doorway, the phone cord stretched to its limit, clutching the receiver to her chest, beckoning wildly.

Lester jumped up. "Ma?"

She was slumped in the doorway, making manic gestures with her free hand. She was clutching the receiver so tightly that he had to wrench it from her.

"Lester Gold speaking," he announced in his best reportorial baritone.

"Lester? It's Naima Johnson."

His knees buckled, but spry old Minnie was steps ahead of him, as usual, and she jammed a chair under his butt as he sank.

Naima. He closed his eyes and the dashboard of the truck floated into view, the trembling needle of the speedometer close to 60 as he sped down the dark highway after the Blue Note, windows down, her songs revolving in his brain.

His compass needle began to waver and then spin, as if the moon had come loose from its moorings and swooped down to earth, crashing hard, disrupting the tides, the winds, the shorelines. He bent over, clutching his knees, bearing down into this reality: Naima Johnson was calling. Some weird magic had ahold of him, commandeering his tongue, issuing a decree: *speak only the truth.*

"I can't believe you're—"

"—Just listen. I'm calling from a pay phone, okay? Your ma is listed—"

"I'm—we're—having breakfast. On Saturday." He was reduced to stating the obvious.

"Yes, well, I have some information that you need to hear. Something I overheard, actually. And . . . it's . . . very important. One thing, though, you didn't hear it from me, okay?"

"Yes, right. You never called. I mean, why would you? Call me?"

"So I work at the Blue Note. It's a club on—"

"—I know it."

"The other night I was waiting tables, and there's a back room, you know, sort of private, and certain regulars use that room a lot. Anyway, I was serving this one table and I heard something."

He struggled to concentrate. He couldn't yet process that it was really her. His brain raced ahead, bookmarking the moment: she had called, and now nothing would ever be the same.

"So you used to work at Louie's, right? If I remember."

"Yes."

"Well, he was back there with his cronies, the usual folks. And one of them says to Louie, 'The Havesons aren't cooperating. We may have to give them the same treatment that Gold's got.'"

"What? Wait, say that again."

"I have to go."

"But—"

"Lester!" Her voice was urgent. "Listen to me. Watch your back."

She hung up. He whirled around and slammed the receiver into its cradle. "Ma!" he shouted.

Minnie had her hands over her ears, as if she couldn't bear what he was about to say.

It was three steps to the front porch, if you took those steps in leaps and bounds—and then he was on the sidewalk, and she was yelling down to him, but all he could give her was a wave before he was in the truck and rolling into second gear.

An hour later he pulled up on Colonial Avenue in front of Lillian's for their "appointment," as she liked to call it. He had driven straight to Pops' place after Naima's phone call, but though he pounded on the door incessantly, no one came. He had walked down the block and called from Santo's phone booth, but no one picked up.

In keeping the date with Lillian he was taking the first step in a careful plan—one clue at a time, each one painstakingly deciphered. But now new information had come from the most unlikely of sources, information that could not be discounted. But what did it prove, exactly? He thought of calling Havesons, but he and Santo had just broken in to their store. How could he face them now?

He walked up the driveway of the unassuming three-story with a screened-in front porch where he had once studied Cicero with the woman who was now Charles' wife. Lillian came to the door in orange palazzo pants and a white peasant blouse with a swirly pattern. Her frosted hair was pulled up in a disheveled bun.

The wall-to-wall carpet was now mustard yellow and the spider plants had been replaced by a huge ficus tree that was crammed against the patio doors. He wasn't sure but the furniture seemed different too—a Prussian blue couch made a semicircle, and the only other chair was molded white plastic.

The couch was Command Central, and Lillian seated herself at its center, marshaling her paraphernalia on the coffee table in front of her. For the first time, Lester could see a twinship between the mother and daughter. An animal hunger. Not sexual, but some inhuman need he couldn't name.

He strode nervously around the room, trying to process the phone call. He debated whether he could say anything to Lillian, and finally decided on an abridged version. "You know Naima."

"Salim's sister. Works at the Blue Note."

"Yes. I . . . received information that she may be in danger." It sounded so formal, but he didn't know what else to say—he couldn't mention Louie. Everyone knew him.

"You must go to the police," she said firmly.

He hesitated. "Thing is, I have reason to believe they could be involved."

She gave him a sharp glance. "*Involved*? I don't know what you mean." She was busily scraping marijuana seeds into a pile with a dollar bill, when she seemed to get it. "*Oh*. You mean, the brother being falsely accused, that sort of thing."

"Yes, exactly."

"Well, then, go down to the Blue Note and talk to her. Warn her."

Lester cleared his throat. "I was thinking that was the best plan. I thought I'd go tonight."

She stopped what she was doing and studied him. "What exactly is the danger?"

"Well . . . it's her boss. He's kind of a criminal element, you know? And she heard something."

"At the Blue Note?"

"No. No!" He had stupidly given her too much information. "She works . . . in a clothing store. It's where I got these new threads," he said, brightening. He modeled his jacket—the one with the elbow patches, the one he had worn to the Blue Note. And he was wearing a long linen shirt with patch pockets and his new boots. He was dressing a little groovier these days, and had grown out his sideburns. "I buy all my clothes there." To himself, he made a vow, a vow to an amorphous God he evoked only when he was desperate: *please keep her safe. If you do, I'll wear these clothes every day from now on and I'll never wear anything else, until she's free, until Salim is free.* It was a lunatic promise, he knew that, but he was in no position to second-guess himself.

He resumed pacing the perimeter of the living room. "I'm not really the Merry Prankster type. You dig?"

Lillian nodded but did not look up. She was carefully unscrewing the lid of a small glass jar that sat on the coffee table. Lester took a few steps closer to see the contents: a brackish brown mass, stems and bulbs. Lillian fished out a porous chunk and held it up. It was curled like a fist, and he could see the spongy interior. "What's that stuff called?"

"Psilocybin. The Mesoamerican peoples used it centuries ago, as a route to the divine. The shamans, the medicine men. All cultures have some conduit to the divine. Perhaps you're familiar with the Elusian Mysteries—secret rites and ceremonies—"

"—Just tell me what it is."

"It's a fungus, a psychoactive agent." She glanced up at him. "Sit down. Stop that pacing. You're giving off bad vibes."

Lester perched on the unforgiving edge of the white plastic chair and began tapping his foot. She looked up at him, bemused. "Do you trust me, Lester?"

He stood up and began to pace again. "Actually, no. Not really."

She emitted a dry husky laugh. "Let me put it this way. I'm a very experienced guide in this sort of . . . journey. Fear, on the other hand, is not a guide. For this to work, you'll have to dispel fear."

He stood over her. "I heard . . . I heard—you don't really remember anything when you're tripping. It can seem like the most important thing of all time, but then it's gone."

She put some of the brown substance in a little white and blue bowl with a Chinese pattern. "I can assure you that what you will experience is expansive, not contractive, and I can tell you that it is highly likely that the effects will linger, perhaps even for a few days."

"Days, huh? I gotta go to work tomorrow."

She handed him the bowl, nodding. "Eat that."

"I'm gonna need a chaser," he said ruefully, as he began to chew the acrid bitter mass.

Lillian watched as he grimaced. "Go out to the kitchen, and bring us a couple bottles of Tab."

He went out and got the drinks, setting them on the counter that divided the kitchen from the living room. Then Lester stopped and stood still. That voice—where was it coming from?

Big mama, big daddy, we're layin' it down. Gonna climb the magic mountain.

He accosted Lillian. "What is that?"

She rolled her eyes and said with exaggerated patience, "The radio?"

Lester looked around wildly until he spotted a transistor radio sitting on the counter behind him. He grabbed it and turned up the volume.

Sure as the buffalo once ruled the plains we gonna hear some righteous tunes tonight—some prayers, *all you good people. Prayers for the fallen, for the good and noble men railroaded, run out of town. My brothers and sisters, I am counting on you.*

It was Salim, Salim's voice coming over the radio. Lester turned to Lillian. "My God, it's his radio show. Santo told me about it. He said . . . nobody could hear it . . . but I'm hearing it! Are you hearing it?"

She nodded and gave him a bleary smile. "Who?"

"Far freakin' out. I *heard* that shit."

Lester began to pace excitedly. It had to be a sign, as if Salim were here with them now, prodding them along, providing clues. He went back over to the radio and fiddled with the dial, but all he got was static. "Okay," he said to Lillian. "Maybe now's a good time for us to review what we know before you go all Flower Power on me."

He could see her resisting the impulse to laugh at him. She leaned back and stared at the ceiling for a moment, and then presented a more serious expression. "He was white. A young white man."

"Yes, I remember from before." Lester slowed his pacing and clasped his hands behind his back, as if he were cross-examining a witness. "Jew?" Minnie's long-time obsession with the Hasidim had seeped in a little. Maybe she had been right all along. "How white?"

"Swarthy."

Swarthy could mean anything. He decided to go for the hair, since Salim's hair was so distinctive—the big auburn Afro, just like Naima's. "Did he have an Afro?"

She rolled her eyes. "I *said* white." She crossed her arms and gave him an I'm-losing-patience-with-you look. "His hair was long and . . . tousled. Straggly."

"Straggly," Lester repeated.

Lillian gave and exasperated sigh. "Lester, come over here."

He went over to where she was sitting on the couch and stood there, his hands on his hips. The sleeves of her blouse were grey now from tracking through the cigarette and marijuana ash heap on the coffee table. Behind her head, a slender grey plume wafted toward the ceiling, and he wondered if perhaps she were on fire. He wouldn't put it past her. Her mouth was a smear of charcoal, and scribbled lines were etched around her eyes. She was growing smokier, more opaque, and he felt himself becoming transparent, like one of those models in anatomy class that you could see right through to the red arteries and blue veins.

He forced himself to stand still. "I don't feel anything. Are you sure this stuff works?"

She smiled and winked at him.

Her pupils were pinpoints, as if she had receded into a netherworld, a nocturnal place where eyes were unnecessary, where vision was so deep it had nothing to do with optometrics.

"What if we could communicate telepathically?" she asked. "All of us, whenever we wanted. Streams of information are soaring past us at every moment, on clouds of digits or letters."

He went over and lay on the rug, admiring the pulsating striated bands of green and yellow behind his eyes, and then watched as a few orderly rows of buzzing bees tried to climb into a hive. He discovered that conversation was unnecessary—he was able to communicate without speaking, just as Lillian had suggested.

"Let's play a few hands of Gin," she said.

He agreed, sending roots down deep at his place on the carpet, hands folded on his chest, eyes closed. After a few minutes, Lillian spoke.

"Would you like to discard, Lester?"

"I would," he intoned.

She paused and he imagined that she was studying the card. "Ace of clubs. An auspicious choice. Why, you've won. Gin. Your hand has won."

Thick curls of incense permeated his nostrils and now the radio was playing in his head.

Wild thing, you make my heart sing, you make everything . . . groovy. I wanna know for sure.

He stood up and did a Jules Feiffer pirouette, and then found his hips, settling into some approximation of what he'd seen on *Hullabaloo*. Lillian joined him, doing a languid frug, her skinny arms accelerating, churning up the smoky haze. He remembered when Flora would put on music and fling herself about the room in gazelle leaps. Sophomore year she'd taken a freestyle dance class for Physical Education credits, called "World Beats," and she'd insisted he come. He'd trotted around the room doing laps as she hunkered down or sprung up with arms flung wide. On the last night, they'd brought in some African drummers, and the room had gone wild. Lester and Flora had ended up dancing a frenetic *hora* with a bunch of the other Jews.

Lillian's arms were snaking in slow motion, her voluminous silk sleeves like flags fluttering above him. He tuned back into the radio. A flute and a marching drum. He knew this song.

And I see the robins
Perched in barren treetops
But just like the peace sign that vanished in our dreams

It was Naima's song, one she had sung the other night at the Blue Note.

And now . . . it's win-*ter*
It's winter in A-*mer*-i-ca
And all of the healers have been killed
Or been betrayed
Yeah, but the people know, people know
It's winter, Lord knows
It's winter in America
And ain't nobody fighting
Cause nobody knows what to save

Save your souls
From winter in America

But he, Lester, *was* fighting. Hadn't he subjected himself to Lillian's Merry Prankster schemes? He crawled across the carpet and lay beneath the coffee table, studying the panels on its underside, admiring the parameters: this coffin fit him perfectly.

Lillian's voice penetrated his consciousness. "Would you be mad at me if I told you you were a silly boy?"

"I wouldn't be happy about it," he said solemnly. He rolled his body across the rug until he had emerged from his coffin. "What . . . are you saying—"

"—your mother and the others, they should have known better—"

"—You can't blame her . . . I was the one—"

"—You were coerced."

He sat cross-legged on the rug, staring up at her, parsing her words. He shook his head, trying to dispel the raiment trails attached to her voice—the words kept exploding into colors, especially the words he didn't like. *Boy. Mother. Coerced.*

Why had she waited to confront him until this moment? She wasn't in her right mind, and neither was he.

She was on to another subject now, as if she had no idea that she had confronted him only a moment before. "Ross is a good man, and I enjoy his company, but you see, he's quite close to the centers of power. You see the allure?"

Her teeth were stained a teak brown from tobacco, and her pupils had been blasted into craters. He could see it now: She was his comrade-in-arms. There was no question that she had been through a tour of duty. It was flaking off her, and she was crumbling under the weight.

She said nothing more for a while and then she began to babble a stream of nonsense. It could have been the keys to the kingdom, but he wouldn't have known it. Just when he had given up on the idea that he would go on a trip, he felt himself descending.

"I have some strawberries in the kitchen." As she spoke the words, a plate of whole strawberries materialized, the stems still on. He watched as Lillian closed her eyes and bit into one, her ashy lips reddening as she ate.

"Mine too," he said, and it was as if someone else far away were saying it, saying it for him, speaking from a place on high, where regular mortals could not go.

And then the voice intoned, "Strawberry fields forever." In speaking the words it placed him there, in a strawberry field, even though he did not know there were strawberry fields, and yet this one was exactly right: it had been painted in all the right colors.

"My Dino, he's in paradise."

Lester felt suddenly panicked. "What, *dead*?"

"Very much alive."

"Santo said that dude disappeared."

"Santo?" she said, with a derisive smile. "What does *he* know?" She reached for another strawberry. "Dino, he's become invisible. It was his choice. He reached a level of mastery that the ordinary human mind cannot comprehend. And so he cannot be apprehended by us, but he communicates with me regularly. He's here with us now."

Lester glanced around the room. A weak shaft of sunlight had infiltrated the closed drapes. What she was saying was absurd, but his rational mind had receded, and he had succumbed to a new reality: what Lillian spoke blossomed in him as pictures in a movie. Now he saw that Dino had turned into a prophet with a long gray beard, and was camping out in the backyards of the Burg. There he was skulking the streets, trying to catch Lillian and Ross in flagrante. In the next picture he was hiding in the yard outside, in the woodpile.

Lester went to the window and looked out. It had begun to rain and he felt sure that Mrs. Cala would attribute the precipitation to her husband: Dino, the Rainmaker. He opened the door and stepped out into the rain. It was obvious that it no longer mattered whether he retained his composure. He flung off his jacket and began to dance and because it was the only dance he knew, he danced the *hora*, slowly, silently, accompanied by a tune that played in his own head. I am a lone Jew, he thought to himself, dancing the *hora* in the rain, and when I am done, I will be free, Naima will be free, Salim will be free.

Somehow he must have come back into the house because when he awoke he was lying on the damp carpet, next to the patio doors, a shard of awareness poking into his brain. The young man with the long tousled hair, the glint of sunlight on plate glass—Lillian's visions were now his too, part of the howling splintered self that had danced the *hora* in the rain.

Lillian was leaning her skeletal frame over him as she exhaled clouds of strawberry-scented smoke. Her face was a pencil sketch—the slash of mouth, the singed lashes. "I know who it was."

He stared into the incinerated depths of her eyes and detected a glimmer.

"I don't know his name. Louie's son."

17
The Big C

As he stepped out his doorway, Lester squinted into the daylight as if it pained him. Which it did. He was convalescing—the trip he'd taken with Lillian had stunned his brain cells into an odd submission. His plan was to go for a walk, a grand perambulation which, he avowed, would require only the kind of slow and fluid moves one might make underwater. On a morning when he should have been beating down doors he was experiencing a new frailty as his resolve weakened. What if the whole business with Lillian was some kind of hoax? She was such a flake. And what proof did he really have?

When he regained his equilibrium he would go into work, but now he could not bear the over-lit bustle of the newsroom: a pack of squirrely reporters wending among the partitions, Amos barking orders, the clatter of typewriters. He was good at his job: investigating, assimilating information, writing the story. His mind naturally calibrated all the twists and turns of a story, and his talents would serve him well, given the new information he'd gleaned. But right now his mind wouldn't land on any of that information—the previous night with Lillian kept dissolving into a mass of mental scribbling he could not decipher.

Louie's son. That would have to be Anthony. Back when he and

Santo worked at the barbershop, Lester had seen the guy nearly every day, but he couldn't place him there—he was a shadowy figure, slipping in and out, using the back door.

Lester had called Pops' number last night after he left Lillian's and let it ring and ring, but there was no answer, even when he called back during Carson. He couldn't figure it out—Pops never missed the *Tonight Show*.

When he set off on his hazy stroll, he hadn't allowed himself to make a plan, but after walking for many blocks, he found himself approaching the station. It turned out that he had had a plan, after all, and he slipped into a phone booth to call Minnie and ask her to meet him. It was only right that she be there when he confronted Randolph—she had stood by her son all these years, as she endured her widow's life: playing mah-jongg and waiting for Lester to come over for brisket.

Lester was confident that he would find Randolph at his desk. Santo had often described his boss's work day: sipping Sanka at 7:30, his gut hanging over his Sansabelt slacks, his face gaunt, his hairline receding. And when he walked through the doors, there Randolph was, just as he had pictured.

He came toward Lester hard and fast, pumping his hand, and firing a bunch of questions. "Well, look what the cat drug in! I'll be damned. What brings you round our way? Can I get you some coffee?"

Lester stood there smiling and taking in the station. The last time he had been here had been the worst day of his life, the day he had given the statement. "I'm just fine," he said, and then shook his head, declining the offer of coffee.

"I hear you're over at the Trentonian." Randolph's light brown hair was greying a bit at the temples and he wore it combed back. His eyes crinkled at the corners when he smiled.

Lester took a breath and started his spiel. "Yeah, I'm working on a story—the Emma Jane Stockton murder. We're investigating that. And I interviewed Mayor Holland last week. Did you know he almost chose the priesthood?" He leaned back against a partition, and his head began to clear. "We're pretty lucky he passed that up, wouldn't you say? Doing a fine job." He smiled to himself, filling in details that Pops had given him.

Randolph blinked rapidly, nodding in Lester's direction, and then took a few steps toward the lobby. "Mrs. Gold. How are you?"

Minnie had arrived, her black pocketbook swinging mercilessly as she plowed past the metal desks.

"Don't give me that rigmarole," she said, shaking a finger at Randolph. "I'd be a lot better if you'd show my son some respect. He's got a very good job, you know. He's working on a very important story, all the news that's fit to print. Someday you'll be glad you know him, you'll be saying, Oh, I knew all along that boy would win a Pulitzer!"

Lester couldn't help smiling. "Bertram," he said, drawing out Randolph's first name. "I'm sure you remember that I was a witness to a crime. And I've got some new information, which means I'll need to review the mug book for that year. Nineteen sixty-eight, as you know."

Randolph rocked back on heels, and then jammed his hands into the pockets of his beige trousers. "Information, you say. Well, first I've heard of it." He smiled broadly at Lester. "I just think—why waste your time? And our time."

Minnie marched forward, planting herself in front of Randolph and staring up at the wide bottom of his blue-checked tie. "Here, he has to ask? Didn't he come down here after a terrible incident and answer all your questions? All day he gives you, all night. Doing his best. My Lester is a good boy, and you must give him whatever he wants."

Randolph took a careful step backward. "All these years," he said, turning to Lester, "you've been content to let sleeping dogs lie. So why open old wounds now, decades after the incident? Have you thought about the family?"

Lester had no idea which family Randolph might mean—certainly not the Johnsons, who had suffered more than any family could bear with their son locked up for a crime he didn't commit.

Minnie marched another step forward. "My son will make a stink. A big stink! You let him do what he wants! He's a good boy."

Ordinarily, Lester would have been reduced to cringing and moaning, but now he just smiled complacently at Randolph, and waited for the next opportunity to address him by his first name.

"Your father—may he rest in peace—" Randolph began.

Lester was galvanized into action by those words, the very words he had heard Minnie repeating almost daily. "He's not resting in peace—far from it! He's turning in his grave! He would never want an innocent man sitting up in prison while the real killer goes scot-free! That, I am sure, would be very upsetting to such a man. A pillar of the community! A businessman, who, I may remind you, always paid his taxes. He never had so much as a parking ticket!"

Lester noted that Randolph was starting to shrink—he couldn't handle being double-teamed. And the other officers were beginning to stare. Lester put his hands on his hips and stared him down. "Let's go, Bertram—get the book. We're gonna spend some time with it right now."

Randolph sighed, but then he headed down the hallway, Lester and Minnie in tow. When the officer ducked into the evidence room, Lester waylaid Minnie. "Ma," he hissed. "I need you to do me a favor. When I say, 'How about that Thurman Munson,' you do your thing, okay?"

She nodded. "Have I ever let you down?"

Lester smiled. No, she never had.

Randolph led them into one of the interrogation rooms, and

Lester paced around for a moment until he was satisfied that it was not the same room where he had given his statement so many years ago. He and Minnie sat side-by-side, and Randolph took a seat across the table. He handed over the mug book, and Lester slowly turned the laminated sleeves, the yellowed pages crackling a bit as he flipped them.

He tried to flip the pages quickly, but the more pages he turned, the slower the pace. What was he looking for, anyway? He'd know it when he saw it. Side view, front view, side view, front view. Some smiled slightly, some were wide-eyed. There were dapper ones and disheveled ones, defiant ones, down and out ones.

Then he came across a kid from his high school class—Wallace Minor. And another—Ezekiel Larchmont. So they were booking black kids back then, he thought, it wasn't just Salim.

And then he saw it—bottom row middle. Anthony, disheveled and angry, his tangled hair nearly to his shoulders. He quickly flipped to the next page, so Randolph couldn't see him hesitate, and placed his finger at random on the face of some beleaguered schmo, as a vision blazed into his brain: Anthony huddled with the other hoods in the parking lot at Trenton High, tossing a butt onto the tarmac, Anthony at the edge of the school grounds, French kissing that hot Italian chick—Francesca? Anthony behind the wheel of a muscle car, the one he had totaled one night out on Route 1. He had come away from the accident with hardly a scratch, but another boy, the passenger, had spent months in the hospital recuperating.

Lester looked up at Randolph and took a breath. "How 'bout that Thurman Munson, huh? I never seen a catcher do what he does—"

"—my God!" Minnie suddenly crowed, clutching her chest, and rising from her seat. "Oy!" She stumbled and then slumped over the table.

Randolph shot Lester a desperate glance.

"This happens a lot," Lester said evenly. "Could you get her a glass of water?"

As soon as Randolph hustled out the door, Lester flipped the page back, slid the photo of Anthony from its sleeve, and pocketed it. When the detective came back in with a glass of water, Minnie was sitting calmly next to Lester. She rose and he followed her to the door.

"Good man," Lester said, clapping Randolph on the arm. "I've got to get my poor mother home right away," he said, as they moved into the hallway. When they reached the main room, where officers and dispatchers sat at desks, and two women typed behind a glass partition, Lester turned to Randolph. "I've got the green light from Amos to write about how you railroaded Salim. I'm going to expose the whole business."

Randolph frowned. "Now Lester, you know you don't—"

"—For what reason does my son come here tonight?" Minnie barked, raising her voice over the din. "He places himself at your mercy."

As always, she played her part perfectly. She grabbed Lester's arm and strode out as if parting the waters, leaving the whole station house helpless in her wake.

They began to walk along Chancery Street, mother and son, arm in arm, neither speaking, as they took in the reality of having spoken aloud what both had kept private all these years. Lester gently tapped the photo in his pocket, and then nodded at his mother. After a few moments, they heard a siren approaching, and both turned, Lester half-afraid that it might be Randolph coming to take him back down for an interrogation.

It was Santo, in uniform, behind the wheel of his cruiser. He pulled over and yelled to Lester, "Get in!"

Lester hesitated, and then turned to Minnie, but she waved him on.

"Ma," Lester said, beckoning to her.

Minnie walked over and took a seat on the bench at a bus stop on the corner.

Lester didn't even try to argue with her—he knew she wouldn't budge. She would remain there, a woman waiting for a bus. He walked over and kissed her on the cheek and she placed a hand on his arm—it was her blessing.

As soon as Lester got into the passenger seat, Santo said, "Anthony's dead. They found him last night at Washington Crossing Park."

"What?"

"I just came from there. Seen the body. Got a needle sticking out his arm."

Lester took a breath, thinking of the photo in his pocket. "I called your place yesterday. Pops didn't pick up. Not even during Carson."

"His kidneys failed night before last. They got him on dialysis up at Mercy. Him and Louie, on different floors."

Lester stared straight ahead as Santo drove the route they'd both taken a thousand times—they were headed to Chestnut Street, Pops' place. "I dropped acid with Lillian Cala." It wasn't a boast, but rather a grim admission that he had undertaken a fraught and terrifying tour of duty, the way one would go to war. "She ID'd him, you know."

"Anthony?"

"Last night."

Lester looked over at Santo for the first time, but he couldn't see his eyes.

"Damn," Santo said, grimacing. "Carol's mom. Stepping up."

"Yeah, she got her memory back," Lester said carefully. "She's a casualty of this thing. It's burned her up from the inside. What's that stuff they give you?"

"Chemo. Louie's full of it."

"Yeah, cancer—maybe she's got it too."

"The Big C, Pops calls it." Santo banged the steering wheel with the palm of his hand. "Do you believe these fucking monks? On TV, burning theirselves up."

"They're protesting."

Santo shook his head. "But you're gonna *die* because of some stupid fucking war?"

"You could say Anthony did the same thing, only in slow motion."

"He's just a stupid shit. He never knew how to do anything easy. Just hit everything so hard. When we was kids, he could eat one of them Hershey bars—you know, the king size—the *whole thing*, when he was, like, four. We have a home movie of him cramming his face. Kid barely made it out of school. If it weren't for basketball, they would have expelled him. I remember when he was in middle school, he set the place on fire. Just a corner, back by the gym, but still. I was maybe five years old."

"What about that kid he almost killed out on Route 1?"

"Sonny Palumbo. Still walks with a cane."

They drove past Columbus Park, where Santo had taken him under his wing, and brought him into the barbershop, and Lester couldn't help but smile to himself. Back before there was anything between them, back when it was easy.

Santo took the turn at Chestnut, and then pulled up in front of the rowhouse, turning off the engine. Lester turned and studied his friend's face. The features seemed rearranged—he saw a mobility he'd never noticed before, as if Santo had been masked all these years, but now his face was raw, exposed.

Santo smiled bashfully and Lester could see his chin tremble. "I told 'em, they touch you, they gotta go through me first. I'm done, I'm tellin' you. I couldn't say nothin', all these years."

"You mean you chose not to," Lester said. "All this time, that bastard was right here, under your roof."

Santo sighed heavily. "I know, I know. I didn't like it, I told Pops, no way. But Louie—"

"—Since when does Louie decide everything?"

"It ain't just Louie, man. Randolph, he radioed me, said I had to take care of it."

"Don't even know what that means."

"That you should have an accident."

Lester slammed both hands onto the dashboard. "Fuck me! *I'm* the putz. I was just down there schmoozing with him, trying to get information. I'll kill that bastard. And Louie too."

"Be my guest. Mercy Hospital, Room 236. He's got maybe two breaths left in him."

Lester tried to picture Louie on his deathbed, but he couldn't make him look any different than he always had—a jowly old man with bags under his eyes, exasperated, tapping the keys of his calculator, his glasses sliding down his nose. And now Santo was saying that both the father and the son were going to die within 48 hours of each other.

"Highly suspicious. I bet he's fakin' it."

"On my honor. If Louie ain't dead in the next couple days . . . I'll . . . turn in my gun and badge."

Lester watched as Santo took his gun out of his holster and placed it in his lap. He stared at the gun, and then studied Santo's face. All the symmetry was gone—it was all right angles, collapsing ruts and crevices. Maybe he had it, too—cancer.

"The Big 'C,'" Lester said, staring down at his own hands, clenched into fists. He thought of his father's hands—clean and strong, the hands of a craftsman. "Yeah, well, in Louie's case, and with all the Bassoni's, the Big C is *consciousness*, man. You *knew*. All this time. You ask me, that's what took 'em down—it killed Anthony, and it'll kill Louie, and Pops too. Maybe they should of thought twice about what they did."

And you too. Lester didn't say it, but he didn't have to.

"He's the one told me I had to shut you up. Louie's been saying for years, 'That Jew kid's a thorn in our side.'"

Lester's hands throbbed from the smack he'd given the dashboard, and he found himself wishing that he was sitting behind the wheel—he needed something to hold on to.

"I'm tellin' you, I had to go to a headshrinker over this. I ain't been right. And this thing, it's bigger than you know. It's more than just Louie. The cops too. And there's money at stake."

"You ask me, it's business as usual. And here's one thing you can count on: I'm gonna expose this thing, I don't care what they want, or what they'll do. Amos'll stand behind any story I write. I'm calling Hafferty tomorrow, we're gonna get a new trial."

Santo nodded glumly and stared at the gun in his lap. "If it makes you feel any better, I'm fucked. I've ratted them out now—to you. I'm probably the next stiff story you'll have to cover on your morgue beat."

"Who gives a fuck?" Lester snapped.

Then he saw Santo put his hand on the gun, resting it there, almost lovingly, the way you'd place your hand on the hood of a car you'd painstakingly restored.

Lester felt a surge of bravado course through him. "Go ahead. You gonna shoot me, just do it and get it over with."

Santo laughed. "I ain't gonna kill you. What's killing you is you got your head up your ass." His long face seemed to be dissolving. "Probably better if they take me out anyways. Anthony's dead and Louie's all but gone, Pops'll go next. It'll just be me. My ma would never forgive me, all these years and I said nothin', and I let you believe—"

In one motion Lester grabbed the gun and stepped out of the car. He hustled several steps to the corner and tossed it down the sewer as Santo raced after him.

"What the fuck?! That's my service revolver!" Santo yelled, but they both just stood there, listening to the clatter of metal against the drain. He turned grimly to Lester, his voice thick. "Get in the house. We're gonna do this thing."

Lester shrugged and started up the steps.

Santo trudged after him, and they faced off on the sagging porch of Pops' house. "Dammit, I gave you a million chances!"

"What the hell are you talking about?" Lester yelled.

Santo began to pace. "I told you, over and over, *leave it, let it go*. But no, you wouldn't. You should of let that jigaboo die in jail! And then you get mixed up with a black girl, for chrissakes. I took you to Havesons! But you didn't get it. For fuck sake, you *grew up* in this neighborhood and you don't know anything. This is *real life*, man. Ain't no degree from Columbia gonna change that. You had your head up your ass this whole time. Why didn't you stay away? Dumbshit, dumb fucking kike. The *Trentonian*? Nobody works for some bullshit rag like that. You shoulda taken a job at the New York Times, and then none of this shit would of happened."

Lester's hands tightened back into fists and he tried to unclench them, but he knew if he did, they would shatter, his whole body would shatter. "Seriously? You're *insane*. How bout, None of this shit woulda happened if you crazy dagos hadn't killed my pop. I mean, you're bringing the crows home to roost, let's start right there. He would of given you the shirt off his back, my pop. Worked harder than anybody. He used to . . . he used to . . . ."

He was crying now and he turned away from Santo to wipe his face. Then he turned back and when he spoke his voice was flat and stifled. "Look, it's simple. I know the difference between right and wrong. I was a coward. And now I'm not."

Santo smirked. "Big fucking deal. You're some hero now? Then you get your ass in there." He opened the door and Lester went inside. Santo led the way up the stairs. "You're gonna search good, you hear me?"

As they came to the top of the stairs, Lester could see into Santo's bedroom, the lava lamp on his dresser, the Mets pennant above his bed, the tangle of clothes on the floor. He knew Santo's room as well as he knew his own. He knew this place, this house—every stair step, every doorframe—and he could have navigated it in pitch darkness. A few more steps down the hall and they were standing in the doorway of a much smaller room, one that wasn't much bigger than a large closet. Dingy walls, a bureau with cracked wood peeling in strips, a twin bed crammed in the corner and above it a poster for *Barbarella* with Jane Fonda in a red bikini bottom and high-heeled boots.

Santo turned to Lester and took a deep breath. "You go in there."

Lester pivoted and stepped off-balance, before righting himself. He hesitated, staring Santo down.

"I'm telling you to go in there. And you search *good*, you hear me?"

Lester strode to Anthony's closet and began ripping through the shirts and jackets, stripping them off the hangers, and tossing them on the floor. Then he attacked the bureau, yanking open drawers. He stopped and stood in the center of the room. A grimy window looked out on a spindly scrub tree growing unwanted and unnoticed in the tiny back yard. A packing crate served as a makeshift bookshelf and Lester riffled the moldy paperbacks—*Siddhartha*, Herman Wouk's *The Winds of War*, *The Onion Field*—to see if they held any secrets.

Santo kept silent sentry outside the door.

Lester tossed everything he found into the center of the room: a transistor radio, a pile of loose change, some 45s, paycheck stubs, military fatigues, dog tags, combat boots, baseball caps, t-shirts, dress shirts, socks, belts. He even ripped the poster off the wall—but he turned up nothing.

He stood again in the middle of the room—he had searched everything, and he wasn't sure where else to look. Santo wouldn't tell him—he knew that he had to find the evidence himself. He could barely restrain himself from picking up the packing crate and hurling it through the grimy window.

He would not look at or speak to Santo until he had completed the task. He got down on his knees in front of the mound of clothes. He began to go through all the clothing, turning out pockets, checking trouser cuffs, and even the linings of the jackets, ripping and shredding the cheap cloth. Nothing. He got up and went back to the closet, got down on his knees and crawled into the back. He ran his fingers along the floorboards, the walls, and the upper shelves. He found a photo of the Trenton Tigers, Anthony in the center, with signatures of his teammates under their names. He ripped it in half and tossed it onto the pile. He tackled the bed, pulling the mattress onto the floor, heaving the box spring aside, yanking the bed slats from the frame. He saw something taped to the underside of one of the slats; even before he had removed the tape he knew what it was, and he gripped it tightly in his shaking hand.

His father's money clip—the one that he always kept in his right front pocket—a small oblong piece of gold, which, Lester knew, Yussel's uncle had given to him. He held it in his palm, tracing the rays of the rising sun engraved on the metal in long strokes. On the back were his initials: JMG. Julius Menachem Gold.

Lester stared hard at the floor as he slipped the clip into his right front pocket. "I've got it."

"Right," Santo said, taking a few steps into the room, but avoiding Lester. He opened his wallet. "It had sixty dollars in it. Here, I want to pay it back," he said, extending some bills.

"Fuck you—I don't want your blood money!" Lester roared, bashing the wallet out of Santo's hand.

Santo backed off and stood in the hallway. "I told him, get rid of it," he said quietly. "But he wouldn't."

Lester reached into his breast pocket, took out Anthony's mug shot, and propped it on the dresser. "R. I. P," he said derisively, and then turned to Santo. "I never thought there was much resemblance."

"What? Me and him, you mean?" He shrugged. "We're a couple of dagos."

"You ain't no better than him." Santo had kept the secret from him all these years, had *worked* at it, dragging him into Havesons in the middle of the night, signing on as one of Trenton's corrupt cops.

Santo turned to Lester, glancing over at him. "Lester, I'll testify. You can put me on the stand. Against Louie, Anthony."

"I never believed it. You got that? Not for a minute. The stupidest thing I ever did was sign that statement. *I knew*. All along, I knew he was innocent." Now the evidence was piling up in his brain. "That's why he went to Vietnam, right?"

Santo nodded. "Louie and Pops made him enlist. 'Til the heat was off. Stupid bastard should of got himself killed over there. Then nobody would of been the wiser."

"But *why*?" Lester asked, as the tears dripped freely down his face. "Anthony. He never had nothin' against my pa. I never once seen him in the store."

Santo looked up at Lester, and then sighed. "You got it wrong," he said gently. "He didn't even know him. Louie, he sent him over there. As an enforcer. You dig?"

"You mean—"

"He wouldn't pay."

"He was killed because he wouldn't pay *the vig*?" Lester turned furiously and thrust his hands in the air, the way he always did when Minnie had pushed him to the brink.

"He was just supposed to scare him. See? Just threaten him. But . . . what Anthony said was Yussel pulled a knife on him, and so he . . . panicked."

Lester could see how badly Santo wanted him to understand, but he gave him only a stony stare. "Of course he had a knife—he's a *butcher*, for chrissakes," he said, thinking of the tender labor of his father's days, the patient bloodletting, the care he took with every carcass. "He was a man of principle. He never would of paid. That's how he is."

Lester closed his eyes and rooted himself. He had memorized every detail of Anthony's room, a boy's room. At that moment he felt younger and stronger than he ever had, and he balled his hand into a fist and lunged at Santo, punching him in the jaw. "That's for the playground."

Santo stepped back and rubbed his jaw, his eyes filling with tears.

"Go ahead, call me Jew," Lester taunted him.

Santo stood there, a condemned man, slowly shaking his head.

"I ain't never gonna back down. My people, we've been despised and cast out for centuries. I didn't think that mattered—for me. But it did, and it woke me up to my own failure. Letting myself be coerced into signing away a man's life. But *you*," he said, stepping back into Santo's space, "you sat on your hands. You took a good man, from his son. You betrayed the best friend you ever had."

As Lester walked out, he caught sight of himself in the mirror on the back of Anthony's door—never before had he seen himself this way: rumpled and slump-shouldered, his arms stiff, his hands trembling at his sides. He had spent his youth, his teenage years, college, practically his whole life trying to make a wrong right. And now it would be Santo's turn.

18

Giant Steps

On a rainy Tuesday afternoon along Route 29 Lester stuck out his thumb and waited for a ride. He didn't think anyone would stop: he looked like a hippie these days—he had let his hair grow down the nape of his neck and his sideburns were more unruly than ever. To make matters worse, he was wearing a cherry red "Free Leonard Peltier" t-shirt, bell bottoms, his tweed jacket with the elbow patches, and Beatle boots. He had topped off the ensemble with a navy-blue beret emblazoned with a red Black Power fist, and a leather pouch slung crosswise across his chest.

The old Ford had conked out about a half mile back and he had pulled it over on the berm. It had been dying for a while now, so as he jumped down he grabbed the silver "D," just in case this was the Ford's last ride. He had found it in the drawer of an old workbench in Minnie's basement, and had dumped it on the console, glancing at it from time to time as he drove around town.

He stuck out his thumb a little farther and smiled broadly, not only because it might help him snag a ride, but because it was the Ides of March and word had come down that Salim would be set free. Today was visiting day at Trenton State Prison.

After a few minutes a guy pulled up in a VW bus, and Lester ran up and hopped into the passenger seat. The driver's long white hair was tied back with a headband and his shades were tinted blue. He wore multiple strands of beads around his neck.

"Well, if it isn't the young Mr. Gold."

Lester stared harder. It was Dino, back from heaven or hell or whatever playground he had disappeared to, working the pedals in bare feet, the long sleeves of his striped cotton tunic rolled back to expose an embroidered leather cuff on his wrist.

"Mr. Cala! That shirt is groovy."

"Thanks, got it in Bombay. Keeps the sun off, but you're still ventilated."

"I was driving my Dad's old Ford," Lester said as he settled in and Dino shifted gears, pulling back out onto the highway, "but it just died, back at mile marker 26."

"Bummer."

Lester began tapping the dashboard nervously. "I kinda got a date?"

Dino extended his right wrist. "Check my scuba diving watch. 'Bout 2:30, I think."

"Scuba? For underwater. No way! That is *hip*, man."

"You're not doing so bad yourself," Dino said, nodding at Lester. "Black power!" he shouted, thrusting a fist in the air.

"I'm dressed to impress," Lester said, smiling.

Dino offered Lester a can of Tab that was leaning up against the gearshift. "Wet your whistle, young man. You out there long?"

Lester took a sip of warm Tab and grimaced. "Nah. You came along just in time." He stared over at Dino. "You can clutch without shoes? I'm impressed."

"Haven't worn shoes in six years. Don't need 'em." Dino rattled the gearshift, easing the Bus into third gear, and it began to shake as it picked up speed. "They got the Concorde now. PanAm flies non-stop to Tokyo. The world ain't such a big place anymore." He glanced over at Lester and nodded. "I been to Timor, Madeira, Rhodesia,

Phnom Penh. Mao's funeral. The Ford Presidency is such a disappointment. I don't trust him, I tell you. Tuetue, we say on Pulua. Means, shake the dust."

"Keep moving?" Lester asked, and when Dino didn't answer, he said, "I'm on my way to see a girl."

Dino reached for a round container on the dashboard that was decorated with a blue sea and green palm trees. He offered it to Lester. "The villagers use the meat of the coconut on their skin to keep it supple."

"Uh . . . thanks," Lester said, as he put the container in his lap. "I guess you don't get too much rain over there in . . . ."

"Hulua." Dino turned toward Lester and grinned. "A girl? You're on your way to—"

"—Yeah, I have to tell you, it was Mrs. Cala, she put me on the right track." Lester cranked the handle to close the window—rivulets of rain were trickling toward the passenger seat. "Hulua? Where's that?"

"Tulua. Polynesia. Have you heard of communes, Lester?"

"You mean, like the Manson family?"

"Well, the fact is that we humans aren't meant to be monogamous. Our hearts are free. Have you read Gurdieff?"

Lester remembered the name—he had something to do with the Square Pegs, the people who Lillian turned on with. Her words from that night came floating back to him. *Dino, he's become invisible. He reached a level of mastery that the ordinary human mind cannot comprehend. And so he cannot be apprehended by us, but he communicates with me regularly.* He remembered it now—something about a Fourth Way. *We're all just walking around in a waking sleep, like automatons.* He couldn't see it then, but she was telling him exactly what he had done wrong all these years. He had been a sleepwalker and it had taken him all this time to wake up.

"I think . . . what she taught me, was . . . how to—"

"How not to be a square?" Dino asked, and then tossed his head back and shouted, "Hah! I was just . . . I was a *square*, man! On Tulua, they sail these huge canoes, filled with warriors, the drums playing. Navigate by sextant, just the stars and the sea. I've been initiated now. I got an honorary doctorate from the Hulua tribespeople. Been acculturated in the ways of the greatest people on earth. I only came back to get my wife. She's coming with me."

Lester had given up trying to pinpoint geography; every time Dino mentioned the place the pronunciation changed. "You mean—"

"—She's the one—"

"—But I thought—"

"—You are referring, no doubt, to a certain carrot-topped interloper."

"Ross. I thought he—"

"A means to an end."

Lester began to wonder if Lillian had perhaps sacrificed more than he even knew. And Dino, he was just like her. They were both blasted open—Lillian in her caftans, Dino with his mushroom cloud of white hair.

Lester began to beat out a rhythm on the dashboard, keeping time with the raindrops. "Yeah, man. *Square*—I was as square as they come! All boxed up in my rational mind. Get this! My best friend, he kept it all from me, all this time. And now he's a cop and he's gonna testify against the syndicate." He rummaged in the leather pouch he was wearing and pulled out the money clip. "See this?" he demanded, holding it out to Dino. "I carry it with me, used to belong to my Dad." He drew it back and began, as was his habit, to trace the grooves in the gold. "See how these rays, they're to the *right* of the sun? That means the sun is rising. You dig?" His hands had begun to shake and he stuffed the clip back into his pocket. "Louie's dead, and Pops too. They went within a couple days of each other. They did a bad deed, and that could not go unpunished, and so they been dying all this time—see. They *knew*. They knew all along. The Big C, it ate 'em up from the inside."

Dino nodded gravely, but kept his eyes on the road. "Lester, a truer statement has never been made." When he spoke again his voice was low and Lester had to lean in to hear. "We loved Julius. Never bought my corned beef from anyone else. Of course, Lillian was a vegetarian." He glanced over at Lester. "You were a good boy, Lester. Carol passed her English test because of you. What a good study partner you were. Your mother raised you right."

Lester nodded, and then he reached into the pocket of his jacket, found the silver "D," and dropped it on the tray of the dashboard. "Hey, this'll make a nice keychain."

Dino glanced over and nodded.

"If it makes you feel any better," Lester said loudly, "Santo, he's ruined. He lost his job."

Dino looked over at Lester, his eyes soft. "Does it make *you* feel any better?"

Lester shifted in his seat. "Nah. I wish it did, but it doesn't."

"That boy, the basketball player—"

"Anthony?"

"He got my daughter pregnant—I shoulda killed him then. Julius would still be alive today."

Lester closed his eyes for a moment. The rain had let up and there could be no doubt of what he had heard. "What?" he said, opening his eyes and staring at Dino. "Nobody tells me jack-shit around here!"

"She was thirteen. Had the baby. Michael. We're raising him on Pulua. Sweet kid. Speaks five languages. Brown as a nut."

"That's why Santo—"

"Always hated that kid—"

"—But if it was Anthony, then who—"

"—Bad seeds both of them."

"Did he know—"

"Well, we had the boy baptized at St. Asaph's before . . . before . . . ."

"You *kidnapped* him?"

"Now that's pretty extreme," Dino said sternly. "I wouldn't put it that way."

Lester smacked the dashboard with the heel of his hand. "Jesus, those dagos took me in. *Why*? Did they think they could get to him through me?"

"Who?"

"My dad."

The Bus seemed to be taken over by Lester's revelation—it began to shudder and rock and then slowed to a halt as Dino steered onto the berm. Lester wrenched open the passenger door and jumped out onto the gravel.

"Shit, we got a flat."

Dino hustled around, barefoot, and stood there in the rain as the bus wheezed and steamed. "Only truly reliable mode of transportation is oxen—they simply never break down."

Lester stood there nervously as the cars zoomed past, and then tapped his wrist. Dino glanced down at his space-age watch. "2:47."

"Man, I gotta book. Sorry! You'll be okay? I can't miss this girl—I've waited seven years for this!"

Dino gave a slight bow and made a steeple of his hands. "Tuetue, my friend," he said, and walked over to put his love beads around Lester's neck. "You need these more than I do."

"Righteous!" Lester yelled, as he took off running down the berm. Harlan had told him that visiting hours ended at 3:00, so if he ran hard, he might still make it.

The prison parking lot was huge. He raced up to it, disheveled and panting, and then stood there staring up at the turrets as a huge American flag snapped in the wind. He turned slowly, searching for any sign of her, and when he spotted her, just as she turned and saw him, he stopped short, jammed his hands into his pockets and tried to appear nonchalant.

Her hair was as glorious as ever, and she had on a colorful tunic, jeans, and clogs. As he stood there watching her, she began to walk back in his direction.

"I got stamina. From tennis," he said, as he bent over, panting, trying to draw a breath. He looked up at her. "Nice dashiki."

She gave him her bemused smile, the one he knew so well from the hallways of Trenton High, and the trails and banks of Whispering Pines. It wasn't possible he'd gone seven years without seeing that smile.

He straightened up and tucked his shirt into his jeans. "My dad's truck just died out on 29, and then Mr. Cala picked me up and his VW Bus got a flat! Damn, I almost didn't make it. But I was . . . motivated," he said, grinning broadly.

She nodded gravely.

He turned and checked the guard towers atop the turrets—of course, they were being watched. It was fitting—here where Salim had endured the worst, and Naima had come to attend faithfully to him. The guards knew her, Harlan knew her.

He did a few funky steps and a slow glide, for the surveillance cameras. "Foxy lady, I ain't foolin'." He slipped into the vernacular with her, and he didn't even try to restrain himself. Partly, it was that he knew it amused her.

She could only maintain a somber stare for about 10 seconds before she started to giggle. "I can't believe you're wearing that."

He grinned. "Free Leonard Peltier?" he said, spreading his arms wide. He had dressed in this outlandish way on purpose—dress the clown to play the clown. "I'm celebrating freedom. And . . . and I made a study of the Indians, back in Miss Schrader's History class, ninth grade, actually."

"No, *that*," she said, pointing to his head.

"Oh, *this*," he said, playing along. "This is my yarmulke."

"Is that kosher?" she asked, laughing harder. "Don't tell me," she said, after a minute. "You wanna know if I've been to Africa."

"Why would I want to know that?"

"You think I'm a radical, I follow Marcus Garvey."

"Baby, you could blow up a Brink's truck, call yourself Tania, I'd still be standing here."

Her smile got bigger. "You're pretty hip for such a scrawny Jewboy." She put her hands on her hips. "Patty Hearst—you believe that shit? 15 million bail. Now if she'd been a sistuh, her black ass would be sittin' up at Bedford Hills right now."

He shrugged. "She wanted to play revolutionary."

"Thing is, I want change, I want it in my *blood*—but I just . . . I could never hurt anyone." She tried to smile again, but her eyes showed the hurt. "You know where my brother was the night your father was murdered? He was sitting up at my mom's eating some ribs and watching I Spy."

"I love that show," Lester said wistfully. "Tigers of Heaven is my favorite."

"Is that the one where they go to Hong Kong?"

"Tokyo."

"Yeah, the neofascists."

"They're releasing him. I guess you probably know."

Lester nodded.

"He's gonna move in with me. It's a long road back. They really messed him up. He said being in there was like being on a slave ship for ten years—brutalized and rowing to nowhere. It's not just your freedom you lose, it's your humanity. You've got no choices. The smallest infraction, even just making eye contact, they put him in the hole."

Lester wanted to reach toward her, he wanted to fall to his knees and beg her forgiveness, but he offered what he knew he could follow through on. "I'm gonna write a series on the prison and the corrupt cops. Amos is behind me," he said. "And by the way, I've got a message from him. He says you can write for him anytime."

She nodded. "We're starting our own newspaper. Volunteered Slavery—it's from one of Rahsaan's albums." She gave him a tight smile. "But you should write about . . . whatever . . . you know, raise consciousness. The senseless brutality of your dad's murder. How my brother was railroaded. All these stories need to be told."

Lester gathered up the necklaces that Dino had given him and took a couple steps toward her. "You know, a man just gave me these love beads. Like, not even a half hour ago. And . . . it's funny, but what I want to write about is . . . love."

She reached toward the beads and touched them gently. "I remember how you said—how they cut the animal's—"

"—Traibering."

"—Yeah—to keep it humane. So I knew then—he was a good man, and . . . ." She shrugged and looked at him with a steady gaze. "You're his son."

Lester nodded. "Actually, that's what I hate about the whole thing. Like, he didn't even mean to kill him, it was an accident. He panicked. My dad would never hurt a fly. I bet you he tried to talk that sonofabitch down. You know, I can hear him saying"—Lester marched a few steps across the lot and then back again, assuming an old man posture and a heavy accent. "Anthony, your father, he's a good man! Imagine how his heart aches to have a son who would go to a public place and make threats. That you should bring shame to your family this way."

Lester smiled bashfully at his own performance. "You know, I dropped acid with Lillian Cala." It wasn't a war story anymore—it was a tale of liberation. Like Flora, he was a Freedom Rider now. He grinned harder and then laughed. "Sheesh. You know, Lillian, she came through. I think it cost her everything, but she remembered. She channeled a mighty power and she saw the vision. That's what put me on the track of Anthony. Can I tell you? I just . . . *consciousness*, man. I always thought it was overrated, but, good God, I musta been the dumbest guy on the planet. So much shit has gone down and I . . . I just looked the other way, I guess." He looked at her helplessly. "How come I didn't know?"

"Maybe you didn't want to know."

"But . . . hell, I'm a reporter. I'm always on a story." He waited, terrified that the slender filament which connected them might snap. "I totally understand if you never want to see me again," he said, talking fast and wanting to close his eyes, to just say it blindly, so maybe she wouldn't even respond. "I mean, what I did . . . to you . . . to your family, I can't—"

She shook her head, turning away from him in one quick movement, and he stood there, thinking that nothing she did could stop the green shoots of his love from growing and twining along her roots. But then he reined himself in: this girl, she would never accept that kind of clinging love. Whatever he had to give her, or she him, it would have to be freely given.

She turned back to him and took a deep breath. "I want to hate you, truly I do. But I can't. Cause you saved my life—Sunrise Lake." She smiled shyly. "I mean, you lost someone too. I lost my brother . . . but . . . still . . . I could come here and sit with him, and I could hug him and hear his voice on the phone. But you . . . you'll never hear his voice again."

"There's a boy lives on an island in Polynesia, he just lost his dad."

She gave him a quizzical look and he just nodded—there was no way to explain Dino and Lillian and all they had taught him.

She shrugged. "Look, I was worried about my brother going to Vietnam. It never occurred to me that he could end up on death row."

It had only been moments ago that he and Dino had squared up about being square, and now Lester understood what all those years had cost him. Lillian had been right all along: you had to dismantle the rational mind. He dropped to his knees and yanked the cassette player out of the leather pouch. He had already loaded the tape but his fingers trembled as he pressed "Play." Then he stood up and flung his arms out and began to spin, not a mad dog spin, but more of a Jules Feiffer pirouette. "This is for you, you washint-playing mama, you!"

He stood in stunned tribute as the American flag flapped gloriously on its pole and Coltrane blew his pure notes into the parking lot. "Na-i-ma, my love, you've given me, love I could dream of—"

Her beautiful lips parted, her slender fingers fluttered near her throat, fumbling, absently searching for her heart. "My dad . . . he named me." A single tear glittered on her golden cheek. "How did you know?"

"Coltrane wrote it for his wife, Juanita. Her middle name was Naima too." He nodded, afraid that his voice might crack, that he might cry too. "I listen to it every day. Every single day. I went to the library—you know how they have those listening rooms. It was after the church. And I found they had Giant Steps. You can listen with headphones. Then I bought the record down on Beale Street."

She reached out and gently touched his lapel. "You know something? What really matters. You never once professed your innocence to me. Never once said, I was railroaded, I was a kid, I didn't know, it wasn't my fault."

Lester nodded, thinking of the day in the diner with Harlan, when he had spread all the bills in his wallet across the table, $96.00, the entirety of his first paycheck. He had bet on Salim and now it had paid off, in this very moment. She was telling him: *Lester, I see my brother's integrity in you.*

"You know you're damn good, by the way," he told her. "I came to the Blue Note," he added sheepishly. "Just once. I didn't want to take liberties, but I felt like I'd die if I couldn't see you."

She smiled and held out a long *hmmmm*. "Thought it might have been you. One night, I don't know how I knew, I felt your presence."

He rummaged in his leather pouch once again. "Close your eyes. Hold out your hands."

She hesitated, then smiled, and took a step back, closing her eyes.

He placed the mezuzah from Havesons in her palms and she opened her eyes. "That belonged to my dad. It's the only thing I kept from Gold's. There's a scroll inside there. It was on the wall outside his office ever since I can remember. It's the most sacred thing—and I want you to have it."

She shook her head. "I couldn't."

"No, no. See? It's *protection*," he said, stepping nearer and caressing the smooth case. "It means that . . . all this . . . meshuggah . . . that happened to you, it was the worst thing, like, nothing bad as that will ever happen to you again."

They both stood there staring down at the mezuzah.

Lester spoke softly and deliberately as he smiled at her. "I mean, you might jaywalk. Might lose your keys. Maybe you'll catch a cold. You might even fail your driver's test. But that's all." He wanted to take her hand, but he hesitated. "It's like what you said—do the right thing."

"I said that?"

"Yeah, you don't remember?"

She shrugged. "I say a lot of stuff."

"But . . . but it was probably the most important thing anybody ever said to me."

She gave him her cockeyed smile. "When did I say this?"

"The night . . . after Calvary Baptist. You said it in French, remember?" It was a night he had conjured countless times.

She laughed. "Yeah. Je responderay."

He nodded enthusiastically. "If you can say it in Hebrew, I'll let you drive me home."

She laughed, and then put the mezuzah in her bag as she began to walk across the lot. "C'mon," she said, and Lester followed, keeping pace with her. "Okay, so how do you say it in Hebrew?"

"From one Jew to another, I have no idea."

He hustled ahead of her and opened the driver's side door to let her in, and then rushed over to the passenger side. The rain had stopped and low smoky clouds bunched up over the prison.

They got into her mother's sky-blue Valiant, she behind the wheel, and he in the passenger seat, as evening was settling again over Trenton, the sky streaked with the same violet tinge that had wreathed the spires of Calvary Baptist on that evening many years ago. They headed out of the parking lot and onto the busy lanes of Route 29: soon they would both be home again, and on the way they would pass Yussel's old Ford parked on the berm, the three silver letters still shining in the rain, and Lester would glance over at the girl behind the wheel, and then back at the truck and mutter to himself, *Rest in Peace.*

Acknowledgements

The work of Jim McCloskey at Centurion Ministries, advocating for the innocents who had been convicted of crimes they did not commit, inspired me to write *The Statement*.

Tom Regan listened to me talk about Lester and taught me how to tell his story.

August Tarrier was invaluable with her help editing and writing the story. I cannot thank her enough for her patience in dealing with my passion, brainstorms, and, in plain Yiddish, my mishigass.

Patrick Bernuth, David Botwinick, Eliot Daley, Hannah Fox, Nancy Karlosky, Ryan Lilienthal, Bob Levitt, Sharon Naeole, John Patberg, and Dennis Stark read, commented, and challenged me to "keep digging deeper."

To Ellen, I say "Thank you, dear" for being so honest with your constructive critiques at every stage of this adventure.

About the Author

Inspired by the pioneering work of Jim McCloskey's Centurion Ministry, Stark has supported the work of Innocence Projects and movements to abolish the death penalty.

A Trenton, New Jersey native, Albert Stark began his civil rights education registering voters in Selma and Tuscaloosa in 1956. He resigned as an Assistant Prosecutor after witnessing police testify falsely in court and beat demonstrators at the Chicago Democratic Convention in 1968.

Stark practiced law, advocating for people with brain, burn and spinal cord injuries, and pioneering the use of video in the courtroom. Victories led to safer cars, bicycles, recreational vehicles, industrial equipment, and roads. He is the author of *Beyond the Bar – Challenges in a Lawyer's Life* (2002), *A War Against Terror Through My Lens* (2006) and *Insider Secrets to Winning Your Personal Injury Battle* (2009).

He is married to Ellen and lives in Princeton, New Jersey.

CPSIA information can be obtained
at www.ICGtesting.com
Printed in the USA
FSOW02n2205050516
20119FS

9 781478 770831